EAST END BOYS AND WEST END GIRLS

by

James A Lyons

Cover designed by James A Lyons.

Paperback ISBN: 978-1-915905-83-3

First edition, Spectrum Books, 2026

Discover more books at www.spectrum-books.com

For all the real Wilma's who have come before.

Author's Note

Hi,

Thank you for picking up this book! Before we start, I just wanted to mention three quick things.

Content warnings:

In this novel there are discussions of adoption, the care system, and bereavement. There are also historical discussions of the AIDS crises as some of the novel surrounds drag queens in their sixties looking back on LGBTQ+ life in the 1980s. There are mentions of fictional missing persons cases and death. There is an instance of homophobia/transphobia made by one character in context in the final third, and one homophobic comment in context in chapter one. The novel features coarse language throughout.

AI:

This book was written entirely without the aid of AI. No chapter outlines used AI, no dialogue used AI. No plot points used AI. I am firmly against the use of AI and have never, and will never, allow AI to be used willingly on any piece of work I create. Part of the fun of writing this book was visiting the locations around Soho and imaging how my characters world would look. I also learned a lot more about life in the 1980s for LGBTQ+ people, something that I wouldn't have learned if I'd relied on an idiot-machine to do the work for me.

Indie presses:

Spectrum Books are a small indie publisher. As with a lot of indie publishers, they often take more risks than the large publishing houses and push to raise the voices of authors from underrepresented communities, whether that is related to sexuality, gender, race, neurodiversity, or other. Please support indie presses, and support indie authors like me. The easiest (and cheapest!) ways to do this is to tell a friend about our books, leave a review on one of the many online platforms, share details of our books on socials, and generally like and support us when we talk about our books!

Despite some of the content being difficult at times, this book has an aim to show joy, and that the right people will find you, no matter what. Thank you again for taking a chance on this novel, and I hope you enjoy it!

Many thanks,

James A Lyons

1.

Uncle Eric

I'm not a failure. I just haven't found success. There *is* a difference. A subtle one, but a difference, nonetheless. When I turned twenty I'd made a promise that I'd leave Stonemouth. It's the one seaside town they've yet to close down, but by God are they trying.

Ten hours into the first day of my twenty-fourth year and I have a hangover that could sink a battleship. According to the BBC News clock I'm already five minutes late for my lunch shift. I trudge to the bathroom, my body screaming, desperate to crawl into a dark corner and die peacefully. Bent over the sink, my eyes close tight as I furiously scrub at last night's thick eyeliner. Mum will drop by the café today and she can't catch me in make-up again. She almost exhausted her homophobic insult guidebook the first time. If she knew the truth, it'd be even worse.

"Good morning, you," comes a tired voice from behind me.

I jump, striking my head on the base of the small bathroom wall cabinet, a line of empty shampoo bottles tumbling to the floor. I recall venomously telling Michelle last night that I don't need no man, but another morning, another unknown hook-up emerges from the cesspit of my bedroom. She'll have a field day when I see her at work. I should've left The Old Fire Station earlier and can't recall much after my cheesy garlic mayo chips from Syd's on the way there from town.

Instead of ordering a taxi and sneaking out, my latest overnight guest, a boy with pale skin, a Green Day t-shirt, and blonde surfer hair, grins at me like a cat waiting to be fed. He's an eight out of ten, possibly a nine due to his small, cute forearm tattoos, but even a ten isn't what I need in my flat.

I stare at him via the water-stained reflection of the cracked mirror and he smiles widely as he plays with his shell necklace. "I wondered where you'd gone. Are you okay?" The words come out as a croak. Did we meet at the karaoke bar? Did I even go there?

"Um, yeah, all fine, thank you." I scramble for his name. Jason? No, Jason is the hot new bartender. Michael, that's it. Maybe. "I'm not much of a host, sorry. Dead late for work too."

He rubs my arm with his left hand as I go back to my make-up, the calluses on his fingertips rough against my biceps. "I'll leave you to it, Harri. Have you seen my shoes?"

I stop scrubbing and lean my wrists on the sink. "What do they look like?"

"Adidas Samba. Claret with light blue stripes."

"I've no idea, sorry."

"They were a reissue of the style used in the fifties."

The extra description was never likely to help. My sister is the fashion expert, not me, but they could've caused my trip when dragging myself away from the sofa. "Try the hallway."

He kisses me on my naked shoulder and bites his lip as he slides out of view. "Sweet. I'll message you next week about getting guestlist for the gig."

What gig? What guestlist? Sick bubbles in my stomach as my heartbeat ripples through my eardrums. Nothing good will ever come from drinking five espresso martinis in the space of sixty minutes. If the alcohol doesn't get you, the caffeine will. Twenty-three is firmly in 'old enough to know better' territory. My dry throat does not bode well for five hours making cappuccinos and small talk with tourists. The temptation to pull a sickie is strong.

Other than my now departed conquest, today is the first birthday since my days in the care system where I've felt alone. With my sister tied to her internship in New York, and Callum and Gabe AWOL, I should've expected as much. I haven't seen either of my two flatmates for three days now. They're likely at the curtain call of another all-nighter smelling of weed, cheap lager, and casual heterosexuality.

I stumble to the kitchen and pour myself a cup of ambition (water with a Vitamin C tablet) and plug my phone into a power bank to resuscitate it. My heart sinks at the half-eaten

Colin the Caterpillar being the only company I have – he sits on the kitchen worktop giving a smug chocolate grin. I punch his stupid face and eat his feet, hoping the sugar helps cure me.

Thick sweat engulfs the air in my bedroom, and condensation fogs the windows. I wipe them down with a pair of boxers, unveiling a picturesque view of the bin area for the neighbouring Chinese takeaway. Seagulls flock around the chicken carcasses and fat-laden black bags torn apart by foxes. At least the wildlife has a breakfast loaded with protein. With its one-star hygiene rating, I personally wouldn't eat there.

My phone vibrates in my hand, and I swipe it open, my finger leaving an oily streak across the screen.

"Happy birthday Harri. Need to speak to you URGENTLY. Call me xx."

That can wait until lunch. It must've been gone 2am in Manhattan when Daria messaged. She's never shown a sense of urgency before, not even when we were angsty teens fighting over a shared bathroom.

I kick last night's outfit towards the corner, landing it on the growing pile of washing which has alternated between my floor and bed for numerous days. It's big enough now to hide the half-finished canvases which clutter my living space. My modern abstract artworks are all I've to show for my time on Earth. The odour of every room I've slept in for the past eight years has been tinged with stale paint and turps.

The wardrobe creaks as I force its stiff hinges open, revealing clothes ranging from morbid on the left, through to bright and glittery on the right, as if I'm turning up the saturation as I scan my fashion choices. Daria keeps threatening to 'pimp my gear', but thankfully her latest modelling internship has delayed that torture for ten weeks.

I grab my work shirt from the duller end of the racks, the Smile Café logo making me sicker than the stale alcohol in my throat, but I've no time to waste. Sliding on my trainers, I scoop up my birthday post from the letterbox cage and dart through the foyer into the sunshine.

Jumping off the bus in The Square, the church bells tell me I'm forty-five minutes late. Craig drags chairs into position on the café patio which stands fifty feet opposite, each scrape causing the local pigeons to seek solace on rooftops. My workplace nestles between the vape and gifts shops that signal the decline of the modern-day high street.

I straighten my clothes and walk across the pedestrianised town centre, the bitterness of last night's drink lingering on my breath, no matter how much gum I chew. My phone is vibrating again, but this time it's constant.

"Hey, Daria. I can't talk now." Even family should be banned from FaceTiming before midday.

"Wow, you look dreadful. Why haven't you called yet?" Daria mumbles something further, but the New York traffic drowns her words. Neon signs on towering skyscrapers surround her like an electric aura, and people jostle as they swerve her on the sidewalk.

"I'm in a rush. I'll call later."

"Wait," says Daria. "You're already late. Give me five minutes, please."

Craig is back indoors. I move into a fire exit set back from the street and pray I haven't been spotted. "Fine. What are you up to? Another high-end fashion party?"

"I'm working. It's five AM and I've been up all night," she says between two yawns. "Parties aren't much fun and I still have a morning shoot at the Brooklyn Bridge in a sec."

"Gross. Have you done all the tourist stuff yet?"

"I thought you didn't have time for small talk."

"Sorry, yeah. I'm still not with it."

"I need you to sober up and listen. One sec." Daria shoos away a well-dressed lady who's trying to add blusher to her cheekbones as she sits. Fake bushes border her and a green awning moves gently above. "Have you ever heard of Uncle Eric?" Her voice is serious and her hazel eyes wide.

"Uncle Eric? Is it another of your underground Bronx artists?" The hangover-monkey is thumping the drum far too much for me to consider opening Spotify.

"Uncle Eric is a person, dickhead." Her deep, steady breath travels all the way across the Atlantic. "I got an email, Harri. Mum had a secret brother."

This seems unlikely. Aside from our parents, we have no family. It was always the four of us, until four became three. My right foot shakes at the thought Mum has been lying all this time. "You haven't been touching the fashion industry sherbet, have you?"

"You know I don't touch that stuff. I'm being serious. I got

an email last night. We've been lied to." My head is pounding and I'm unsure if it's anger or the hangover. I grab at my sweaty hair to quell the pain. "Don't panic, Harri, it's okay."

I cock my head. "Who sent the email?"

"Someone called Gloria. Said she lived with Eric and a woman called Wilma in Soho. She must've messaged every Daria Forrester she found."

"Weird."

"I know right. I was sceptical at first, but she said Eric had an estranged sister called Julia on the south coast who'd adopted two children. It has to be Mum, right?"

There's a chance it's a coincidence. "Did she say why they lost touch?"

"Nah, but you know what families are like. You saw the fuss Mum made when I accepted this job."

"A model is a prostitute for designers," I say in my best impression.

"Precisely. I want to believe Gloria is telling the truth."

"Maybe I should invite Eric over for dinner tonight to freak her out. Can you imagine the look on her face?" I'm only half-serious. A pregnant silence hangs on the line, and Daria knots her front curls around an index finger. "Daz?"

"He's dead, Harri. Eric died last week." I let out a long slow breath and Daria dabs at the corner of her eyes with a tissue. She's always been the sensitive type. Even though we aren't blood related, the emotional connection is as strong as any siblings. "That's why Gloria was looking for us. Says she's got something important so wants to meet up."

"Have you replied yet?"

"Of course. I told her I was in America so couldn't do much until I'm back, but I thought—"

"That I have to help?" I say, before she has to hint. It's a strange sensation to mourn someone you never knew existed. I sit on a low wall to steady myself, going through my mental diary. "I'm heading to the Tate Modern in a couple of weeks. I could swing—"

"Can you go tomorrow instead? I wanna find out what it's all about." Her blank expression shows this isn't a joke.

"I dunno Daz, it's my first Saturday off in ages. Also, what if I spend two hours on a bus to meet a random woman and it turns out to be nothing?"

"Gloria is not random, Harri. This is our chance to find out about our past. How many times have we wished that? Also, agreeing to go means you can reject any overtime that prick of a boss tries forcing on you."

"I'll have a think, I promise."

"There was something else which might help you make up your mind." Her face comes close to the camera, her voice failing to hide a bubbling excitement.

"Eric left us a fortune in inheritance?"

"You wish."

"Was he a spy?"

"Listen," she snaps. "I don't have long before I get picked up."

"Sorry, I might be a bit drunk still."

She tuts. "Eric was gay, Harri."

"Get out was he." If he was, then going to London has to be on the cards. I've never been part of an actual gay scene before (Stonemouth's one gay bar does not count). Daria continues to stare through the screen. "Are you sure?" I ask.

"Apparently he lived with someone called Vincent for a bit."

"Daz, I share a flat with two men and they're so straight they're practically rigid."

Daria chuckles. "Okay, what if I told you Eric was a performer in some of London's most iconic and notorious gay bars?"

This is more like it. "Tell me more."

"That's all I know."

I don't believe in fate, but her reasoning is convincing. Having a connection with Gloria and Wilma will create a bond with my 'uncle' and help unravel the confusion which has occupied my mind since the day I walked out of college. It will give me fresh hope, the purpose I've always craved. "Look, send me the details and I'll do what I can."

"I'll email them across in a mo." Before she can continue further, a man in a business suit whispers in her ear.

"Is he part of the FBI?" I ask.

"Martel's my chauffeur. I have to run, but thanks for listening. You've a card from me at home. Love you."

She hangs up before I can say goodbye.

The sound of Stonemouth's bustling town centre filters

back. People, who were invisible moments earlier, brush past me as though I've passed through a timeslip. Behind the large panes of the cafés wide front, Craig stands, the condensation from the coffee machine part obscuring his obnoxious face. I take a deep breath before facing the music.

"Late again," Craig grumbles as I pass into the staff room and throw my bag onto the lockers.

"Sorry," I lie. My contempt for him growing further.

"You know how busy we are with the lunch crowds. Michelle is on her own out there."

"My sister called with some news."

Craig drops a box onto the countertop and wipes his sweating brow with blue paper towel. "There's always an excuse with you."

"It's a reason, not an excuse."

He steps towards me, standing so close that his body odour is stronger than the brie baguettes behind him, his forehead as creased as my work shirt. "Gossiping about fashion can wait until you're on your own time."

I want to put his head through the microwave but my aching muscles don't have the strength. "I found out a family member died." He doesn't need the full details. Craig's face softens a little, but he doesn't offer sympathies, instead turning to fill the napkin containers. I glug a glass of water and head behind the counter.

"How's the head?" Michelle asks as she squirts fairy liquid onto the cups in the sink. "You were well gone before the band even started."

"Fine now, but rough as anything this morning. Is it bad I don't remember them playing?"

"Just as well. You told the bassist you wanted to fuck him." She pinches my cheek expecting a response, but the shame has already spread through my veins. "You kept saying you liked his Green Day t-shirt."

As she busies herself restocking the muffins, I take a cloth and wipe the side slowly, my eyes fixed on the customers in the smoking area outside. After cleaning the same spot ten times, Michelle is back at my side.

"What is it now?" she asks.

"What is what now?"

"You're up to something, I can tell." Her eye contact forces me to stop dead. “It’s not another art show you’re not going to submit to, is it?”

Ever since we were thrust together in a Year Seven drama class, it’s been impossible for me to hide anything from her, even if it’s in my subconscious. We’re so alike I thought she could be my biological sister at one point, so much so in fact her mum had to deny it. “I need to show you something.”

“Is everything alright?” Her hand drops from my arm. “Is it another bad Tinder date? Don’t worry. I’ve been ghosted four times this week. I feel like Pac-Man. I ghosted one myself though cos he looked like you."

“What’s wrong with me?”

“Nothing. Honestly, he could’ve been your brother. Bit taller though, and better looking. No offence.”

“None taken.” I hand my phone across and she wipes it on her stained apron. “Daria called and told me about this.”

After a few seconds, her mouth drops open. “No. Fricking. Way.” An unattractive slurp echoes out as she drinks some of her cold brew as she reads. An older couple sitting near the counter glance disapprovingly. "Are you going to visit Gloria?"

"Yeah." I surprise myself with the speed at which I’ve made the decision. It normally takes me five minutes to choose which pair of shoes to put on in the morning. “Even you have to admit this one is too potentially life-changing to ignore."

"It’s piqued my interest, I guess, but y'know." She breaks eye contact and picks at her new yellow nails as she preps one of her life lessons. "I get you aren’t happy here, Harri, but I don't want you to get yourself sucked in quickly. Your unhappiness won’t magically disappear without real change.”

“It’d help. Gloria could be my ticket away from this shithole,” I say, gesturing my arms around the café. The old couple stare again. “Eric might not be my uncle, but it’s the not knowing that intrigues me. If we’re related, it might start the chain reaction which leads to my life having a purpose."

"And if you aren’t?"

“Then I guess I’ll have to wait for the next life-changing opportunity.”

Michelle raises her eyebrows and takes the cloth from my hand, cleaning the lengthy nozzle of the *CoffeeMaster 3000* with rapid, suggestive hand movements that wouldn’t look out of place on certain NSFW websites I may or may not have bookmarked. She shouts over her shoulder as the machine hisses. “And how many life-changing opportunities are we up to now? Three? Four? Or is this the fifth?”

It's the tenth, but I don't want her keeping tally as well. “This could be the one, Michelle."

“Harri, you said that about the online portfolio competition. And did you enter? No.” She pulls her aquamarine scrunchie from her head, talking with it between her teeth as she scrapes at her messy parting, the roots dark beneath dirty blonde hair. “You need to stop letting opportunities pass you by. You’re due good luck.”

I serve a customer a flat white (basic) and a warm milk (or a *babyccino* as the modern world is forced to call it) and read Gloria’s email aloud to Michelle to ensure I didn’t miss anything important.

She pushes my hand down and nods behind. Craig stares disapprovingly at us from above his copy of *The Sun*. “Pretend you’re counting the flapjacks or he’ll send you to solitary stocktake confinement in the big fridge again.” She thrusts two boxes in my hand and I pile the goods on the metallic work surface, snaffling a bite of a toffee one when no one is looking. “Look, I’ll humour you. Let’s pretend Eric’s your uncle. Will you pack your bags and head to London?”

“I didn’t say anything about moving to London, but never say never.”

“What does London have that Stonemouth doesn’t?” she asks.

“Opportunities!” I reply, embarrassed with how cliché it sounds as soon as the word leaves my mouth. Before she can ridicule me, I wave a hand in front of her. “I mean, like London has art shows and chances to network. I could make a name for myself, stand out from the crowd.”

“Yeah. Another miserable skinny white twink. You’ll really stand out, I'm sure.” That’s an accurate description, though I’m more disheartened than miserable. “You need a plan,” she mutters, before taking an order from some Lycra-clad customers who have steam rising from their limbs.

“I have a plan.”

I lean against the fridge, the coolness soothing my hangover as Michelle squirts caramel syrup into three takeaway cups. “Going to London is not a plan. You need to make a list of things you want to achieve.”

"Such as?"

"What you want from life. You're firmly against more education, you didn't accept the offer to work for my dad, and you flick between ideas like a hyperactive toddler. It's a bit weird."

"I want to be a proper artist." With art, making it, whatever that means, is all I've ever wanted. I was never a child prodigy, due to the fact I bounced around foster families for the first six years of my life like some kind of trendy accessory. The closest I got to being the next Mondrian was felt tips on the walls when alone in another new bedroom. It wasn't until regular detentions with Miss Kennedy in the art block led me to discover a real passion for becoming a creative.

"Three caramel lattes," Michelle calls to the waiting group, before turning back to me, taking my hand in hers. "Art doesn't pay well." As if I didn't know already. "I want Gloria to be good for you but would you even be able to leave Stonemouth? Can you afford to live in London? Will you be able to find friends? What will you do for work? I love you, but you seem a bit, I dunno, lost?"

"Lost how?"

"Since you and Kristian broke up, you don't seem to know what you want. You don't have a Plan B and your Plan A is wafer thin." She emphasises her point with pinched fingers close to my eyes. "I don't want you to move just so you won't bump into Kristian and his new boyfriend."

I hate how Michelle is right. She always is. Kristian does play on my mind, but as I enter my seventh week of single life, the panic attacks are less frequent. When the end inevitably came for the brief fling (as Michelle called it, despite it being a four-month relationship), it was clear Kristian would never be 'the one'.

"But," Michelle continues, "I'm a nosey cow and want to know about Eric, Gloria, and Wilma. It will do you good, uncle or not. If any opportunities come up, I want you to say yes. No slinking away from things. You need to learn to grab the duck by the bollocks, understand?"

"I understand," I reply, even if this isn't a phrase.

She gives me a hug and moves my fringe away from my eyes, allowing me to breathe in the caffeinated scent on her fingers. "Now, are you going to London tomorrow morning?"

"I think—"

She pushes her fingers to my lips. "Duck, bollocks."

"Yes, I'm going to London tomorrow," I say with a sigh.

"Good. Harri, you deserve the world, and we'll work this out together. If London is good, I might even move with you."

I sit in the stockroom breathing heavily, my body craving electrolytes, calories, and ten hours of sleep. The vending machine hisses as a watery cup-a-soup flows into a small mug, before it belches, firing molten chicken-flavoured liquid down my top. Scratching around for a change of clothes, I pull open an old cardboard box of promotional t-shirts from last year's town carnival. I remove a medium from its plastic wrap, a crescendo of self-pity rising at the *'I heart Stonemouth'* logo now emblazoned across my torso.

I gather my birthday cards from my backpack to remind myself someone cares about me. The pink envelope on top is from another ex, Adam. Other than Mum, he's the only person to address me as Harrison. He used my full name to wind me up, as boyfriends tend to do, when I first introduced 'my friend from Sixth Form' to my neighbours at a barbecue five years back. The Glasgow postmark in the top corner gives the game away too, as does the *hilarious* penis-illustrated envelope. His drawings are sickeningly detailed.

Red glitter pours out across the tiled floor as I rip open the card. Adam is an idiot, but there will always be a *what if*? I don't know if this is because I genuinely thought I loved him, because *he* was the one who ditched *me* to go to university, or because he was the first boy who dared to allow my hands to wander in a more southerly direction when making out behind the Co-Op after a sixth from disco.

I brush myself off and return the booby-trapped card to my bag, along with the one from Mrs Higgins who lives across the hall. Hers features a much more suitable-for-work image of an old man fly fishing, despite me never expressing any enthusiasm for the hobby. It's naff, but she did superglue a pound coin inside, so beggars can't be choosers.

"You can't wear those clothes at work," says Craig, pointing to my tatty t-shirt after bundling an armful of dirty aprons into the laundry bin.

I wave my hand towards my dripping uniform on the peg behind. "It'll only be for an hour or so and I'll change back into that."

He perches on the window ledge, pulling a pad from his top pocket and licking the end of his pencil. It's a shame they don't still use lead. "How many times have I reminded you about your punctuality?"

"I'll be back down after I've finished this." I raise my cup to him.

He breathes out heavily to the sky and his face turns a light shade of crimson. "When you get older," he starts, his voice pointed and rough, "you might understand what it takes to run your own business. Actually, you'll be too busy with your painting, I expect."

"I prefer to call it art," I reply, my temple pulsing with anger. "Painting is what decorators do."

He scribbles something and I crane my neck to look, but he tilts the page higher. "I warned you about your timekeeping this morning, and instead of knuckling down, you're stood in front of customers playing on your phone and gossiping with Michelle. There has to be a line, young man, so I don't have any other choice than to make this formal."

"Whatever," I mutter. I should be more tactful, but Craig's proximity forces my hands into fists. I punch on my thigh to disperse the heat in my body.

"Harri, I understand you might not see your future here, but whilst I'm paying you, you do as I say. You're sat here now looking like you're on day two of a stag do, and my floor looks like a poof's dressing room with all this glitter."

If I didn't need the calories, my soup would be over him by now. I remain quiet as he bullet points my indiscretions on the written warning.

"Final chance," he says, tearing the page quickly from the book. I snatch it from his hand and toss it into the bin when he turns his back. "You'll never have a career with your attitude."

I wish they would change the record—managers, teachers, career advisors, parents. We're constantly told to prepare ourselves to spend the next fifty years working for someone who earns more from your productivity than you'll ever earn yourself. A career will not be on my mind today. Today, my mind can only be occupied by Uncle Eric.

2.

The Boy with the Cheekbones

Not many things in life scare me. Heights? A little. Spiders? Not at all. It makes the fact I'm rooted to the spot, absolutely terrified of a front door, even more ridiculous. It's painted a regimented plain black with two rusting brass numbers showing fifty, the zero at a slight angle as if in italics. It almost comes off in my hand when I force it back into position, and I leave it hanging, worse off for my intervention.

The sun beats down on the pavement, yet shadows are cast over me in Gloria's small entrance way in the heart of Soho. No light filters through the half-moon of glass above. The panes are dirty, with thick, beige marks skirting around the edge, and a plaster of masking tape hiding a spiderweb crack forming from the centre.

I've travelled seventy miles to be standing here this morning. If my proverbial glass is half full, a world of information on my family history will be sat waiting on the other side. If half empty, it'll be two confused ladies called Gloria and Wilma. Judging by the litter the breeze drags to my feet, it's unlikely to be a glass at all, more a discarded can of Stella.

I climb over two carrier bags on the multicoloured tiles and brush cobwebs from the panel of buzzers on the right-hand wall. Next to the button for Flat 2, thick marker spells out Gloria & Eric, the dark ink merging into the yellowing background like the fading memory of Soho's glory days.

It's only been five minutes since my arrival, but I'm nervous Michelle's warning of loitering being an arrestable offence is true. I breathe out heavily and run my hand over the bell panel, stabbing my finger on the buzzer. A robotic trill blurts from a dented speaker. Five rings. Nothing. If I've come all this way for Gloria to ditch me I'll be fuming. I arrived dead on 10am, as promised in my email to her last night, and being stood up is my greatest rejection fear.

Even though this is central London, I could well be alone. People walk as if in a dream-like state, many with no focus and no direction. A west end town, but a dead-end world.

My teeth clench at the high-pitched squeal and sterile odour coming from the application of ink on skin at the neighbouring tattoo parlour. The sound runs right through me, so I press Gloria's bell again, harder, and longer this time. After the third ring, it goes silent. I slow my breathing and listen carefully to the subtle movement down the line, leaning into the speaker until the cobwebs brush against my right ear. "Gloria?"

"You're not a Tory are ya?" comes a gruff cockney voice from upstairs.

"God, no."

"Labour?"

"No, I'm—"

"Well which are ya? Not a Lib Dem, I hope."

I let out a sigh. "Gloria, It's Harri. Eric's Harri."

No reply. I bend down and push the stiff letter box open with my fingers, its hinges creaking noisily like old machinery in a disused factory. The scent of a thousand ashtrays flows out as I peer inside. I turn away spluttering, gasping for fresher air.

I can almost chew on the pollution in the atmosphere, the petrol absorbing into my tastebuds, stifling the oxygen in the air. It doesn't have the salty freshness of Stonemouth. I wouldn't be surprised if I returned home asthmatic after a few hours in the capital.

As my choking comes to a stop, I spin back to the flat. A woman stands in front of me, half concealed by the dimness of the hallway. Sweat forms under my arms and drips down my sides as she stares at me through semi-dark lenses. I put on my best smile and give a small and accidentally-camp wave. "Hi."

It might be a warm May morning, but she's dressed in a garish Kermit the Frog Christmas jumper. A half-burnt cigarette hangs loosely near her face, held between two discoloured fingers. Her striking maroon lipstick stains the camel-coloured tip. The eyes coming from under a lank fringe travel slowly from my toes to head.

"You don't look like our Eric," she says, her accent thick

with the ingredients of an East End upbringing.

I roll my eyes. "I'm adopted, remember?"

"He was taller for starters." She takes a long drag of her cigarette, studying me a second time, blowing a cloud over my head. "And Eric were better looking. No offence."

"None taken." I run my hands through my hair to stop her smoke particles from clinging on.

She nods and goes back inside, the door closing with a swipe of her foot as she does so. It clunks loudly as its lock falls into place. My heart sinks and I text Daria this might be a lost cause, but Gloria returns before I've hit send. She's managed to light a new cigarette during the few seconds she was away.

"What's your mum's name?"

"Julia." I mumble. "Julia Forrester."

"Speak up or come closer," Gloria replies. "I ain't got my aids in."

I shuffle forward, the shake in my legs clear. My arm hair rises, and my body flips into fight-or-flight mode. A knot forms in my stomach and my mouth dries. I swallow to help gain composure. "Sorry, it's Julia. You contacted my sister and said Eric might be our uncle?"

She pokes out a bottom lip. "Yeah, probably. Pretty certain."

Is *that* it? The moment I've been waiting for, the purpose of my visit, the pivotal lightning bolt of excitement that will alter the entire course of my life. She's so matter of fact, as if the news is no big deal at all. I guess to her, it isn't.

The cherry on her cigarette glows red, and she hands me an Oddbins carrier bag from the banister behind. "This is for you."

The handles are tied, and it matches the two between my feet. "What is it?"

"Fucked if I know. Eric wanted your lot to have it if he ever…y'know."

I catch her lips curling into a slight smile at the mention of my uncle's name. I tilt my head like a sympathetic parent and hold up the bag. "I'm sorry for your loss." I wanted to be sincere but it comes out more sarcastic.

"Not your fault." She looks over my shoulder and gives a wave.

An older man stares through the windows of the café on the other side of the narrow street. He's tall and thin, dressed in a stained white apron. There doesn't seem to be any joy sparking in the eyes behind his round, thin-rimmed glasses. He nods to us with no emotion as he dries a mug with a tea towel.

"He owns the café across the road," says Gloria.

I assume his name to be Roberto, based on the sign above the plate window, although the O is only a dark circle on a sun-bleached grey background where the original letter has been lost to time. A plastic sticker proudly boasts the café was awarded bronze in the *Evening Standard Dining Awards*, however this was sponsored by Woolworths and dates from 2008. It could be 2006. It's difficult to tell even from this short distance.

Having not eaten since boarding the 6.30am National Express, my stomach rumbles at the mere thought of food. Before I can ask Gloria if she has a teabag, kettle, and barrel of biscuits, loud stomps come down the staircase behind her. Someone who can't be much older than me jumps down the last three steps, faltering slightly when we make eye contact. He quickly looks away, cautiously throwing a leather jacket over his slim fitting Bob Dylan tank top and resting large sunglasses on his razor-sharp cheekbones.

He's trouble I tell myself to stop it showing externally how annoyingly attractive I find him. He'd be the perfect man to prise my cold, drunken hands from the Grindr app. My mind jumps to multiple nefarious conclusions about why he was inside this building. He must've been dropping off drugs. No, that's not fair. He must be Gloria's (much, much) younger lover. Lucky cow.

The boy lights a cigarette, the spark from the match glinting off his silver Rolex, before he stares in my direction from behind his lenses. If he were on the dancefloor of The Old Fire Station I'd be making a beeline for him immediately. He's exactly the boy I've described to Michelle during our many 'ideal man' chats. And Bob Dylan? He has taste, too! I look to the clouds and whisper a thank you to Eric.

"See ya later, Gloria," Cheekbones says, his eyes fixed on my shoes, but mine on his face. He kisses her cheek and I lean back until I'm pressed tight against the wall. He squeezes past closely, hopefully deliberately, his divine floral aftershave a stark contrast against the smokiness of the entrance hall.

"Don't forget, I need the money by sundown," Gloria calls after him as he paces across the street. He waves a dismissive hand over his shoulder, his mid-length hair bouncing as he spins. My gaze follows his tight trousers until the crowds swallow him.

"He's another gay," Gloria says, pointing at him with her cigarette. "I attract 'em."

I look at her sideways. "How did you know I was gay?"

"I didn't. I meant as well as Eric." She looks me up and down. "Although it don't surprise me with the way you're dressed."

Maybe wearing tight jeans and a studded belt does not make me as incognito as I wanted. "Um, do you mind if I came in?"

She throws her cigarette by my feet and stubs it out, her knee clicking with each twist of the sole of her pink fluffy slippers. "Why?"

"To talk about Eric." My words hang in the air, as if there is no trust. I hate to beg, but I fall into it anyway. "Gloria, I need to know what he was like, I've travelled for miles, I'm hungry, thirsty, and in need of a cushioned seat."

Gloria's face brightens after a few seconds. "Give me twenty minutes. It's a shithole up there and the Doctor is coming over to drop off some supplies."

"The Doctor?"

"Dr Graham. Used to be my gynaecologist. He's retired now but we like to keep in touch. It's better now our meetings don't require my feet in the air and me being treated like Sooty." What starts as a chuckle rises into a piercing cackle, only stopping when she coughs on the tar being brought up from her lungs. She spits a globule of gunk into the gutter and straightens her jumper. "Sorry," she says. "Go keep yourself lively, grab yourself a coffee or summat."

The door slams, and the brass zero falls to the floor before rolling into the gutter. Despite her blunt approach to conversation, there's something about Gloria I like. I don't know what *it* is, but there is *something*. I put Eric's gift bag into my backpack and spray my armpits with deodorant to stop the sweat which already clings to the cotton of my Bowie t-shirt. Another rumble from my stomach sends me straight across to the café.

The bell inside the café chimes as I enter, the sound echoing off the walls. They're bare aside from two large, laminated menus hidden partially by strands of dying pot plants on a shelf. The menus are faded from years of sunlight, and they hang at odd angles where the tack has given up the fight. Unsurprisingly, I'm the only customer.

Roberto stands behind the counter with a long metal spatula raised in his hand, remnants of egg encrusted on its once shiny surface. Next to him, a younger, shorter girl with dirty blonde hair looks into the distance. They look like a modern-day, east-end equivalent of *American Gothic*.

"One latte and a bacon sandwich, please," I say, trying to sound chipper. My enthusiastic approach does not transfer across the keep-warm. The girl turns without speaking, grabbing a frying pan from the metallic hook above the hobs. Her 'over it' expression is one I've worn many times during shifts at Craig's.

"Normal milk or oat?" asks Roberto. His voice, like Gloria's, is estuarial and gravelly.

"Oat, please." I've always been a semi-skimmed, green-top kind of kid, and fear Soho has gentrified me already. After paying twice as much as I would back home, I take a seat at a square table by the window to keep a lookout over Gloria's. Groups of language students, all marching along with matching backpacks, block my view at regular intervals, but I manage to catch a glimpse of The Doctor handing a leather bag to Gloria.

As they stand chatting, the waitress slaps a well packed bacon sandwich on the table, along with a smorgasbord of condiments. I lift the lid of the bun and squirt a solid amount of ketchup onto the crispy bacon. It's so burnt I might need its dental records to identify it, exactly the way I like it. I devour the sandwich in record time, swiftly drinking half the coffee to wash it down. It tastes like heaven.

"Another?" asks Roberto, standing next to me and pointing to my cup. I give him an affirmative nod. When I turn back to look across the street, I'm shocked to find someone sat at my table. The boy with the cheekbones has appeared out of thin air, staring not into my eyes, but at my body.

"Hey. I'm Harri, nice to meet you." I offer a hand, but he doesn't flinch. The spitting of oil from behind the counter is providing the only sound, the atmosphere becoming immediately awkward. "I love Dylan, too."

"Dylan?"

I nod to his t-shirt. "Bob Dylan."

He looks at his chest. "Oh, yeah. *Ashes to Ashes*, right?"

"That was Bowie?"

"Bowie?"

I open my jacket slightly to show him my own top. It's not exactly the fairytale beginning to our relationship, but perhaps a work in progress is better. I could take him on dates and educate him on the Gospel according to Ziggy. We could lay in our bedroom on a warm Sunday afternoon, his head on my chest as we listen to the new vinyl's we've picked for each other from the record shops of nearby Berwick Street.

"Why are you here?" His voice is soft, but the words still appear tinged with a threat. His fingers drum on the table. Two taps, then three. "Who sent you?"

"I know Gloria."

"I've never seen you before. I don't trust you." He stands from his chair and his thigh collides with my shoulder as he passes.

"Wait!" I call, not wanting to lose my future dream weekend plans. He stands still, his right hand on the handle. "I was wondering, did you know Eric?"

Cheekbones releases his grip and moves back opposite. He pulls the seat out slowly and I gesture to show I'm more than happy for him to rejoin. "I did, yeah. Everyone knew Eric."

"I didn't. But he is — rather, was — my uncle. Although we never met." I fold my arms across my body and stare at the crumbs scattered across the tabletop. "Gloria emailed my sister a couple of days ago, trying to find us."

"You don't look like him."

Roberto slides a fresh coffee down, and I take a long sip to save me explaining this statement for a second time this morning. "What happened to Eric, if you don't mind me asking."

"He'd been on the decline for a while," Roberto says.

"Looked a lot older than his age," adds Cheekbones.

Roberto nods. "Was only late sixties. In daylight he could've been ten years older, though he spoke as if he were still in his twenties. Mentally he was. It happened last Monday. Was opening up here and Gloria ran across in a panic. Found him on the bathroom floor with a face covered in shaving foam. The ambulance was here within minutes of me starting CPR, but…" he tails off.

Cheekbones' hands are now tucked into his sleeve, his right hand over his mouth. Roberto rubs his back to comfort him, but he too is fighting off tears, swallowing regularly.

"I'm glad he wasn't alone," I say.

Roberto lets out a small chuckle. "Eric was never alone, believe me. He was a one-man party. Where he went, others followed. He nearly left us last year. Massive heart attack in the Lord Nelson halfway through a rendition of *I Will Survive*. Sounds morbid, but I think he'd have preferred to have gone out centre stage with a bang, every time."

"Did he sing often?" I ask.

"Every week." The words hang as Roberto stares down the street into central Soho. "The soul of this place has gone with 'im."

"Was he a good performer?" I crave for there to be someone else with creative flair in my family.

Roberto smiles and closes his eyes briefly. "Best cabaret act I've ever seen. Every week since the early eighties he did something around here. If a bar didn't have him or his friends performing then it was not a bar worth going to. They were the foundations of everything here today. Tough times though, very tough."

"Are his friends still here?"

"Who knows," he says, shrugging. "Most of the good ones upped and left when they thought they were getting too old for it. It wasn't exactly idyllic round here back then. Lot of nastiness to deal with. There were some horrible people for sure. Riots, graffiti, torching."

"Why? People only wanted to have fun, didn't they?"

"Look, um, sorry, what's your name?" Roberto asks.

"Harri."

"Look Harri, another time, yeah? I'm too busy for it all now. It was a different era was Soho in the eighties. The community is still on edge these days. You've seen the race riots and the transphobia in the news. We can't let history repeat itself."

I nod silently and look around at the empty café, understanding his want to be left alone. Part of me wants to dive deeper, but Roberto's and Cheekbones' sunken demeanour shows I can't. It's only been five days since Uncle Eric died after all, and it's clear the pain is still raw.

"Is Wilma about?" I say to Cheekbones as I stand and throw my backpack over my shoulder.

"Wilma?"

"Yeah. Is she in the flat?"

Cheekbones looks at me as if I'm stupid, his head tilting slightly to the right, and he scratches at his floppy black hair. "Eric *was* Wilma."

I sit back in the chair quickly, my bag knocking the ketchup to the floor, firing liquid across the tiles like a murder scene. "You mean Eric did drag?"

"Of course Eric did drag." He laughs sarcastically at my apparent stupidity. "Everyone knows Eric did drag."

"Wilma Cockburn, the Queen of Old Compton Street," calls Roberto from behind his counter.

I can't wait to tell Michelle about this. We used to have regular Drag Race watch-a-longs when I first moved into my flat, back before the boyfriends came and ruined everything. My mission has flipped on its head. I'm no longer here to find out about one person, but two.

A smile comes across Cheekbone's face as he watches two boys walk past hand in hand. His side profile is even more attractive than his front. His jawline is sharp, and his skin glows from the sunshine that's pouring in. He scratches his arm, and I catch a quick glimpse of a tattoo. I may not know his name, but I love the extra air of mystery this brings.

I stand a little too close to him and take a deep breath. "Do you maybe want to go for a drink sometime?"

He glances at me briefly, but turns back to the window without answering, just a gentle shrug of his shoulders. I guess not all ducks are ready to have their bollocks grabbed. Outside, I look along D'Arblay Street, wondering how life would've been for Eric when he was my age. There would be fewer nail bars in this quarter of Soho for starters.

Many of the buildings nearby have been repurposed as offices, but the small stained-glass panels in their upper windows and the faded murals on brickwork evidence their place in a more vibrant past.

I dart across the road, carefully avoiding the Deliveroo cyclists and taxis, and dodge the charity hunters with their clipboards who have gathered near Gloria's like alligators around a Serengeti watering hole. As I'm drip-fed information about

Eric, Soho's gravitational pull catches me and drags me towards its burning core, invisible feather boas tightening around my arms to lock me into place. I promised Michelle I wouldn't make any rash decisions, yet I fear it's too late to turn back.

Eric, and Wilma have departed, but they must be kept alive or Soho will slip ever further from its heyday. My brain blends the excitement and sadness of the moment, wanting to be part of the scene, but fearing I've arrived too late.

For now, The Queen of Old Compton Street has left the building.

The Queen is dead.

Long live the Queen.

3.

Take To The Streets

The communal hall inside Gloria's building is even dirtier than her doorstep. Each stair groans from underneath a frayed carpet as I follow her up to Flat 2. The once magnolia walls could do with a fresh coat to cover the scrapes, and scratches run all the way from top to bottom. The whole place is crying out for an air freshener to hide the scent of ash.

"Welcome to paradise," Gloria says, kicking the door open, the force causing fragments of wood to dislodge from the already splintered bottom corner.

The fumes of fresh paint on canvas which hit me like a cricket bat are comforting and reinforce coming here has been the correct thing to do. The flat resembles an art studio. More care has gone into the artworks leaning against the far wall than the upkeep of the main front room itself.

The curtains are heavy and drawn, but the tears in their fabric allow some light to illuminate a slice of dust hanging in the air. It's still and claustrophobic, like the atmosphere of a museum, as if the residents have got up and left, leaving behind only strange clues to their lives; a collection of mismatched furniture, a small desk covered with notepapers, decapitated Barbie dolls nailed to the wall. A shiver runs down my spine.

"Harri is an unusual name," Gloria says as she follows closely behind, kicking clutter out of her way with a swipe of her slippers.

"It's short for Harrison. The nurse who found me was a big Beatles fan."

"Why didn't she call you George, then?"

"I like it being a bit more unique."

"It must've been difficult for you," she says. "Be thankful you and your sister have those unique names. Made it easier for me to know when I'd found the right person."

I move my way around the room before the conversation starts resembling a therapy session. I didn't come all this way to unravel my past. It's the past of those who have lived *here* that I need to add meat to the bones of.

"How many people did you email?" I ask.

"Only about five. Your lot answered first. Thought it'd take me ages to find you, but I'm glad it didn't."

Along the mantelpiece, an array of dusty trinkets clutter the surface. I can't guess as to how old Gloria is, but the room reflects the elements of her personality I know so far. Slightly chaotic and hard to read. She clearly taps into the sentimental value of everything, but it's juxtaposed by being captured in a building that's breaking at its seams.

Mould is scattergunned down the walls, and the ceiling is dim with a nicotine hue. It makes the bright and bold art in front of me even more prominent. I move close to the most striking pieces; three large, square Pop Art style artworks hanging above the sealed fireplace. The words *TAKE TO THE STREETS* are emblazoned in a bright painted font in the centre of each, backed by slabs of primary colour base layers. From where I'm standing, the individual brush marks reflect a moment of time spent in creation.

"Don't touch them, they're still wet," says Gloria. She makes a heaving noise as she lowers herself into an armchair, its cushions moulded around her body. She rests her arm next to multiple coffee-ring stains which are embedded in the white leather material, the chair resembling a caffeinated Olympic flag.

"These are great. Simple, but great." I mean it too. I've always thought more is more, but the clarity of these works jumps from the canvas.

"Glad you like 'em. Eric weren't keen on Pop Art."

"Did he paint?"

She smirks. "Performing was all he did. Those are by Jack."

"Jack?"

"The kid with the arse you couldn't stop staring at."

Cheekbones. I nod, running the names Harri and Jack through my head, debating if they could be written together on a wedding invitation. I move away and take in some other pieces but keep getting drawn back to Jack's creativity. "How long have you lived here, Gloria?"

"Coming up to forty-five years now. Seems longer though. Problem with living in a twenty-four-hour city is you never get any peace and quiet."

A nearby police siren echoes through the room as she leans back and lights a cigarette, her eyes closed but tilted towards the ceiling. "It's gonna be strange here without him," she adds, gesturing towards the empty space at the right-hand end of the sofa.

During the brief silence of contemplation she brings on, I drop my bag onto a stack of fashion magazines and take a seat on a stool near to her. "What was Uncle Eric like?"

She opens her eyes and smiles, giving me a flash of her yellow teeth. "The best. Not sure what I'll do with the room I have here now. I don't want to hit seventy-five and be rattling around on my own, blending my food like an idiot. You would've liked Eric."

"Are we similar?"

"No, but he was likeable. He didn't have an enemy left within the M25. What did he leave you anyway?"

I take the carrier bag from my backpack and rip it open, releasing a puff of stale air. Inside there's a small purple headdress, like a fascinator, but homemade and as camp as Christmas. Glue is visible beneath the fake emeralds which run around the circumference of its rim.

Gloria leans forward in excitement. "Christ, I ain't seen that in years. Thought he got rid of it."

"What is it?"

"Wilma Cockburn's original crown."

I turn it in my hands before extending it with an outstretched arm. "You should keep it." It might be cheaply made, but the emotional value is much higher on Gloria's side than mine.

"Absolutely not. He made it clear, that bag was only for the eyes of a relative. I never knew exactly what he was planning, but despite everything, family was important to him. He regretted not reaching out to you and Daria a few years ago. He deprived himself of getting to know you both, and you both with him."

"Am I allowed to know what happened for them to fall out? Mum has never mentioned Eric before."

"It's not my place to reopen those wounds, Harri, I'm sorry. You'll find out eventually, I'm certain of that, but for now, it's your turn to take the crown."

There might be someone back home who could frame it for me. It'd brighten up the landlord-approved white walls of my bedroom, a splash of colour making them seem less clinical and depressing. Then again, would removing it from Soho be right? "Are you certain you don't want to keep it with the rest of his stuff?"

"Knowing my luck, if I kept it, he'd come back and haunt me."

"Would that be a bad thing?"

She lets out another small cackle. "Guess not. Wouldn't be as lonely I 'spose. Is there anything else in your bag?" I pull the sides open to show there's nothing left to reveal. "Well at least you have summat to remember him by."

The problem is, I don't. Yes, I have the crown, but I can't remember someone I never met. I don't have any tales of his time on the scene, no family stories from celebrations or days out. I've nothing but his cardboard regalia. In the right hands, this would be a treasured item, but to me it looks no more meaningful than the school projects I did whilst at Stonemouth Academy.

I rest the crown on my head, hoping to spark a connection. It fits snugly, and only a few of my ginger hairs get caught in the plastic gemstones.

"You look like a pillock," says Gloria from over her lenses. "Then again, so did he most of the time."

"When you emailed I thought Wilma was another flatmate."

"Would be cramped with three of us. Nah, Wilma was

the even more fun side of Eric. Him and the other queens used to be such a laugh together." She takes an extended drag and then props herself up slightly as she stubs it in the ashtray. "The Dragnificent Seven. Everyone knew 'em."

"I wish people liked me as much as that."

She gives me a glance. "I said they were well known. I didn't say everybody liked them. Most did though, to be fair. Where they went, the gays flocked. They were like a queer Henry the Hoover, sucking up any crowds within spitting distance."

"What were the other queens like?" Another cigarette comes out the box. "Do you always smoke so many cigarettes?"

"Do you always ask so many questions?" she replies without missing a beat. She strikes a match before tossing it aside into an empty mug.

"Sorry." I lean back on the stool until I'm resting against her bookshelf.

"It's alright. Jack's been on at me to try vaping instead, but he's still on these occasionally too, and surely this week I'm allowed to keep at least one vice. As for the drag lot, you missed out. Absolute riot every weekend with the five of them."

"Why were they called The Dragnificent Seven if there were only five of them?"

"That was part of the joke. They could've been huge stars, however times were different you see. We had to keep ourselves more underground. Out of sight, out of mind and all that. Even when they were at their peak, the demand from certain club owners for a bunch of flamboyant homosexuals weren't exactly sky high. Round here was alright, but less safe elsewhere."

Gloria tips the contents of her ashtray into the soil of a yucca plant in the corner, and then hands me a shot glass from the mantelpiece. I use my t-shirt to remove the layer of dust sitting at the bottom. She pulls two miniature bottles from down the side of her cushions and I hold out my glass as she pours shots of rum.

"To Eric," she says as she tips her head back and downs the content of hers.

"To Eric," I repeat. My throat burns immediately and I press my tongue against the roof of my mouth to stem the rising vomit in my throat. "What were Wilma's stage outfits like?" I croak.

"As if someone had dipped a mannequin in glue and dragged it through Barbara Cartland's wardrobe."

"Do you have any of them here?"

She sits back down. "Nah, he got rid of them all at a charity shop. Can't believe they accepted them as no one would wear some of those clothes during daylight. Might have a few pictures though if you're interested."

"Extremely." It'd be nice to put a face to both sides of his persona.

"There was usually someone with a camera at the big shows and the Pride marches. It wasn't as easy as it is these days with you kids and your mobile phones recording every second of your life through a screen. Back in those days, we lived our lives rather than document them.

"Bit hypocritical considering you have a mobile sticking out your pocket."

She tucks it out of view. "Touché. But you have it easy, believe you, me. I know how much kids like you can access with a quick swipe or tap. Phone sex in my day would require lubing up the receiver on my mother's old rotary whilst she was pottering around the garden."

Gloria lets out a groan as she heaves herself out the chair, stumbling past and opening a small door opposite to reveal a cupboard stacked with junk. A mop bucket, a game of Buckaroo, and multiple shoe boxes are tossed between her legs like a dog digging a hole. "Did you eat yet?" comes a now muffled voice.

"I had a bacon sandwich across the road," I reply.

"You definitely ain't blood related to our Eric then. He was the first vegan I knew. He used to joke the only flesh he liked was the thighs on show in the front row. Told me his diet would be good for his heart. I told him it wouldn't. I ain't happy at being proved right, of course."

I study Jack's artworks again, keeping my distance from the mutilated Barbies that are disrupting my thoughts. "I did ask for oat milk in my latte."

"Oh I don't care. Be thankful he ain't here or he'd rap

your knuckles. He was so vegan he wouldn't even come to Turkey with me last year." I laugh, but the look she gives around the door shows she isn't joking. "Was gonna get my tits done," she adds as she departs from view again.

Once she's deep in the closet, curiosity gets the better of me and I explore more of the flat, trying to get a sense of the environment in which Uncle Eric lived. Compared to the box front room, the kitchen could be straight from a new build. Going through the plastic strip curtain is like entering a portal to a different world.

The chrome fittings reflect the light from several exposed hanging bulbs, and the shelves brim with life from a selection of houseplants. There's even a mini herb garden in an old fruit box on the windowsill. The fridge is well stocked, and the smoke and emulsion fumes are replaced by the scent of the fresh linen drying on the metal fire escape outside an open back door.

"Mind if I make a coffee?" I call out into the void.

"No need to shout," Gloria replies as she reappears as if by magic, the curtain half draped over her shoulder. "There's some good instant in the top cupboard. Make me one while you're at it." She removes two mugs from a wooden tree and drops a bag of sugar next to me. "Three spoons, please."

The spoon inside is clumped with beige caramel, a build-up from not being washed. As the kettle rattles in its holder, Gloria stares out the window, looking down to the alleyways of Soho below.

"Did you find any photos?" I say, noticing she's empty-handed.

"No, which is weird. He always stored sentimental stuff in the glory hole. Used to be with his contact books, but they're in the front room so he must've moved the pictures. The only thing he's got in there is his old jazz mags." I turn my nose up, not wanting to think about them. "Was a big fan of Miles Davis," Gloria adds.

Waiting a little longer for the photos will do no harm. It gives me a reason to come back, and I can be much better prepared now I know the kind of person Gloria is. I was too quick to judge her upon my arrival this morning.

What I thought was rudeness when we first met across the doorway was caution on her side, built from years of living semi-nocturnally amongst the neon lighting and greasy paths.

She's softened quickly, and even gives off the odd hint of motherliness in brief flashes. For her, she needs someone like me around too. I may not be Eric, but I'm technically family so I can be an ear for her to chat to if required.

I sniff the milk in the fridge, and pour it into the mugs, passing one carefully to Gloria. She takes a sip and then grabs the sugar back out the cupboard. "Three spoons as in heaped spoons." Once fully glucosed, she drops the spoon to soak in a jam jar, also housing a ramshackle collection of old paintbrushes.

"Do you paint yourself?" I ask.

She nods whilst taking a drink. "Prefer painting other people though." There's her laugh again. "I'm taking part in an exhibition down Whitechapel way currently as it happens."

"How long is it on for? I'd love to come along. Being exhibited is a dream of mine."

"Only 'til Thursday. You can come for the press night this evening if you want? The Doctor dropped off some wristbands."

"Thanks, but I don't have anywhere to stay. Also, I've got a train booked back to Stonemouth."

She downs the rest of her drink. Mine is still too hot to sip. "Stay over if you want. You can have Eric's old room. He don't have use for it anymore."

There's no way I can spend a night in my dead uncle's bedroom. Based on the rest of the flat, there's only a fifty per cent chance the sheets have been changed since he woke up last. "Maybe another time."

Gloria is back looking out the window, occasionally leaning over and tearing some decaying leaves off the top of the mint plant sitting between her and the outside world.

"Did Eric still talk to his drag friends?"

"Nah. Best part of three decades since they were together. We used to discuss them, about what they're up to now, and he did make an attempt to find them. It's probably why the photos are missing. It's as if he knew his time was gonna be cut short."

"He had a heart attack last year, I heard."

She nods. "Amazing what a defib can do to your attitude. He didn't have much luck with his search as far as I'm aware. The only one we know for definite is up north somewhere. Manchester, I think."

I'd hate to lose track of my friends. Although I'm hardly with the biggest crowd of people, it's unthinkable we'll drift apart. Me and Michelle are attached at the hip most days, so I've no idea how we could go from something so strong to being virtual strangers. I look down to the small mews housing below, imagining how this area would've been back in the eighties.

How did Eric lose touch so badly with those closest to him? He was anything but introverted and they performed together for years. Them not being at his funeral doesn't sit right.

"Gloria, can I try and find the other members of the group? If he'd have wanted me to."

She turns to me slowly. "Are you sure? Don't want you getting yourself disappointed if nothing comes from it."

"It'd be worth a shot."

"Wait here."

I stay in the kitchen, swilling the coffee around in my mug whilst listening to her rummage around the front room, stopping when she shouts. "There ain't a book on top of the fridge is there?" I stand on a chair and move the junk mail, but there's nothing. A look of confusion spreads over her face. "He used to have two books. Can only find the one. Even if they no longer talked, they deserve to know he's kicked it."

"Should I invite them to the funeral?"

Gloria shrugs. "Some might come. Some will wanna make sure he's dead this time."

"Bit morbid," I reply.

"It's the truth," replies Gloria. "Look, I want you to take this. This is one of Eric's contact books. There's another somewhere with a lot more in but he's probably stashed it away in a cubby hole with his poppers and whips."

I hope she's joking. I take the book from her and flick through the first few pages. The names which jump out prove this will be vital. There can't be many people called Ivana Saltyrim or Princess Thigh-Ana who weren't part of his crowd. Sadly, Eric's writing stops abruptly halfway through after only three queens have been named. "This will be a great help, thank you."

"Don't get too excited. There ain't much to go on. Also, it all went downhill between the queens a while ago, and even if you do find the others, they might not want to get involved. They've all moved on, and if that's what they want, you're gonna have to respect it."

This reality check is what I need. I tend to get involved in some projects for far longer than is healthy and chasing the dream of finding Eric's fellow queens might cause more harm than good if I'm not careful. "You said there was someone up north?"

"Thigh-Ana. Ivana was near the Docklands at one point, too." She stands right in front of me and holds my wrists with cold hands. "After what happened between us all, I'll keep my distance, just in case. As I say, Eric did some of his own investigating, but not sure how far he got. I reckon he was doing more behind my back than he let on. Now, are you sure you want to commit?"

"I will commit, Kermit," I reply, immediately hating myself for saying it. "I need a purpose in life, and this could be it."

"Good. Keep me updated, alright. You're welcome here anytime, as long as you give me a heads up first." Gloria scratches at her arms and moves across the flat with a nervous energy. "I best get a shifty on. Gotta be at the gallery to do some setting up by three. I've a load of errands to finish off once Jack's been back. Sure you don't wanna come with us?"

I do, but time is against me. "Next time, thanks. If I find anything, I'll email you. If you find the photos, can you send them across?"

"I promise, scouts honour," Gloria says, giving me a mock salute, before she throws items into an oversized handbag. “Finish your coffee while I get ready. Now, I ain’t saying I’m gonna get involved, but if you’re looking for somewhere to start your journey, try the Lord Nelson.”

I put the contact book in my bag as she purses her mouth in front of a small pocket mirror, a fresh layer of fiery lipstick being briskly applied. As she leaves the room, I sit back on the stool, staring once again at Jack’s art.

These people belong in a completely different world to the one I’m used to, and my God do I want to be a part of it.

4.

Convergence

The Soho sunshine is bright and sobering when compared to Gloria's dim flat. I'm no longer hungry, but my stomach cramps from developing nerves. I doubt the Lord Nelson is open yet, judging by the other closed pub opposite. Even at a quarter to eleven, Gloria's 'twenty-four-hour city' claim appears not to be entirely accurate. It's far too early for a pint anyway, which is a shame as having one would calm me a little. I grip onto the straps of my backpack, trying to steady myself.

Berwick Street is an obstacle course of bollards and parked delivery bikes. Office workers dart with bags of pastries, and tables outside independent coffee shops slow my progress further as I weave my way to Old Compton Street. Near the food market halfway down, a strong wave of déjà vu bounces through me. I know I've never been here before, but the architecture and high rises seem familiar and comforting.

"Sample?" comes the voice of an elderly man to my right, his face leathered from exposure to the sun. He holds out a large tray containing bite-size squares of baklava. I thank him as I take one, discarding it in the cart of a passing street cleaner. Now would be an inconvenient time for my pistachio allergy to make an appearance.

I rifle through my pocket for some loose change and swap it for a large orange. The shot of Vitamin C will do my immune system the world of good. As I peel down a narrow alleyway, I'm blocked by a clipboard being waved in front of my nose.

"Wanna help stop knife crime?" asks a small kid in a blue windbreaker. Two further bluecoats stand behind me wielding clipboards and I become a prisoner in a pubescent prison.

"'scuse me." I push through them, causing one to stumble over some scaffolding and land near a newsagent's window.

"It's two quid a month," says lead bluecoat. He hits me on the arm with the clipboard. It's the same line they always use, but two pounds is often all I have to my name. His friend brushes himself down and approaches me again, but I keep my head down until I'm spat out into Soho proper.

A sex shop across the cobbled street is open and a few men lurk in the shadows browsing. I never knew people dared to visit those shops during daylight, but I guess it's my small-town modesty rising to the surface. Maybe getting a baguette, bag of crisps, and a butt plug is no rarer than me picking up a Tesco meal deal in Stonemouth.

Old Compton Street is a captivating place. It's vibrant, atmospheric, alive. The air full of laughter, locals relaxed in each other's company. Many gay couples pass hand in hand, stopping to peruse menus. Compared to home, it's a parallel universe. I can't recall seeing any queer couples holding hands there. I never dared hold Ben or Kristian's with Mum on the prowl.

Everything is freer here, not stifling and suffocating. Gloria and Eric made an excellent choice in making this place their base. Sadly, all this doesn't make the Lord Nelson any more open when I find myself on the wrong side of its locked doors. It's small and unassuming from the outside, narrow, but reaching four storeys high. A large rainbow flag drifts quietly in the morning breeze above my head, the edges torn after being exposed to the elements for many seasons.

The Oxford blue front of the establishment is hiding what looks to be a long and thin venue inside. I push my face to its plate windows, the glass cool against the tip of my nose. All lights are off and towels drape over the beer pumps like hooded figures. The stools are upturned on a stage at the back, and the fruit machine facing the entrance is dead. The tranquillity is in contrast to the bustling street.

For a place which allegedly accommodated raucous parties with The Dragnificent Seven, it's underwhelming. It should be grander, a bat signal calling out to any homosexual within a ten-mile radius. It's early, so perhaps it all changes when the sun goes down. Despite the teen charity muggers roughing me up, I regret not booking a later train home so I can experience Soho by night.

For now, there's nothing I can do. I'd sit on the floor and contemplate my next move if the ground weren't sticky. I widen my stance, keeping my Docs away from the rainbow-coloured grease which snakes from a pile of bin bags. The thick waste liquid oozes across the pavement, dripping into a partly blocked drain. Flies buzz around my head, their sound mimicking the needles of the tattoo shops. As I stare inside the Lord Nelson, hoping it will come to life, the clack of heeled ankle boots approach to my left, coming to a halt a couple of metres away.

"We can't grab that drink then. No one will be here for at least another hour," comes a familiar voice.

Jack echoes my stance, his head pressed against the glass, hands tucked into the back pockets of his jeans. His cheekbones catch the sun, and his skin is unblemished. No sweat is sticking his hair to his forehead like mine. I pull up the front of my t-shirt to hide the shaving rashes flaring around my collar line. I knew I shouldn't have used an old razor to remove my patchy stubble this morning. Then again, I never expected to meet someone like Jack.

"Gloria said you were heading to an art show," I say.

"I am." He gives me the hottest side-eye without his head losing contact with the window and stares at my chest. I only thought people this attractive existed on the discovery section of Instagram. As he scratches the back of his head, his low-necked t-shirt reveals a hint of collarbone. "Gloria told me what you're up to."

"Well it isn't going well so far," I reply, looking again into the empty pub.

"Can't say I'm shocked."

The silence is heavy and the way he keeps eyeing me

isn't welcoming. The adrenaline builds in my legs, ready to move quickly if the situation becomes unbearable.

"I dunno if I'd have gone in if this place was open anyway," I say eventually. "Never been to a proper gay bar before, especially on my own."

"As in, not a gay bar in London, or as in never ever?" He furrows his eyebrows as if trying to figure me out.

"We don't have them in Stonemouth. Well, we have one, but it's underground and full of big mirrors. It's only a gay bar by name anyway. Usually full of drunken hen parties."

"That's the worst," Jack says. He takes out some gum but doesn't offer me any. "Happens round here from time to time, but luckily not as bad as it was."

"How long have you been coming out in Soho?"

He chews for a few seconds in contemplation. "About six years now but been around the area for longer. I look younger than I am and the bouncers were too wise to let me sneak in underage. Anyway, I'm gonna get a coffee."

I stand straight. Coffee will help me focus.

"I'll see you around."

His flat delivery sounds more of a threat than an invite. I can't let it go. I can't let *him* go. I follow a step behind as he jumps off the kerb in front of a bike. The rider slams on his squealing brakes. As the cyclist remonstrates, Jack ignores him and continues towards the café.

"I'm Harri, by the way," I say to his back.

"You told me that already," he replies over his shoulder. "Gloria said it's cos of George Harrison, right?" He opens the door of a small café but lets it swing back in my face. I remain outside as he laughs in conversation with the barista, clicking his fingers constantly. This environment is more natural to him, unlike for an outsider like me.

As I stare, my chest tightens with the realisation I've developed a mild fascination. I can't afford to get hurt by another boy this soon after Kristian, and especially one I know barely anything about. His dismissive demeanour shows he doesn't care for me in the same way. He's only using me as a tool to kill time, or act as a spy for Gloria. I attempt to appear nonchalant as he steps back onto the street.

"Oat milk latte?" He sits next to me on the windowsill.

I smile and take the recyclable cup from him, swapping it between hands to stop it burning my skin. "So you were paying attention in Roberto's, then?"

He doesn't reply, instead knocking back one of two espressos. I've never been into non-alcoholic espressos myself. Coffee should be for enjoyment, and the pleasure shouldn't be completed in two seconds and one gulp. It's the same with alcoholic drinks (with the exception of Tequila Rosé – drinking acidic milkshake has to be done as quickly as possible).

"You intrigue me," Jack says, shuffling a little away. "Why do you want to find the drag queens?"

"It's what Eric wanted," I reply.

"You won't succeed, y'know." Someday, someone will have belief in me, but Jack's lack of eye contact proves it won't be him. "Maybe you should forget the whole thing."

"Why? I could be on the right track."

"You're already too many steps behind." He downs his second drink. "How many times have you been to Soho?"

"This is my first time. Doesn't mean I can't help though. I'd love to know why you think I can't do this."

Jack crushes the cups in his hand, pulling apart the sides and allowing coffee dregs to drip to the floor. "When Gloria said she wanted to reach out to Eric's family, I was expecting someone different to come."

"In what way?"

He shrugs. "Older, I guess. Everyone in my world is older. I suppose it comes with the territory when you join a collective of artists who're at retirement age. It's hardly a youth club."

"Well, I can't change when I was born. I'm determined though."

"So what's your plan?" he asks. "Sit here and hope they walk past?"

"I'll figure it out. I'll write to the ones I know first."

"Eric already did that, Harri. Eric did that and failed." His voice is curt, the syllables sharp.

"He's dead. Things are different now," I snap.

"And that's why you should keep your distance. Give the people who cared for him time to grieve. This is real life, not some game."

I remain on the ledge as Jack types on his phone. A therapist would explain my anger at his lack of belief stems from the rejection in my early life, but the helplessness bites each time someone dismisses me as not good enough. It's as if I'm trying to run through mud to escape the barriers I've caged myself in.

The attraction evident moments ago has faded. I don't do the *bad boy* schtick. "Where are you off to?" I ask as he steps off the pavement.

"To see Mark."

"Who?"

"See. One step behind. He owns the Nelson."

"You mean you know him?" I chase after Jack, waving apologetically to a taxi driver as I almost slide across his bonnet. Jack buzzes on a door between the pub and a trendy Japanese restaurant. One thing for certain is you'd never starve here.

"Hullo?" comes a jaded voice on the intercom.

"It's Jack." Immediately, the latch clicks open and the door becomes ajar. Jack stops before entering. "What do you want from me?" he says, looking at my shoes.

"Can I come?"

Jack smirks and pushes the door wide. "See you around, Harri."

This is all pointless. Michelle was right. This is not life-changing. It was me living in hope that something would stifle the relentless circular boredom of home, but is this reality a valuable substitute? I don't know what I've done to make Jack see me as enemy number one, and no one here knows me. I'm nothing but an extra in everyone else's play.

Old Compton Street has a continental vibe, albeit one without an architecturally stylish square to cast your eyes over. The outside seating areas are mostly full. I'd join them, but the eyes of everyone nearby appear to be fixed on me as if I'm a time traveller, clearly out of place in their world. I quicken my step, trying to escape their gaze.

This is not my natural habitat. Maybe an earlier train home is required.

As I check out a selection of pasta on display in a small Italian delicatessen, I'm nudged in the back. I spin around to find the three blue coats stood near me. "I promise I don't have any money, sorry."

The largest of the group moves to the front and stands far too close for comfort, my eyes watering from his powerful Lynx odour.

"Gonna push us over again?" he says aggressively.

"If you do, I know someone who can mess you up," says the dark-haired boy at the rear.

I brush them off and seek solace in a compact sandwich shop on the southern side of the road. It's busier than Craig's place, and the art on the walls is bespoke, not picked on a whim from a Cash 'n' Carry purely because it has a coffee bean on it. Tall fridges hum as they chill a well-stocked sandwich selection, and carrot and lemon cakes sit proudly on the counter, perched under glass domes.

The teen boy behind the counter is attractive, with bright hazel eyes and a floral tattoo on his defined biceps, half hidden beneath a fitted black polo. Any tingles forming slowly burst and fade when I spot Kristian on his name badge.

I ignore Eric's veganism as I bite into my overpriced chicken mayo baguette, having taken a seat on a tall, plastic stool looking onto the Lord Nelson. The meat is rubbery, but the food isn't the most important aspect of this stakeout. Jack will have to emerge eventually. When he does, I'll be ready to stalk him. If he's tracking me, then it's time to play him at his own game.

"Anyone sitting here?" A man stands beside me. He's dressed in a waistcoat and smart trousers, a flat cap covering his greying hair. I haven't ever seen someone wear a kravatte unironically in real life before. I nudge the stool, and he sits, picking the tomato from his toastie. His breathing is heavy, interspersed with a clearing of his throat between each bite.

This is definitely a lost cause I type, firing off the message to Daria. She reacts with a sad faced emoji, and then goes back offline.

"Why so glum?" says the man, wiping his tanned, wrinkled face with a napkin as the overhead light glints off his nose ring.

"I'm okay," I reply.

"So what makes it a lost cause?" I store my phone in my backpack, angry at the invasion of privacy. "Date gone wrong?"

"I'm fine, I promise."

He raises his eyebrows and slides his plate away, before leaning forward on his elbows, his face resting on steepled fingers as he studies me. His fingernails are rough, dirt lodged under most.

It's only Jack still being with Mark making me stay. I need to shut out the distractions around me. I'm determined to prove Jack wrong. If that means getting the creeps from someone for five minutes then so be it. I drink my juice slowly, trying to ignore his presence.

Michelle was right. My plan is wafer thin and it's already been torn to shreds. All I have from my time in London is a tattered notebook with the contact details for a few of Eric's friends. It's a start, but there's no guarantee they're correct. Once I've broken free from Soho I'll make it my first mission to write to them. So what if Eric tried this approach? So what if he failed? This time it could be different. His death will help twist their bracelet-laden arms.

"I've not seen you around here before," the man says, now further into my personal space. His breath smells of parmesan and bits of rocket lodge between his surprisingly immaculate teeth.

"I'm visiting friends," I reply, staring at my drink.

"Who?"

"You wouldn't know them," I reply.

"Try me. I've been here since the eighties."

I look at him, and he has a half-smile on his face. "Do you know The Dragnificent Seven?" It's worth a shot.

"Of course."

"Do you know where they are now?"

He leans back, moistening a finger and using it to dab at the crumbs on his plate. "There's one up east."

"Docklands?"

He looks at me with his head cocked. "That's right. Owns a pub in Limehouse I believe."

"Do you know which?"

"The Dog and Bucket. Why do you wanna know about them?"

"I'm writing a history on gay rights in Soho," I reply, surprising myself with how easy the lie comes. "I know they were a big part of this area so I'd love to find them."

"I wouldn't bother. Most people from those days have gone. Your text was right. It is a lost cause."

"Thanks for the tip," I say, scraping the seat back.

"No need to run off. We can talk about something else instead."

I'm sweating again. The relaxed atmosphere of Soho is a mask for its confrontational undertones. I look towards Kristian as he glides across the floor behind the counter with ease, not flustered as the queue mounts.

"I enjoy modern art too," the man says, and I snap back into his net. His blue eyes have a sparkle attempting to pull me in like a whirlpool, used many times before to get his own way, no doubt. His voice sinks into a whisper. "I've some nice pieces in my flat if you would like to take a look sometime?"

There's nothing I want less than to go to this stranger's lodgings. "I don't know anything about art."

"*Convergence*."

I sigh. "What?"

"Your phone. You have *Convergence* as your wallpaper. People who don't like Pollock don't have his art as a background. I'm disappointed you went with that one, though. *Mural* is much more appealing. A bit more uniform, if such a thing could be said about Pollock's work."

I've been caught out, but it doesn't make a trip to his flat any more realistic.

"Magento. Pleasure to meet you. If you need any inroads for your art, ask for me."

"Ask where?"

"Anywhere." He gives me wink which sends a shiver down my spine. I need a proverbial bell to save me, and thankfully, it comes just in time. Jack is back on the street. He leans casually against the soot-coloured wall and flicks through a small book of papers.

"Nice kid," says Magento, nodding in his direction.

"I barely know him."

"He's always getting attention. Gorgeous bone structure. He moved into the same building as a friend of mine recently, so I am seeing a lot of him."

"Is it a big house?"

The man tilts his head. "Bedsits above a massage parlour."

Jack sucks on a vape and blows a spiralling cloud to the sky. When he spots me, he quickly looks the other way. He takes another drag and lets out a visible sigh before heading to the café. He enters with some force, causing the door to bounce off the spring on the skirting board.

"Alright, Mags?" Jack says as he stands between us. "You're not trying to fuck Harri now, are you?"

Magento raises his palms. "We were talking about art."

"Did he invite you to his flat?" Jack asks me.

"Wait, you two aren't…" he tails off, waving a finger between us.

Jack's face contorts with disgust. "You know I don't date."

The beat of my heartache taps my eardrums.

"I didn't think you did friends, either," Magento says, pointing at me.

"We're acquaintances, not friends," Jack replies.

"Can we go?" I ask. Magento is making my skin crawl, a thousand invisible cockroaches clambering up my body. I scratch at my arms but it doesn't help. Jack nods his head and I stand swiftly. Magento gives me a final grin as I dart out, a grin that I won't wish to remember.

Jack is already walking away and I half-jog to catch up. "Where are we going?"

He doesn't stop but calls over his shoulder. "*I'm* going to Gloria's."

"Magento told me Ivana works in a pub."

"The Dog and Bucket. I know."

"How do you know?"

He strides forward again and my left calf burns as I keep up, the pain shooting down into my ankle. Jack slaloms through tourists with ease, leaving me to fall further behind as I swim against the tide.

"Are you always like this?" My voice is filling with an anger usually only reserved for Craig.

"You can talk," he replies, finally turning. He holds his hands to his cheeks as he looks skywards. A vein is pulsing on his left temple. "You're like an annoying puppy, biting at my ankles and not leaving me alone."

"I want answers, Jack. I need them, actually. It's okay for you. Everything is fine in your world with your art and your connections. Eric was my uncle after all."

"You didn't give a shit about him when he was alive!"

"I would've if I could've. Only finding out about him yesterday doesn't mean I don't have a right to be part of all this."

"All what?" Jack says, raising his voice. "Why do you care about his friends? He didn't bother to try and find them until it was too late. They lost touch for a reason. When you meet the queens you might wish you never had."

"Maybe I'll go to Limehouse and see Ivana now."

Jack leans against the wall of a theatre and runs his hands through his hair as he holds the papers between his closed knees. He clicks his fingers again, and the rhythmic pattern builds in speed. Two clicks, followed by three. Over and over. He only stops when he speaks. "Listen to me Harri, why can't you realise you might not be the first to have tried helping Eric get the band together? Before he died, I tried too."

"And what happened?"

"Nothing. No letters were answered or phone calls returned. To them, The Dragnificent Seven is the past, and that's where they want it to stay."

"Give me a chance," I plead.

"Pass me your phone." I do as he says, like a puppy. I hate myself for being such a sap. "My number is in there. Prank me so I can have yours. Let me know when you've proved me wrong." A small laugh is audible as an undercurrent to the flow of his words.

"What if I find them? Would you want to be involved?"

He sucks on his vape slowly, playing with the silver chain around his neck with his free hand as he stares intently at another gay bar opposite. He kicks the wall gently with the sole of his shoe.

"I'll text you when I have something," I say.

"*If*." He may be trying to talk me out of finding the queens, but he's smiling slightly. I don't care about what he says, his expression shows he can't let The Dragnificent Seven go so easily.

"I'm off to Gloria's. See you around," he says. He walks again, heading towards a small, square park. This time I let him go. I've done my chasing. If he isn't ready to admit he's interested in continuing the hunt, then that's his problem, not mine.

I find his number in my phone. To my surprise, he's added a heart emoji after his name. I fire across a smiley face and stare down the street as he disappears from sight.

I cannot wait to prove him wrong.

5.

Cottage Pie

Seven days and no queens. After the whirlwind of London last weekend, I strapped myself in for an onslaught of information. Instead, my phone has been quieter than usual. I've been constantly checking my letterbox for a reply to the four letters I posted last Sunday, but that remains barren.

The posties are the latest people to get irritated by me taking on this challenge. They talk dismissively every time they can't escape my building before I ask about my post. I check my email inbox again now; nothing except the usual spam. Even if a drag queen told me to piss off it'd at least confirm my letters had arrived.

Contact with Jack has also been a desert of tumbleweeds, anxiety hitting as I wait for his reply to my many messages. Even my dreams have been gate-crashed by caricatures of our last interaction. My messages haven't all been about Eric either, with my questions about his exhibition also bringing silence.

The large box of blue towels is caving a little under my weight as I blow the surface of another bland, out-of-date, chicken and sweetcorn cup-a-soup in the café staff room. The almond croissant I've taken from the condemned box is stale, and the pastry flakes onto the floor. Craig wanting me to bin everything left over makes sense now. The pastry is dusty and the almond paste coats my teeth with an oily film. Rain taps at the window on my left, the April showers delayed by a month, but they're soon drowned out by a flushing toilet.

"Need you downstairs," grunts Craig as he exits the solitary toilet cubicle, doing up his belt and revealing an overhanging gut beneath his stained work shirt. "Heaving down there today."

"I'm on break for another five," I tell him, focussing my attention on the free TV magazine from his tabloid. The hand dryer drowns out my words, but I don't care enough to repeat myself. My enthusiasm for working here has declined to such a state I could happily slip out, never to darken the doorway again.

Craig glares at me as he pulls a tray of mini quiches from the cooling racks before disappearing. I only took this role, on Michelle's advice, as a way of helping save for further education alongside paying my rent. With no pay rise in the eight months I've been here, and my college dreams on hold, why should I push myself more than required? The final written warning hangs over me like a dark cloud, but even this does not spur me to give further commitment.

As I invest myself in the terrestrial movie listings, the peace of the stockroom is broken again, this time by stomping footsteps rising up the staircase. Michelle's heavy breath is audible well before she comes into view. Beaded sweat drips down her forehead, exposed from her scraped back hair, and she's biting at her lip piercing.

"You alright?" I ask as she stumbles towards me with red cheeks. She pulls up her sleeves and sits beside me, the box beneath now at breaking point.

"Your mum's downstairs and she knows."

My face remains expressionless. "About me being on the verge of a sacking or because of the disgrace I made of myself in The Old Fire Station last night?" Another solid consumption of coffee tequilas led to a stumble off the stage, the resulting kerfuffle seeing me banned for a week.

Michelle sighs. "She asked why you were going to London last week."

"London? What did you tell her?"

"I played dumb, as promised. I tried to tell her you were busy doing stocktake to give you some time, but she's refusing to leave."

"How do I get out of this one?"

"Blag your way through it, I guess. She can't prove anything." She removes her apron, using it to dry her face before throwing it towards the laundry bin across the room. It clatters against the metal side and drops to the floor.

"Won't you need that?"

"Nope. It's four. Only you and him on close today."

"Don't fancy staying to help, do you?"

"Becki is doing my roots after I'm done here and then I have to get to the scout hut for my weekly weigh-in. Hoping to get my two-stone certificate tonight. Might get a chippy tea to celebrate."

I rest my head on her shoulder. "You're smashing it."

"I'd murder for a doughnut."

"I've got some here to bin if you're desperate." She sticks up her middle finger. "Can I come with you? I can't stand this place."

"Becki is doing my roots after I'm done here, and then I have to get to the scout hut for Brown Owl duties. It's Baking Badge night too, so dinner will be a pile of shite scones."

I rest my head on her shoulder. "I've got a box of scones here if you wanna have them. Can't be any worse.' She sticks up her middle finger. "Can I come with you? I can't stand this place."

"You know you can't. Anyway, you've only got two hours left. Staying up here won't make the situation with your mum any easier." She stands and fumbles for her locker key. "At least the café is full of tourists - if anything does kick off, no one can shout at you."

Reluctantly, I leave Michelle as she changes into her lightest pair of shoes and descend the spiral staircase leading to the prep area. I peer through the porthole window at Mum as she waits at the end of the counter. Her face is painted with anger under her newly re-dyed hair, her fingers drumming the glass countertop at 120bpm. I take a deep breath and push through the swing door.

"Hey, Mum." I'm casual, hoping to calm her. She doesn't answer, instead pulling out a chair at a table in the corner and throwing her shopping bags on to the neighbouring seat. My shoulders slump. "Won't be a sec, Craig."

Craig virtually has steam coming out his ears and his face is bright red from his chin all the way to his receding hairline. He's making a mess on the stainless-steel table as he fights to keep up with orders. "I could *really* do with you pulling your finger out, son."

All this is his fault for starting a click and collect service. I said last month it wouldn't work but now is not the best time to gloat. Despite his protests, I slide out from behind the counter. Mum is staring at me from the other side of the queue, eyes fixed as I walk across and slide into the seat.

"Nice to see you," I say.

"What were you doing in London last week?" she snaps.

"At an art show in Whitechapel, looking at the history of Pop Art."

She looks back suspiciously. "That's what Michelle said too, word for word."

"That's because it's true," I lie.

Over the past six years I've become a master at lying to Mum. Her poor grasp of technology means I can back up any claims with fake photographic evidence. She doesn't need to know the photos could've been taken at a different time or downloaded from *Pinterest*. The ones I snapped of Jack's art in Gloria's flat will be vital.

"I received a letter this morning," Mum says, leaning forward as if this is a police interrogation. "What does the name Dai White mean to you?"

A get out of jail free card. My shoulders relax, and the vacuum-like pressure in my head dissipates. "I can promise you, one hundred per cent, hand on heart, I've never heard Dai's name in my life."

"Tell me the truth, Harrison." Her eyes are wide as if a wolf hunting prey.

"Scouts honour," I reply, holding my palms up. "I've never met anyone called Dai."

She looks at me through narrow eyes, her left fist clenching at having not caught me out. Dai White was not listed in Eric's contact book.

"Is there anything else you wanted? I've got work to do." I stand and put my apron string over my head.

"Sit."

I take out a cloth and wipe the sugar debris from the wooden tabletop and lower myself back down.

"If Dai White does contact you, you need to let me know, okay? He's a nasty piece of work."

"I will. Thanks for the warning. Who is he anyway?"

Her face softens a little, although her mascara is now caking the crow feet corners of her eyes. "He's a friend of the family from a while back. Caused a lot of harm to your dad and me back in the day. I thought we had heard the last of him, but then out the blue, whose letter should I open at six o'clock this morning?"

"What did he want?"

"To tell me to stop whatever it is I'm apparently doing. He wants to reawaken old family wounds. He said I've sent you to spy on him." She looks off into the distance over my shoulder. "He told me you'd been sniffing around Limehouse last weekend, hassling him about someone we once knew."

Even now she can't bring herself to mention Eric's name. "Whitechapel Road was as far east as I went."

"Promise?"

I nod. She offers me a square of Dairy Milk from her pocket, and I stick it between my molars and gum. "What did happen between you and this Dai?"

"Not now, Harrison, okay? It's all water under the bridge."

"Doesn't seem that way. There's something you're hiding from me."

It's Mum who's now uncomfortable. She bites at a hang nail on the edge of her new veneers, resting an elbow on her other arm. "He said some things which carried weight, like he could be telling the truth."

Dai White is connected to Eric, but how? My immediate thought is Roberto. I trusted him. He wouldn't grass me up when all I wanted was to get to know my family, would he? Whoever he is, Mum is being too reluctant to share her secrets. Seeing her uncomfortable is spurring me to dig deeper.

"I dunno how I can stay away from someone if I dunno who they are. We don't have connections with London as far as I know."

"Look, Harrison, it's complicated okay. Everyone has a past, and that's where it will stay." She pulls her coat tightly over her cleaning uniform and lifts her umbrella from the porcelain stand. "We've a nice life together, us lot, don't we. Let's focus on that. We've all come a long way."

"I don't understand why you're being so secretive. It must've been important enough for you to storm over here and accuse me of being a liar."

She lets out a sigh. "I apologise, okay. If you receive anything from Dai, come to me immediately. Being involved with him and being involved with this family are two mutually exclusive things."

I remain silent. Her desire to leave quickly shows I have her on the ropes, yet I don't have the skill or information to deliver a final body shot to get to the truth. I could ask about Eric outright, but this situation requires a more tactful approach. Something is in motion and it can't be stopped.

Mum's shadiness has made my passion to find the drag queens rise to the next level. I need to reveal my own family's past and only those in the capital can help me do it. There's clearly a treasure chest of secrets which the queens have the key to.

Mum slips into the downpour, her umbrella springing wide. "I'm cooking my famous cottage pie tonight if you're free. Nothing special, just something warming. Come and catch up. It's lonely being in the house on my own."

She waves over her shoulder as she jogs slowly towards the bus stop in The Square, water from the puddles splashing up her laddered tights. Electricity fires through my nervous system, and I can't wait to make my next move.

By putting my head down to focus on the remainder of my workload, I was back in Craig's good books, and it wasn't even 6pm by the time I arrived home. Callum had been festering on the couch, grunting a hello as he ploughed through a kebab. It resembled roadkill and smelled twice as bad.

Dirty plates and cups filled the sink, and when a random girl came out of the bathroom halfway through yanking her underwear over her thighs, my mind was made up. I couldn't spend another evening in that place. Not tonight.

The buzzer to Gloria and Eric's flat is answered on the second ring despite it being so late. I'm in desperate need of a towel, my t-shirt damp and sticking to my torso. The rain on my hair is running into my ears and the sound of Soho is washed away, as if I'm submerging myself from the questions and cottage pies of home. The notes I hastily made on the train are likely smudged and indecipherable.

Lights from nearby bars reflect their neon glow from the puddles forming in the potholes peppering the street. I crouch in the flat entrance as groups of well-oiled revellers stagger past. Those who pay me attention do so only with a quick disparaging glance. I'm not dressed smartly and full of gusto like them, instead cowering, craving a hairdryer and a charger for my phone.

A metallic crash comes from inside the entrance hall, and above the noise of the few passing cars, I pick out the odd swear word being muttered in Cockney. After hearing someone (or something) being told to fuck off, the door opens and Gloria stands before me.

Her hair is in rollers, and her fake polyester kimono glints from the light of her trademark cigarette. She gives it one final inhale before it spirals past me, fizzing to its death in the gutter. "Could've given me more warning," she says in the welcoming way I'm becoming accustomed to.

"Any chance of a cuppa?" I reply, beaming widely. She nods her head towards the stairs. I wipe my shoes around the junk mail on the coarse mat and manoeuvre my way past the buckled bicycle laying in the alcove. "I was gonna come tomorrow morning, but my flat was disgusting."

"Must be bad if you prefer this place."

The water pooled inside my Docs makes each step on the stairs sodden. The front room is bare now the bright artworks are no longer on display. It's claustrophobic without them. The Barbies remain nailed above the fireplace, like a Toys R Us crucifixion, and one has the addition of a dart sticking out of its arsehole.

Gloria shuffles through the room, throwing a towel at me as she enters the kitchen. "I've done up the spare bed for you. There's softer towels on the dresser and some spare hangers in the wardrobe. Hairdryer is in the top drawer. Help yourself to whatever you need. It ain't the Ritz but it's better than a kick in the bollocks, ain't it."

"Cheers." The click of the kettle coming to life echoes off the kitchen tiles and I poke my head through the plastic curtain. "Um, where's the bathroom? Sorry."

"Down the hallway. Your room is on the far right. I ain't got much food in but we can get some chips or summat if you're hungry. Failing that, I've got some cheese. Might have to scrape the mould off first."

"I'm fine on both counts, thank you."

The door to Eric's old room digs into a plush blue carpet as I force it open for the first time. The baby pink paint is broken up with large film posters, the characters from *Priscilla* and *Little Miss Sunshine* forming a crowd around me. I straighten the frames so they sit level, brushing the dust from my fingers on the new cotton bedsheets.

I hang my wet clothes along the top of the warm radiator, thankful my spares remained dry inside the carrier bag I tied them in. The window's heavy wooden frame judders as I pull it open, and the noise of a helicopter chuttering in the low clouds fills the room, its searchlight pushing through the drizzle.

I sit in front of the dresser and pick up the towels from the surface, brushing away the powder escaping from the half-used pots of blusher and eyeshadow underneath. The brushes laying at their side are mushroomed, positioned exactly where Eric had left them.

The mirror has a large crack down its centre, but despite the distorted reflection, bags are prominent under each of my eyes. This is the first chance to rest since leaving for work over twelve hours ago. Hopefully, a shower will fix me.

Eric's room can't be more than ten feet square, and the double iron-framed bed will be cramped compared to my king-size. It's like moving in with The Borrowers. Although my flat in Stonemouth is bordering on the condemned, at least it's airy and spacious.

I lay back on the bed in my boxers, resting my head on a soft towel and take a few deep breaths to reset my mind. Low clouds pass in front of the full moon. I use the sound of taxis travelling over the cobbles down below to form the rhythm as I inhale, exhale, until I'm back in sync.

When I reopen my eyes, my attention is drawn back to the dresser. On the top right is a small Polaroid. I shuffle on my knees down the bed, reaching to pull it from the gum fastening it to the wood.

Staring back at me is Eric. He's fragile. Not bone thin, there's some muscle beneath his tight outfit, but thin, nonetheless. Despite the heavy make-up, he has the same eyes as Mum. They're catching the spotlight shining from above the stage, and his stare into the camera is as real as if he's sitting across from me now. In the space below the picture, the caption is faded but visible.

23rd April 2022, St George's Gay, Lord Nelson.

I've never seen a still image seem so alive. It's as if Eric is going to climb out from the photograph and burst into song, strutting around his old bedroom. I can't pull my eyes away, transfixed by finally seeing who he was. A fire rises in my stomach, the determination to fight on ignited.

The sofa is comfortable, and the tea warm. Gloria rests a selection of biscuits on the arm next to me, and then retreats to her usual spot, her ashtray filling up nicely.

"Have you seen Jack this week?" I ask.

"I've seen too much of him if anything. Been some long hours at the gallery."

"Is he okay?"

"He's great. Sold those pieces you had your eye on last week. Nice grand or so for each in his back pocket."

That's more than I'll ever make from art. "He hasn't messaged me all week."

She laughs. "You'll get used to that."

"Have I done anything wrong?"

"You need to give him time." She snaps a biscuit in two and eats half slowly. "It's cos you're new. He don't deal with change as well as others. He blows hot and cold more than summat that blows hot and cold, but that's why I love him. Don't take it personally, he'll be back. He was singing your praises this week."

I stop, a custard cream half submerged in my drink. "Are you sure he was talking about me? He hates me, Gloria."

"Nonsense. He finds you intriguing. And he told me about going to Limehouse."

"I didn't go to Limehouse," I reply.

"No, he did. Went up Wednesday night after *Corrie*."

A twinge of excitement ripples through me, but why has he left me in the dark? I'd be lying if I said I hadn't been talking about him too. Michelle has warned me I owe her a pound for every time I say his name in the future. Having him only in my thoughts has made the lack of contact unbearable.

"Did he tell you what he found?" I ask.

"Not a sausage I'm afraid. No news is no news with him."

The tick of the clock counts through a fifteen-second silence. I dip a bourbon into my tea and swallow it in one go. "We haven't got anywhere with the search. I wrote to everyone and had no replies."

Gloria is focussed on the television and doesn't answer. She's fully engrossed in a news story about a missing teenager, WilliamBosnich, last seen leaving an event at Bethnal Green Working Men's Club. It's hard to gather all details with the volume on zero, but Gloria's eyes are fixed on his image.

As it flips to the sport, I put my cup down. "Gloria, do you know Dai White?" She shuffles in her chair and stares at me with a concerned expression. "I'm assuming that's a yes."

"How did you hear of Dai?" she asks.

I fall into the cushions deeper and fold my arms across my body. "He wrote to Mum."

"When?"

"This morning."

Her cup is put on the floor at pace, its contents jumping out onto the magazines nearby. "Do you have the letter?"

I give her the thumbs down. "Mum told me about it at work. I've not seen it. She told me if he contacts me I should ignore him."

"I bet she did."

"He said she needed to keep out the way too."

Gloria moves and crouches in front of me. "You need to be careful, Harri. Your letters last week have clearly ruffled some feathers. Someone in Eric's book is out to get you, making you a scapegoat for all the trouble in the past. We need to tread carefully."

"Well surely that's easy enough. We can take extra care around Dai. Which queen was he?"

Gloria leans her head into her hands at the mantlepiece. Her left leg is shaking, but I'm not sure if it's from upset or anger. "Dai was a hanger on, brought in by Eric. They were in a relationship for a short while towards the end of their run."

"Well, hopefully I can steer away from him. I can focus on the queens, get them all onside first."

"It's not so simple." She comes and sits next to me on the sofa, placing a bony hand on my exposed knee. "None of this will be simple. Dai hasn't been around for over a decade."

"You mean he's dead?"

She shakes her head. "Prison. He got fifteen years. If he's writing, it means he's back."

6.

The Duchess

The scent of burnt egg engulfs Eric's bedroom like a nuclear fallout. When I force open one eye, a light cirrus smoke cloud is creeping across the ceiling and out the narrowly opened window. The hands on Eric's Mickey Mouse alarm clock split its face in two. 9.15am is too early to surface on a Sunday morning, however no sleep can be had with the sound of pans clattering on the other side of Gloria's wafer-thin walls.

The film posters on the wall rattle with each clunk of kitchenware. I always thought old houses were meant to be sturdier. I wrap the bedsheet around me like a toga and drag myself down the hallway.

"Sleep well?" Gloria asks. She passes me an instant coffee as I lean on the doorframe of the kitchen.

"Woke a couple of times with the sirens but otherwise, yeah." I had a long sleep despite the bed's creaky frame. The stress from the arguments with Craig and accusations from Mum drifted away across the Soho rooftops

"You'll get used to the police soon enough. Eric used to say he had better sleep on the benches of Soho Square after a heavy night." She adds a splash of milk to the saucepan and starts beating the eggy mixture heavily. "Anyway, come grab yourself some toast, you need to fill your stomach. Looks like you're wasting away."

I pull the cotton tighter around my naked torso and take a seat. The newly risen sun reflects its glow off neighbouring skylights, creating dancing patterns on the Artex ceiling. I slather butter onto two thick slices of granary and allow Gloria to ladle a heavy portion of scrambled eggs onto my plate. They're slightly grey, but the brown sauce will hide their flavour.

"I was thinking in bed last night about you," Gloria says, waving a ketchup-coated knife in my direction as she drops down opposite. "Writing to these queens doesn't work. I know you're disappointed but it was worth a shot."

"Would they listen to you?"

Her laugh confirms it's a ridiculous question.

"So what now?" I say, shovelling a forkful into my mouth.

"You need to take it up a level. The queens have always been quick to lean towards the dramatic. They're sat in their houses being all *woe is me*, too stubborn to do what's right, too far up their own arseholes to realise some things are worth rediscovering."

"And I'm the person who can win them over?"

She nods. "Some of them, anyway. You need to try convincing them to come back for the funeral."

I swallow a particularly yolky portion of my breakfast and try unsuccessfully to suppress a burp. "I guess I could phone them. Explain who I am, why I'm here."

"It'd save time to go in person."

I throw my fork onto my plate. "I can't afford to. It cost me forty pounds for a single yesterday to Waterloo. My wage might allow me to get to Swindon but no one needs to end up there."

"Driving would be a lot easier, y'know," she replies, adding eight twists of salt over her breakfast.

"That would cost even more. Anyway, I haven't passed my test and you don't have a car. Not to be a stickler for the basics, Gloria, but they seem vital components."

"I might not have a car, but I know someone who does. Get yourself showered and meet me downstairs in ten minutes with an overnight bag."

Slightly unnerved at the plan she's hatching, I devour anything edible in front of me, unsure when I'll next eat. Gloria acts oblivious as I side-eye her whilst I scrape the leftover residue from my plate into the bin. I want to meet the queens, but don't want to risk my life doing so. Either of us behind the wheel would be lethal.

When I stick my head outside, Gloria is perched on a footstool on the pavement, leant back against the entrance of the tattoo parlour. She's barking into an old mobile phone being held at arm's length. I've not seen anyone use a flip phone in real life. Daria used to beg our parents for one when our age hadn't yet hit double figures, but when they had relented, smartphones were flooding the market.

"No, I said ten. You're the one saying eleven," she says, before snapping the phone closed and lighting a cigarette. She offers me one this time, but I refuse. "Got a new three-piece suite coming. Been wanting to upgrade for ages but Eric said the one up there was as comfortable as a buxom bosom."

I agree with Eric. Their sofa might be stained with wine and have more rips than Edward Scissorhands' gloves, but the cushions are soft. "How will you get it up the stairs?"

"Roberto said he'd help. That was him on the phone."

I look across to the café and Roberto gives me a cheery wave. Once again, he has no customers. Many people are out enjoying the morning sunshine, but they don't go through his front door.

"Now, have you got everything you need?" Gloria says, removing flecks of dirt from my shoulders with her hand as I sit on the floor beside her. Her bracelets clang together in my ear with each swipe of her palm.

"How would I know? You've not told me where we're going."

"A road trip, like I said. And I ain't going cos I need to be here for the sofa. It'll only be for a couple of days."

As exciting as an adventure would be, I get a shock of guilt when Michelle and Stonemouth come to mind. That's new. "I'm meant to be working tomorrow morning."

Gloria takes hold of my hand, giving my thumb a gentle rub. "If you cared for Stonemouth, you would've bought a return ticket. Have Eric's room for as long as you need. No rent until you get some money."

I give her a smile. She's got me there. Craig won't miss me. I'll be replaced by another kid in desperate need for cash before my dirty apron even reaches the spin cycle.

"There's a cool bag at the bottom of the stairs with a packed lunch and a bag of Jelly Babies for the journey. The orange bag is a tent, just in case."

I get flashbacks to my Duke of Edinburgh trips with school, curled up in a sleeping bag, cowering from driving rain on the Gower Peninsula with no protection other than two bits of carbon fibre and a frayed piece of canvas. It got so bad that me and Gary, my camping partner for the week, plotted a route to The Mumbles on the third night, but never followed it through. Gary cried on the final day due to being homesick and exposed to nature. He only calmed down after I reluctantly read a *Narnia* book to him until he'd fallen asleep. I've not been able to see the word Aslan since without coming over in a cold sweat. Gary's in the army now, God help us all.

The quiet Sunday Soho street scene is obliterated when a noise resembling a gunshot explodes from around the corner. Those walking to the local church services grab their nearest and flinch behind cars.

"What the hell was that?" I stutter, shrinking back inside the entrance hall.

"Your lift," Gloria replies.

The splutters of an engine grow louder, causing a flock of nearby pigeons to fly off coordinated as a vehicle enters via Berwick Street on two wheels. When the smoke from the exhaust settles, a VW Beetle skids to a halt in front of me. It's been painted shabbily with thick pink stripes across its yellow base, a large black crown emblazoned across the bonnet.

"Oi oi!," shouts Jack out the driver's window to Gloria as he slings his bag onto the back seats. He then clocks me, his face dropping. "Why are you here?"

"I could ask the same thing," I reply. This is a setup. I look to Gloria, but she smiles back with satisfaction and quiet pride.

She taps the roof of the car twice. "Harri, this is Eric's

old hag, The Duchess. What do you reckon?"

Moving around the vehicle, I spot at least three flaws which will cause The Duchess to fail an MOT. I'm already fearing for my safety. The back left window has been replaced by transparent plastic, hastily sellotaped to the bodywork, and the exhaust pipe is being held together with what looks like a glittery belt. Most of the original metal around the perimeter is bronzed with rust.

"This is a death trap." I brush some dirt off the boot, causing more paint to flake off in my hands.

Jack pushes the driver's door wide. It bounces on its hinges, creaking like a derelict swing. "She's a bit old and knackered, groans a lot, and might spit every now and then, but she's got a heart of gold."

"Her and me both," replies Gloria.

He kisses her on both cheeks. "You're gorgeous, Gloria, you know that. You can be up the front with me, and he can be in the boot."

I don't want to be in the car at all with him. I do another walk around the vehicle. The back tyres are worn, borderline illegal.

"I'm not coming," says Gloria. Jack fails to keep his whispered expletives inaudible.

"I didn't know it'd be you and me, either," I tell him.

Gloria takes our hands and holds us closer. We still fail to make eye contact. "Now, you two be careful, okay? I'd love to join you, but you know, my sofa and all that jazz."

"I promise I'll drive slow," Jack calls as he lets go and stretches into the air, his v-lines being revealed above the waistband of his Calvin's.

"You wouldn't be able to go fast if you tried," I reply, trying not to stare at his stomach. I hate myself for even entertaining the idea he could be the one for me, but one glimpse of his body is enough to convince someone as shallow as I am to jump in and buckle up. I need to learn to think with my brain and not my dick. Gloria throws the tent at me and it flies into the road, metal pegs spilling out into the littered gutter.

"Will someone at least tell me where we're going?" I beg.

"Manchester," says Jack.

"Any particular reason?"

"In the notebook it said Richard lives in Burnage."

"Richard?"

"One step behind, see? Princess Thigh-Ana. He runs a quiz night on Sundays at a place called The Coaching House. I booked a table for it this evening, so we best get a move on."

"How do you know this?"

"Google exists."

I let out a sigh. "Would've been a lot easier than writing."

"Even so," says Jack, spitting on a tissue and wiping dead bugs from the wing mirror, "we can't rely on sending them an email now. I need to sort this face to face."

"We," I say firmly. "This is as much my search as yours." Despite the warmth of the morning, the atmosphere becomes frostier with each passing second. "Is Richard expecting us?"

The look I get back from them both shows he isn't, causing a wave of doubt to encroach.

"Richard is a good person," says Gloria.

"Are you *sure* this is a good idea? What if the old wounds haven't healed?"

"He drifted from us, wanting a quiet life nearer his sister. He never fell out with Eric. Despite what you expect, sometimes you lose the friends you said you'd keep. Often, you find new ones when you don't expect it." She nods towards Jack, who looks at her like she's just pissed on his Weetabix. "Now, stop hanging around. Give me a call when you get past Wolverhampton."

Jack jumps back into the front seat, and Gloria kisses me on the cheek. With one psychological drama after another coming in waves, I reluctantly open the passenger door with a clammy hand, my heart skipping slightly faster than usual.

The seat is low, and once my seatbelt is in, my head is level with the glovebox. "Are you insured on this thing?"

"Stop worrying," replies Jack, starting The Duchess' engine on the third go. "Here." He passes me two pillows from the footwell behind and I stick them under my backside until I'm equal in height. "Are you always this nervous?"

"Maybe I was made to watch too many stranger danger videos in care," I reply sarcastically.

"Well I promise I'm not gonna kidnap you and bury you in some dark and mysterious woodland like that girl with the blonde bob."

"Tabitha," I say. A shudder runs from my head to my feet at the thought of the TV being wheeled into the dusty common room during summer school. When told through a flickering screen, her kidnap story was terrifying. I know it was only bad acting portrayed through a 1970s VHS, but she's given me the creeps ever since. "The first time I saw Tabitha was on an outing with some other children in care at Maplewood."

Jack sits up. "In Oxfordshire?"

"Yeah, the old country house. Do you know it?"

"I've heard of it."

I've not thought of those days for a while now. My memories are like quick film cells of a long-forgotten home movie. "It had a play area in the garden and an orchard where we were shown how to pick apples."

"And Tabitha."

"And bloody Tabitha," I say, laughing at her for the first time in my life.

Gloria taps on Jack's window and he battles with the stiff rotating handle to lower it. "Drive safely, boys."

Jack gives me a smile, and strokes my knee, causing my breathing to stop. "We'll be alright." The gearbox grates as he struggles to find first, every bump in the road transferring vibrations up my spine. The speed we pull off at is closer to a moped than a Formula One car. A final backfire spews a cloud of petrol smoke to signal our departure.

As we approach the west of Luton, the rain sets in. The wipers squeak with each swipe, but at least the silence is no longer present inside the car.

"Did you bring a waterproof with you?" asks Jack, as he cleans condensation from the inside of the windscreen with a Paddington toy. Despite only having one eye and half his face being covered in mould, Paddington is likely in a better mental state than me. "I might have a spare mac. With luck, the weather will clear as we head north."

Jack looks across in time for a large drip of rainwater to fall down the neck of my t-shirt.

"Christ, how the fuck am I getting wet *inside*? This car is a legit heap of shit."

"No swearing in front of The Duchess. Where are your manners?" Jack punches my knee with his gear-changing hand. "There's a hole above your head. Rust, probably. Here, take this."

He bends towards me, spitting chewing gum onto my lap. I take it gently between my thumb and index finger.

"Stick it in the gap and it should hold for a couple of hours."

I look up to the ceiling, a second drip hitting me directly between the eyes. I jam the gum in the source, but it does little to stem the leak and a wet patch forms on my left leg. "It's no good, we need something better."

"There's some services coming up, I'll swing in there. Do you have an umbrella?"

"What do you think?"

"There might be one in the boot with the rope and shovel I need for when I murder you, *Tabitha*."

"Don't even joke." I stare through the passenger window to hide my smile at the thaw in his attitude. Our wedding is back on the cards.

We pull off the M1 and navigate the labyrinth of slip roads leading into the services, pulling up close to the entrance. The rain continues to patter on the roof but this doesn't deter Jack from jumping out and throwing a yellow raincoat on. Within seconds, a scream pierces the air. I look out and a terrifying clown is staring back at me, his face covered with thick make-up which is slowly running down his cheeks like blood, dripping onto his oversized collar.

"What do you want from us?" Jack shouts as he crouches near the boot, his arms up like a boxer in a defensive stance. All his confidence and bravado has been washed away in the storm.

"I'm raising awareness for *Therapy With a Toy*," says

the clown. "It's a local charity for underprivileged children experiencing life difficulties."

I use the car to keep a barrier between us. "Sneaking up on people in the rain dressed like a Poundland Pennywise is unlikely to get people on board."

"Nor is calling a charity a name with the acronym T.W.A.T," adds Jack.

"We're Britain's twelfth biggest children's therapy charity," the clown replies, but my enthusiasm for support has dwindled. Jack's even more so, and he bounds off across the car park, not looking back.

I've never been a fan of service stations. They suck any hope out of you the moment you pass through their automatic doors. The music is at the annoying level where it's hard to pick out anything other than drums and bass, and the artificial lighting makes the place seem fake.

The kid behind the burger counter wipes the till point down whilst staring into the distance. A children's birthday party taking place on the largest table isn't helping his mood, I'm sure.

"We should grab some food," Jack says flatly, watching the kids play with their fries. "There's still three hours of driving to do."

I get a croissant and a coffee and sit at a table which gives a stunning view of the lorry park. The coffee is bitter and grainy, but it keeps my hands warm.

Despite being three chairs to choose from, Jack slides in next to me, his thigh pressed against mine. He takes his chicken burger and devours a quarter in one bite. "I picked up some sealant from the minimart for the car roof. Ten bloody quid!"

He pulls the small bottle out of a carrier bag and I spin it in my hand. It states it's waterproof, but this might not be true when applied by a couple of cowboys like us.

"How long were you in care for?" Jack asks.

As usual, my shoulders retract at his question, but I appreciate him starting a conversation. "Nearly seven years."

"Did it affect you?"

"Can't remember much of it before the adoption. My parents tried to integrate me with the other kids, but I always felt like an outcast. Always felt I was different, y'know?" Jack nods along as I speak. "My mum can be alright now, like, to an extent. We don't always see eye to eye but that's the same for everyone I assume."

"How often did you visit Maplewood?"

I shrug. "A few times. Four, maybe five. It's gone now."

"Closed?"

"Derelict, I heard," I say.

"Did you destroy it?" he says with a laugh, abruptly stopping when he catches my glare. "What about your birth parents?"

I expected this question next. This question *always* comes next. I play with the flakes of pastry scattered on the table in front. "They were never traced."

Jack picks out some onion cautiously and lays it on his tongue. "That's horrible, sorry."

"And one of my foster mothers died. Even if I wanted to trace my real parents I'm not sure Mum would be pleased. She's warned us off before. It's why her not telling me about Eric is so painful."

"Have you asked your dad about him?" Jack asks.

I look to the floor, shaking my head. "Road accident. Six years back."

Despite what Mum would think, I have weighed up the pros and cons of starting a search into my birth family, but never once followed it through. Daria did some research shortly after Dad passed, but it soon became too overwhelming. The free trial emails from *findmyancestors.com* always sit in my inbox for a few days before I delete them.

"Does your Mum have any other siblings?" asks Jack.

"Can we leave it?" I hate to cut him off, but I can't face it right now. We sit for a moment in silence. The weather outside has taken another downturn to such an extent the wind is causing car alarms to blast out. At least The Duchess will be keeping quiet. The clown enters the foyer, wiping his stupid shoes on the hessian mat and shaking his wig dry next to the arcade. We both focus on him as he lowers himself to the floor.

"What about your family, Jack? Are your parents in London?"

"They live in a five-bedroom house in Wimbledon." His voice is almost robotic as if their upper-classness bores him.

"Must cost a bit," is all I can reply.

"At least seven figures." He slurps through the ice at the base of his cola before tapping on the end of his straw. Two taps, then three. "My dad is Kenneth and he's a wealthy businessman, funds educational programmes. My mother is Deborah. She works at the tennis centre."

I stretch my legs, my knees clicking after being sardined in the front seats for eighty miles. "I mean this in a nice way, but if your parents are minted, why the hell are you living above a grotty massage parlour and taking someone you barely know across the country?"

"I want to be independent," he replies. "I wish I could be like my parents, but I never did well at school. My parents are the type who believe money can solve anything. Dad said I could've had a job in his London office one day."

"Didn't fancy it then?" I say, trying to lighten the mood.

Jack laughs to himself at the thought. "I've got better things to do than walk around in a suit shoving half my earnings up my nose on a Friday night. I was on the fringes, never settling in, never finding my true voice. Not until I found art, anyway. Art makes me feel like I belong."

Again, I'm thrown back into Miss Kennedy's art-based detentions. I want to tell Jack all about them, but don't want to act like I'm stealing his thunder. "Gloria showed me some of your work last week. I thought they were great. You must be proud."

He shrugs. "Not the most someone has paid me, but it means my landlord isn't on my back for a couple of months, and petrol is covered for our adventure. I've a grand put aside for the trip."

"I'll pay for some too," I reply, calculating how much of the three-hundred pounds in my account can be siphoned off. "You got any brothers and sisters?"

"Two sisters. Maggie and Lisa."

"Like the Simpsons." He's heard this joke hundreds of times judging by his silence. "How about pets?"

"Noodles. R.I.P."

I wait for him to elaborate, but he focusses on the burger, grease dripping down the flat lettuce and onto the paper wrapping. I want to have this slightly talkative Jack for the rest of the trip. It's preferable to the version of him I met last week, yet something still tugs at me whenever I allow myself relax into his company.

"Why didn't you tell me you went to Limehouse last week?" I ask.

His eyes open wide as he chews, reflecting the sterile strip lighting of the burger joint back out. "Oh, shit, yeah. I got there and Ivana don't work for him. Never has. Landlord said he knew nothing of them."

"I thought Ivana was the landlord?"

"According to Eric's notes they were. Means we can't fully trust all the info we've been given."

I nod, but still unsatisfied. "You didn't answer my question. Why didn't you tell me you were going?"

"I was scared of making things harder for you." I turn away slightly. "Listen, Harri. I did push the point when I was there, but when I hinted towards the subject for a third time, one of the regulars snapped a pool cue across the bar. I legged it as I thought he was gonna kill me. Scary bastard."

"He sounds less Lily Savage and more Randy Savage," I say.

"Randy Savage?"

"Someone's never watched classic wrestling on YouTube."

Jack stares for a couple of seconds before going back to his food. "This bloke, though, he was at least a foot taller than me, bald and with a scar running from his left eye all the way down to his mouth. He was frothing as I ran to the DLR."

"Fingers crossed we have better luck with Richard."

"It can't go much worse, can it? Anyway, eat up. We need to make tracks soon if we want to sort somewhere to stay."

"We have the tent."

Jack doesn't answer, instead pulling his collar up to protect his neck from the rain. He holds it tight as we shuffle towards the exit. Our clown friend is now half-costumed, slumped on the floor and pouring water out of his comically large shoes. Jack offers him a small toy from his carrier bag as a signal of peace, which he accepts with a nod.

Inside The Duchess, my footwell now holds a small lake, the piece of gum floating around the surface like a stricken yacht. I flick as much water out onto the tarmac as I can, whilst Jack squeezes sealant into the holes above my head. It's a slapdash attempt, but the drips subside slightly. The improvement here is not relayed to the rest of the car, however. Once again he fails with the ignition for the first two attempts.

"You're gonna have to give me a push," he says with a wry smile.

"Good job I have grip on these Docs."

Handbrake released, I push on the slimy boot as Jack holds the driver's door. We look like the world's most amateur bobsleigh team. Remarkably, after fifty yards we pick up some pace on a small downhill and Jack jumps in, firing the engine into life. I run to catch up, bowling myself into the passenger seat before we head back onto the open road. Next stop: Manchester.

7.

A Kiss on the Nipple

The final three-hour stint of the journey north took over four, and when we pull into the newly laid car park of The Coaching House, my stomach pulses through starvation. I grab my belongings from the boot, pain shooting through my calf muscles and my spine unfolding now I'm free from The Duchess' claustrophobic front seat.

"We're in luck." Jack walks around the car park, occasionally squatting and stretching his arms like a gymnast warming up to vault. He grabs his fake Louis Vuitton holdall and points to the ground floor windows. A digital sign, the type usually seen flashing in the fried chicken shops of Stonemouth, advertises empty rooms, alongside information about the late-night Sunday karaoke.

"As long as I don't get put above the function room, I'll be happy," I say. "Last thing I want tonight is to try and sleep whilst someone is belting Celine Dion out of key."

The timber-framed hotel has a white marquee erected over the patio area, the top stained green from the debris of large trees that climb above. It'd appear more upmarket if the eight-foot-long vinyl signs advertising sporting events weren't draped from its wooden picket fence.

"We'll take whatever room is available," says Jack. "Beggars can't be choosers. I'm not camping, and if you expect me to drive anymore today then you've another thing coming. I need a pint."

"What if it all goes a bit pear-shaped like it did for you in Limehouse?"

"It won't. I have a gut feeling."

"Probably all the Jelly Babies you ate when we hit Greater Manchester."

Jack sticks his middle finger up, but I'm inclined to trust he's right. A negative attitude won't get us anywhere. A little faith in the project is the least I can do to repay him for driving halfway across the country.

"Welcome to The Coaching House," says a pre-recorded voice from above as Jack presses the bell on the reception desk. A lady with a beehive and blue glasses stands behind a plastic screen, giving us a cheery wave. She points to the phone at her ear and gestures to two armchairs nearby. The walls along the corridors which splinter from the reception display modern art, and Jack studies each in depth whilst I sit and eat a Mars Bar to muster up some energy.

The textured wallpaper and peach carpets give the hotel a retirement home vibe, but even so, it deserves more than the two stars the RAC plaque behind the counter is showing.

Through the double glass doors to my right, the bar area is busy. Half the tables are full of patrons tucking into large, delicious-looking meals. I'd murder someone for a curry. My stomach rumbles again, and my mouth fills with saliva.

"I'm sorry about that," says the receptionist. She tucks a strand of hair behind her ears and smiles, revealing a gold tooth. "Welcome to The Coaching House, part of the Hologram Hotels Group." Her accent is thick and Gallagher-esque. "How can I assist you today?"

"We were wondering if you've any rooms for tonight please?" I lean on her desk, crossing my fingers behind my back. Jack, again, was right. The tent needs to remain firmly in The Duchess' boot.

The receptionist makes a few clicks on an old laptop, comparing notes with a large leatherbound binder to her left. "Double bed okay?"

I look at Jack, wondering for a brief second if it could work. "I think two single rooms would be best."

"Oh, yes, sorry. One should never assume." The receptionist screws her mouth slightly as she taps away.

"Sadly, no singles left tonight. There's a party in the garden. Couple celebrating their golden wedding anniversary."

"In that case, twin is preferable, please."

More clicking, and more leafing through the binder follows. "We are extremely busy this weekend," she keeps saying. "Gary Barlow is in town too, you see. Let me check for cancellations."

"The sign outside said there were vacancies," I reply, practically begging.

She looks at me out the corner of her eyes. "I always forget to change that."

Jack is running his fingers over a sculpture, taking pictures from all angles. As soon as he looks my way, I wave him towards me. "They have great art here," he says. "Are the rooms sorted?"

"You're in luck," say the receptionist. "We've two available. The Marilyn Suite is a beautiful twin with a private bathroom at one hundred for the night."

"Any singles?" asks Jack.

"Your only other option would be the Honeymoon Suite," says the receptionist. "Obviously, this is a double room, but it does come with complimentary champagne and chocolate strawberries. It is a little dearer at two hundred."

"Aren't the golden couple staying there?" I ask.

"They haven't slept together for twenty-three years," she replies, before lowering her voice to a whisper, "but I didn't tell you that."

"The Marilyn Suite is great, thank you," says Jack, fumbling in his pocket for his wallet.

I spot a picture of a dog tucked inside, a place normally reserved for a family photo. I assume this is the late Noodles. The picture looks like it was taken for a dog food advert in a magazine, not taken himself. Jack folds it away, before taking the binder. As he's writing his details, he looks up. "The quiz is still on tonight, isn't it?"

"8pm sharp," replies the receptionist. "Would you like to book a table?"

"Already sorted, thank you."

"Richard will be happy. He always worries no one will

come to his drag events, but every time they're packed out."

"What time does he get here?" I ask.

She does a weird backward nod towards a doorway next to the printer. "Richard, you've got your first quizzers already." Her eyes reconnect with mine. "He probably isn't in the office. He's having terrible trouble with his back passage today. Council haven't collected the bins again so it's filthy."

She's wrong. From the doorway, a queen strides into view. His tall wig reaches high. One arm is stretched against the frame, the other on his hip. The dress is mermaid green with dashes of gold like individual lightning bolts. In his mouth, a long cigarette holder sits empty. His dark eyeshadow makes his ocean-blue eyes pop from their sockets. Everything in my peripheral vision is sucked away.

The queen strides elegantly across the reception in ruby red, knee-length platforms, before sitting side-saddle on the desk. He clicks his tongue twice as he looks us up and down.

"Hi boys." His voice is sugary sweet, but as rich as cocoa. "Princess Thigh-Ana, absolute delight for you to meet me."

"Hey," says Jack. He beams, nudging me in the ribs with a bony elbow.

"Hi, hey." I can only stutter, my left leg shaking. This is real. The Dragnificent Seven are real and one-quarter of the remaining members are stood in front of me. I want to scream, cry, shout, laugh and do a stupid little dance all at the same time. I need to say so much yet I can't say anything at all. My entire body has frozen.

Princess Thigh-Ana stares intently, only twitching when they catch Jack's eye. After a split second they shake their head and lean closer. "I've not seen you boys here before."

"We've never been," says Jack.

"We drove up from London especially," I add.

"I'm glad word of my star quality travels. Are you hungry?"

"Starving," I reply.

"We've a happy hour from 6pm. Half price cocktails and a quid off the lager. I'm more of a Bacardi girl as you can tell. The lager tastes like rat piss, but you have to give people options, don't you? If you treat the bar staff nicely they might give you a decent head. Derek will put on a marvellous spread for you both."

"Sounds great," I say.

"Now, this lady is busy, but don't run too far." He taps the cigarette holder on my nose gently. "I'll see you tonight, boys. Please don't get too drunk before the quiz." He gives a wink, and then struts back out of sight.

Every inch of our room is covered with photographs of Marilyn Monroe. She adorns the coasters, the bathroom mats, and the curtains. Even the wallpaper has her face on it. Maybe we should've chosen the Honeymoon Suite. The beds are firm, the television has Freeview, and a selection of shortbread is packaged next to the retro-electric kettle.

I sit on the armchair in my complimentary fluffy dressing gown, hugging my knees. Jack's whistling drifts from the bathroom, before he spits and the whirring of an electric toothbrush starts.

Outside, the sun is low, the long shadows of the trees fading into darkness as they stretch across the park opposite, the skeletal football goalposts slowly turning into ghosts of the night. A group of kids play below, bowling through bad light at three stumps scrawled in chalk onto the red bricks of a nearby garage. As a tram squeals to a halt at the end of the street and workers trudge like ants along the footpath towards *Coronation Street* terraced housing. The window frames the scene of a real-life Lowry.

As the first streetlights burst into life, the photo of Eric flashes into my mind. I'm determined to grab the duck by the bollocks and tell Richard our story this evening. Christ, Michelle. I haven't called her.

"This will do nicely," says Jack as he comes back to the bedroom with wet hair and a towel wrapped around his lower half. I try to distract myself but find my eyes drawn to a long scar down his right arm. It runs from elbow to wrist, his dark tattoo keeping it partly covered.

"That shower is amazing," he says, flopping onto the nearby bed. "It's a dream of mine to have a bathroom like that."

"I thought you'd have bigger ones at your parents'."

"Oh, yeah, three bathrooms at theirs. My room was large with an ensuite and room for a sofa."

"Why would you swap that for a bedsit? I'd kill for one of those. My sister would prefer a walk-in wardrobe though. She's got more clothes than Primark."

He sits up, leaning back on his elbows. "What was it like growing up with her?"

"Alright, yeah. Probably the same as you and your sisters."

"Oh, mine argued a lot. One reason I moved out as soon as I could. Mum wanted girls and I know she was disappointed with me. Then the twins came along and they were spoiled more than I ever was."

"How about your dad?"

He stands and pulls a pair of boxers up beneath his towel. "I'm not here to talk about my family."

"You were the one who brought them up," I protest.

"I said I don't want to talk about them. I'm off for a pint."

Moody Jack is back, wanting to be left alone, not allowing me to cramp his style by following him around. He pulls on a Gucci shirt, selecting a neckerchief from his rucksack to finish his look before sitting on the edge of the bed texting.

I desperately want to go downstairs with him but force myself to stay. I throw myself horizontal on the second bed, staring at his back. Tomorrow I'll reminisce of the luxuries Marilyn offered us when we're hauled up in a tent eating pot noodles, drinking from plastic cups, and urinating behind the nearest bush.

Not wanting complete peace, I grab the remote and flick through the channels. All BBC channels are unable to connect, so I settle on an old black and white movie whilst I dig out a change of clothes. It's only when I recognise Tom Holland in spandex that I realise it isn't a flick from the forties, but the latest Spider-Man being played through the knackered television. I hit the top of the box as the picture crackles, the fuzzy outline of the Holland's arse not bringing me joy on this occasion.

I jab a button and it jumps to a travel documentary. Dexter Buchanen, aka Britain's Hottest Man (as voted for by myself), is sampling wine in Bordeaux. Between the screen-snow, sporadic images of the vineyards of France come in and out of view.

Jack pokes in his earphones and throws on his leather jacket, lifting the sleeves to his elbows. As he's halfway out of the room, the telephone rings. "Who's calling us?" he says, panic in his voice.

I shrug and pick up the receiver. "Hello?"

"Hello, it's Rebecca from reception. Is Mr Montague there, please?"

"Sorry, no Mr Montague here," I reply.

"Wait!" says Jack, but the receiver is already replaced. "Who was it?"

"The receptionist."

"Jack Montague, nice to meet you," he says, his tone frustrated.

As Jack redials, I style my hair in the bathroom mirror. It's dry and brittle, and bags are forming under my eyes. At least I can get a decent night's sleep, karaoke pending.

"We have to go downstairs," Jack says, appearing behind me in the mirror as he taps the back of his phone case.

"Is everything okay?" I reply, looking at him via the reflection.

"Richard has requested our company in the snug."

"Does he know?"

"I don't know how he could. No one knows about this. I'm happy to go if you need some alone time."

"You were the one who wanted to be alone," I say. I take my aftershave off the shelf and spray it liberally. "I'm perfectly ready to face this. The sooner I can tell Richard who I am, the sooner we'll know if we're wasting our time or not."

I try to figure out Jack's tattoo. It looks like a letter T inside a diamond, with exact vertical symmetry. Maybe it's a band logo or some obscure artwork I'm not clever enough to be accustomed with. There's so much we need to learn about each other, but it's difficult when only one party is willing.

"Hurry up, then," Jack says, nudging me in the back. He holds the room key in his teeth as he pulls his jacket tight, causing my heart to fire another electric pulse through my body. I punch at my arm to stop it. I don't have the capacity to allow those thoughts into my mind.

I wait on a sofa in the snug, my hands shaking from a cocktail of nerves and excitement. Small bookcases stand where fruit machines should be, mini bowls of pretzels central on each table. I study Jack as he stands at the bar, a mixologist preparing our *Walk of Shame* drinks. Hopefully, the alcohol doesn't go to my head this evening. We've a long road ahead of us, and the fewer speed bumps we encounter, the better.

As my eyes follow a well-dressed couple across the room, the artwork on the far wall stops my gaze. Across the four yellow Pop Art pieces, the words *Take down the system* stand out in royal blue paint. I was taught protest art was born and raised in London, fighting the establishment from their own foundations. The art education I've received in Stonemouth has now proven to be lacking.

"Here," says Jack as he passes me a tall, multicoloured drink. He opens a bag of peanuts but doesn't offer one to me, instead concentrating on his phone.

I take a sip through the curly straw, nearly taking my eye out on the small umbrella, the rum striking the back of my throat instantly. "That's strong," I cough.

"It better be for eight quid."

I stir it a little, praying Richard arrives soon to ease the tension as the rainbow liquid swirls, the ice clinking against the edge of the thin glass. But what if his arrival makes things worse?

"You need to cheer up," Jack says.

"I *am* cheerful. Just worried this could all go wrong at any minute. What if I need to escape?"

"Alright *Ask for Angela*, calm down."

I wonder if Jack's always been this much of a dick-head, or if he has saved it all up especially for me. I take my mind off the thoughts of my purpose and scan the walls again. "For a tired hotel in the middle of nowhere, the art is surprisingly good."

Jack sighs but looks up from his phone to where I'm pointing. "No way!" He slams his drink down and stands immediately. "They're so similar to yours. I thought you'd like them."

"Like them? Harri, they *are* mine."

I chase him across the room, leaving our drinks behind.

"I exhibited these at a show last year as part of the *Arts by the Thames* festival that creep Magento organised. I even did a talking head for Channel 4 cos they were doing some documentary on art in Britain."

"How have they ended up here?"

"The owners bought them, I guess."

"It was me," comes the treacled voice from behind as an arm slips over both our shoulders. Jack quickly shrugs Princess Thigh-Ana off. His outfit has changed, and we're presented with a six-foot-tall blonde bombshell.

"Modelled on the real Princess Diana revenge dress," says Richard. "Think of me as the Queen of Tarts." He looks incredible, although the people's princess never wore as much blusher, and I've never seen a picture of her with penis-shaped earrings. "I fell in love with these paintings instantly and they had to come home with me. Richard Hathaway, he/him, lovely to meet you properly."

I sit on a chair, itching at how us two and The Dragnificent Seven have had a connection all along.

Richard moves in front and rubs his hand down a frame as he smiles at Jack. "Do you mind if I talk in my normal voice?"

"Go ahead." Jack says.

"Thank God," he replies in thick Mancunian. It breaks the enigma slightly. "Speaking like that is hard to keep up all night." He sucks up some water, gargles it, and spins towards Jack. "I knew I'd seen you before. Your face was familiar when you arrived. It took a bit of time to place you, but then it hit me like a paddle across the arse. I got these last year after seeing you on the television. Do you still dabble with art?"

"All the time," replies Jack. "I've just finished an exhibition in Whitechapel with my latest pieces."

"I might have to buy some more," says Richard. "The power they have. Such an impact."

"My latest have sold unfortunately."

Richard strokes his chin and looks back at the art. "Shame. Another time. Would you both like a kiss on the nipple?"

I assume this is a cocktail and not a formal request, but with his cocked eyebrow, I can't be certain. "We've got drinks but thank you."

"Harri needs to speak to you," says Jack and I shoot him a look. I'm not sure if now is the right time.

Richard tucks his wig behind his ears and straightens his fake breasts. "Make yourself at home. I'll be with you in a momentum."

I sit on the sofa, my legs bouncing nervously. The drink is doing nothing to steady me. Why couldn't Jack keep his mouth shut?

"Come straight out with it," says Jack as if reading my mind. "I ain't doing all the legwork for you."

I wish I could work him out. It's like being away with Jekyll and Hyde, or Hannah Montana and Miley Cyrus depending on your taste. Richard strides across effortlessly in his heels and sits in the nearby armchair. He raises his bright drink. "Cheers. I should be asking Jack more questions, but I'm too intrigued about why you wanted to speak to me. It's ever so mysterious, and I *love* a mystery."

I swallow hard and lean forward, focussing my attention on a small stain on the carpet. "I wrote to you last week but I'm not sure if you received my letter."

Richard frowns. "I sadly don't get much fan mail these days, including yours. Did it contain anything valuable? And did you send it here?"

"No, it was somewhere in Trafford."

He waves a hand at me. "Darling, I've not lived there for a couple of years I'm afraid. It was a nice flat, larger than the one in Burnage, but the football fans walking by every other week was unbearable. Used to find them pissing on my petunias on a regular basis."

"Where did you move to?"

"I've a gorgeous room here now. I can keep my *Moet et Chandon* in a pretty cabinet, I can access the jacuzzi in the guest spa, and the park over the road was ideal for me to walk Minnie."

"What breed?" asks Jack, disrupting the flow.

"Sausage Dog. Yappy little shit, but a shame you never got to meet her."

"I used to have a dog called Noodles," Jack replies.

"What happened to him?"

"Her. Died when I was sixteen. We buried her under an apple tree in our garden."

"Sounds a peaceful place to rest."

The bartender brings over a tray of lime-green shots and places them in the centre. "Three *Spit Roasts*," he says with a sigh.

"Add to my tab, darling." Richard downs his quickly, and then passes one to us both. "So this letter, what was it? Happy for you to share in private if it's embarrassing."

"It wasn't fan mail," I reply, downing the shot for courage. "It was about someone called Eric. He used to be in The Dragnificent Seven with you."

Richard jumps up in his chair and claps his hands together. "Bloody hell, are you serious?"

"One hundred per cent. I'm his nephew."

Richard studies me for a moment, trying to work out if I'm telling the truth. "He was taller than you," he says eventually.

"And better looking, I know."

"I adored hanging around with Wilma. Well, used to anyway. It was chaotic, but there was a lot of love between the pair of us. How is the old sod?"

I shuffle slightly. "I'm afraid he passed away a couple of weeks ago. Heart attack at home. Sorry."

Richard blows slowly out from his puffed cheeks and falls back into the cushions. The spark within him fizzles and his face drops. "You've knocked me for six a little. I'm sorry. We hadn't spoken for some time as you may know, but I do recall our days in Soho kindly. Are you religious?"

"I only went to church for Harvest Festival," I reply.

"Fair enough. Just wanted to check that you didn't want us to form a prayer circle or something."

"Is that what you want?" asks Jack.

Richard shakes his head. "I've always been more Benny, Bjorn, and Elton John than Matthew, Mark, Luke, and John. Have you been told about the time me and Eric got arrested in Trafalgar Square? Or the time we put up a barricade outside the Lord Nelson. Happy days."

I lean forward. "I dunno any stories at all. I only found out myself when his flatmate emailed me."

"Not Gloria?" His eyes widen again. "I'll have to tell you *all* the gossip. I was closer to her and Eric than the others. We used to drive to the gigs in this clapped-out old Beetle, singing to the chart shit on Radio One."

"The Duchess?" asks Jack.

Richard chuckles. "That's her. How we didn't die in her I'll never know."

"I was thinking the same this afternoon," I say. "My knuckles are still white from hanging on to the door handle for dear life."

Richard's mouth falls open again, staring at me in a stunned silence. "You aren't telling me The Duchess herself is here?"

"In the car park," says Jack. "I can take you out for a drive later."

Tears form in Richard's eyes, and he dabs at them with a handkerchief. "Look at me being a silly old git. The Duchess symbolised our lives for many years. Days you never thought would end, with people you never thought you'd lose. You don't know what you've got 'til it's gone, as someone once sang."

Richard clicks his fingers to the bar and three more shots are brought across. Gold this time. He passes them round and raises his to the sky. "To Wilma."

"To Wilma," me and Jack respond.

Gin. There's a lot of gin in this. A tinge of the Parma Violets too. I press my tongue to the top of my mouth to allow myself to breathe through it.

Richard spins the glass around between his fingers. “The problem with getting older is that the time you spent going to weddings is replaced with time spent at funerals. I haven’t missed Eric’s, have I?”

“The date is still being confirmed,” I say. “He would’ve loved for you to be there. I’m trying to track everyone down from the old days.”

He stands up and straightens his dress. “Some of us left on bad terms, do you know that?” His voice is tinged with caution.

“I do,” I reply. “I’ll understand if you don’t want to open old wounds.”

“Who have you found so far?” he asks.

“Only you,” says Jack.

“We’re doing a road trip to gather the troops, so to speak,” I say.

He nods, and then sits quickly, a wide smile coming over his face. “When do you leave here?”

“Tomorrow,” replies Jack.

Richard has a glint in his eyes and places a hand on my knee. “Is there room for a small one in the back of The Duchess?”

8.

Debbie Harry's Perm

I'm in the bathtub of the hotel ensuite with no memory of the pub quiz. Richard stands above me, aiming the shower head at my shirtless torso, ice-cold water battering my body.

"Christ, my head hurts," I say as I push myself up. My muscles are equally as painful. "Have I been hit by a bus?"

Richard looks at me with his eyebrows raised. "You'll feel like that if you sleep against the taps all night, although it could've been your insistence to taste every cocktail on the menu. Last I saw, you were asking the young bartender for a *Cheeky Finger*."

My final recollection of the night was standing on a chair telling everyone within earshot I thought they were great. Everyone except Jack. He'd disappeared sometime before. I climb out of the bath, only making it to the toilet, where I sit with a towel around me on its closed lid. "Did I make a disgrace of myself?"

"No, darling, you were fine. Although, you owe me eighty quid for the bar tab." He moves into the bedroom, using the oval mirror to reapply a fresh layer of eyeshadow.

"Can we sort it later?" I call after him.

"As it's you, but I do need the money eventually. The events world is not cheap. I've promised to give five hundred quid to a Nigerian prince on Wednesday."

"Sounds like a scam."

Richard pokes his head back around the corner. "I

hope not. His cover of *Purple Rain* is second to none. He's headlining the Eighties weekend at the end of the month."

A shiver runs down the length of my body, my legs shaking from the alcohol leaving my bloodstream as I trudge to find my clothes. The beds are made, mine with my backpack sitting on the top against a swan made from fresh towels. My eyes close from the glow of the artificial light above. The curtains are open, but the weather is being stereotypically Mancunian.

"Where's Jack?" I ask.

"Sitting in The Duchess. Check out was an hour ago." Richard throws a t-shirt at me as he exits the room. "Meet you in la reception in five, okay?"

The excitement of the nomadic lifestyle we entered yesterday has had its shine removed. I'm hoping I didn't declare my love for Jack or say anything else stupid. The pounding in my head increases at the twenty missed calls from Michelle and Daria flashing on my phone. It must be serious. With the hangover giving me a touch of Dutch courage, I bite the bullet and call Michelle. It takes her a good half minute to answer.

"Where the hell are you?" she whispers, her voice echoey through the speakerphone.

"Manchester. Long story."

"Jesus, Harri. You were meant to be at work two hours ago."

I knew I should've messaged her before I skied too far down the slippery White Russian slopes. The panic affects my coordination and I tumble to the floor with my legs stuck halfway into my jeans. "Can you tell Craig I'm ill?"

"I did. He told me if I lied again he'd sack me too."

"I'm sacked?"

"Not officially, but you will be the next time he sees you. He hates your guts."

I scramble onto the bed and grab the phone. "I'm sorry mate, genuinely."

"I bet you are. I've got to work all day with him now. You know I can't stand Mondays."

I take it off speaker. "Where are you? Your voice sounds all weird."

"In the big fridge out the back. Look, I love you okay, but you need to get a grip. One minute you're here, the next you're in London, and now you've run off to Manchester."

"I found a queen though," I say. "And they said they want to come with us."

"Yeah, great, but it doesn't make my day any better."

"It isn't my fault," I say, begging to keep her on side.

"Kinda is. I guess you want me to lie to your mum when she comes in?"

"Please." She'd kill me if she knew I was here.

In the background, the fridge door clicks. The line muffles, but I can pick out Craig's voice complaining to Michelle. His tone angrier than normal. I can picture his salami-red face, steam coming out his ears.

In the next moment of silence, Michelle is back. "Call me later, okay?" The final words before the call abruptly ends. I text Daria, letting her know I'm safe. She responds before I can put the phone in my bag.

"I have amazing news. Call me tonight! Don't forget!!! xx"

I check the drawers of the hotel room for any discarded belongings and head to the car park. Jack is sat in the front seat of The Duchess, staring intently at the trees opposite. His fingers drum a frustrated beat on the steering wheel. Two taps, then three. I put on my best *I'm sorry* face.

He raises his eyebrows. "Just get in."

Richard is laid across the backseat in a maroon smoking jacket, his legs curled on top of a giant suitcase. I guess expecting a drag queen to travel light was a ridiculous thought.

"Sorry I was a mess last night," I say to Jack. He forces a smile as he drags Paddington across the wing mirror but otherwise ignores me. For once the ignition works first time and I strap in for a long journey.

The Duchess weaves through two miles of built-up streets, houses built years before for local factory workers. The headlights bounce off the greasy surface, the wipers doing their best to keep the water from the screen. The aircon smells of antifreeze, and, with the building heat and the choking of the engine, I fall back asleep.

When I awake, there are two immediate facts. Firstly, I'm alone in The Duchess on the edge of a ploughed field. Secondly, it stinks of shit. Not a faint and stale whiff carried on a breeze, but fully blown, melt-in-the-mouth, steaming manure shit. I kick open the car door and climb out. The smell is stronger out here and may be causing the fog surrounding me. A short distance away, the ghost of a small, converted farm building is visible, alarmingly with our bright orange emergency tent erected on its squared front lawn.

I trudge down its steppingstone path, trying to avoid the dirt below my soles. The green front door has two pairs of filthy wellington boots standing to attention against its frame. Through the oval window, I can make out the shadows of two people, Richard's faint voice being carried down the hallway.

With no doorbell, I slam the lion's head knocker four times. Within seconds, it opens a fraction, and half of Jack's face is visible.

"You're alive then," he says.

"I was having a sleep."

"It's nearly 4pm, Harri. We should've been on the road hours ago so we're camped up for the night. Want some food?"

I follow him down the hall. The floor is polished, and my socks slip as I try to keep up. A dark staircase leads off to the right, but we pass and enter a farmer's kitchen. A plate of freshly baked fruit rock cakes sit on a patterned dish in the centre of a circular table, one that's far too small for the size of the room.

Richard is laid back on a chaise longue in front of the French doors, dropping grapes into his mouth like Cleopatra. "Oh, darling you're awake. Now, I know what you're going to ask." I open my mouth, but he cuts me off by flicking a grape at me. "You're going to ask if the cakes are for us. Yes, and yes you can have one. Cream and jam in the fridge. Pot of tea on the aga."

Saliva fills my mouth, so I take one and slice it in half. "I was actually gonna ask where the fuck we are, if you must know."

"Irene's," Jack says.

"Who?"

"Irene," confirms Richard. "She was a friend from the London days, and in a stroke of luck, she messaged me last night letting me know her husband had recently died."

"Not exactly what I call lucky," I reply. I take my rock cake to the table and sit at one of the two chairs.

Richard takes the chair opposite, sets a crossword in front of him, and points a jammy knife in my direction. "It is actually. I left some boxes here when I moved into the hotel. They're like little time capsules. Photos, articles, everything Dragnificent that might be good for you to see. Irene has gone to an antique fair down in Tenby to sell some of her husband's possessions, so said we could come over and take what we need."

I polish off my food quickly and pour a fresh tea from the novelty teapot. "What's this Irene like?"

"Very similar to Gloria, except she's in her eighties. Irene had enough of London after she got kettled in at Euston Station during the Olympics, so moved out here. It's a shame really. She was a real risk-taker, one of a kind. Bright pink hair, multiple piercings, and a large tattoo of Debbie Harry on her inner thigh. She sent a pic of it with her message yesterday, actually."

I take Richard's phone and see a faded and wrinkled Debbie Harry staring back at me. It's so high on Irene's thigh that her unruly pubic hair has given Ms Harry and unexpected perm. I decide against a second cake.

"So what's the plan?" I ask.

"Stay the night here," Jack replies. "And before you ask, there is only one bedroom, hence us having the tent."

"There is a pull-out in the front room but it doesn't have springs and needs disposing of," adds Richard. "I told Irene I'd take her bed."

"Is she not coming back?"

"Not 'til the weekend. Irene will stay at her sisters in Wales tonight to get some sea air."

On the table, yesterday's newspaper lays open on the racing pages, various horses circled in heavy pen. A pair of thick glasses and a man's wallet sit on top, betting slips poking out from its leather interior. Then there is the opened tin lunchbox on the side, cling-filmed sandwiches, and a bag of ready salted on show.

"When exactly did her husband die?" I ask. I almost don't want to know the answer.

Richard looks up from his crossword. "Yesterday." I stare at him, but he furrows his brow. "What?"

"Her husband died yesterday?"

"Yes."

I look to Jack, but he can only shrug. "Sorry, am I the only sane person here? He's barely cold and she's god knows how many miles away cashing in on all his stuff?"

"She never did like clutter," Richard says with a smile. "That's why we should take the boxes. My back is killing me, if you pardon the pun, so if you and Jack don't mind grabbing them from the loft that would be an enormous help."

The loft smells like an old flannel, the dim bulb in the centre swinging after Jack's head collided with it as he pulled himself up. I feel weirdly seasick and sit on a pile of boxes with Richard's name on them. They immediately sink and I topple backwards onto the dusty boards. Jack, on the other hand, drops onto a torn armchair, a cloud of dirt filling the air under his weight.

"Where do we even start with all this crap?" he says.

I climb back onto my feet, tilting the lightbulb to illuminate a corridor of plastic storage containers. "These look to be ornaments."

Jack joins me, and cracks the lid on the nearest, before pulling the newspaper away from a spherical object. An ornate ginger jar lands in his hand, its lid crashing into two on the floor.

"They must be Irene's," I say.

"No doubt these will be at a car boot before long."

"Jack, you go down and I'll throw Richard's boxes to you."

"You're stronger than me," Jack replies, grabbing my left bicep. A rush of adrenaline floods my veins. He holds on for longer than is necessary, but there isn't a chance in hell I'll shake him off. "I'd only drop them."

The loft stands at the top of the dark staircase, and I

balance on the edge of the top step as, one by one, boxes are thrown from above. Not wanting to fall to my death, I try to remain focussed, but this is made harder when Jack leans over the hatch shirtless, his pecs and shoulder muscles glistening with sweat.

"Only about five to go," he says. Speak Harri. Stop staring and speak. He breaks into a smile. "Cup of tea after this I think."

Personally, I think it's more of a Diet Coke break that I need.

Once the last box is down, we take them to the front porch. The Duchess sits on the edge of the field, clearly too small to transport our haul.

"Maybe we could attach that horsebox to it," says Jack, still shirtless and clearly thinking the same.

I give him a side-eye. "She can barely carry the weight of three people. You saw how it struggled getting out the pub car park with Richard's suitcase added."

We take a seat on the stairs, and again, Jack's reluctance for body contact has vanished. His leg is pressed against mine, despite the extra room on his side. We call Richard, and he floats down the hallway.

On arrival, his shoulders drop and he bites his lip. "I didn't mean those ones. Sorry."

"We ain't taking these back up," I say.

"Absolutely not," Jack agrees.

"Burn them." Richard pulls a box of matches from his pocket and tosses them across. "Irene has set up a bonfire in the back field, so it will be doing her a favour."

"Are you sure you don't want anything from them?"

Richard lets out a long, twisted laugh. "Many years ago," he starts, "me and a few of the girls decided to set up a summer-long fundraising campaign. I spent hours locked up in my room, calling various councils and landowners trying to get a sponsored walk off the ground. Those are all the t-shirts we had made. Fifteen hundred of the buggers."

"You mean no one turned up?" I ask.

"Oh they did!" Richard sinks to his knees in front of us. "We put Oliver in charge of the marketing. Now, I'm not being cruel, but he was a little…how can I say this in a politically correct manner?"

"Thick?" says Jack.

Richard nods. "Definitely a few sequins short of a ballgown, put it that way. I said time and time again to ensure the text was correct, and he assured me time and time again that he'd written it carefully. But then the t-shirts arrived."

"And you couldn't use them?" I ask.

"No. I did think about asking the councils to check but decided that a sponsored charity *wank* beside the Thames might be frowned upon by the tourist board."

Jack uses my thigh as leverage as he stands. "Where's the petrol?"

Richard sighs and pulls the tape away from one of the boxes. "Poor Oliver. I do miss him. 13th January 1987."

As dusk falls over the farm cottage, Jack strikes a match and a river of fire flows to the base of the giant bonfire. It crackles and spits at first, but soon the flames lick the sides the of old and splintered pallets. The black smoke from the boxes we recovered is dense, burning not being the most environmentally friendly way of disposing of the t-shirts, but neither of us have the time and energy to check if Sue Ryder or the British Heart Foundation can make good of them. We did take one each to wear though, and I know everyone else in our situation would do the same.

As the flames roar, I sit next to Jack on the broken sofa bed, which Richard said was good to go as well. There is a chill in the air tonight, but the warmth of the fire does its best to battle against it.

Jack swings his legs over the arm of the sofa, his head lying next to my legs. He's turned towards the bonfire, his body semi-foetal.

"We should've brought some marshmallows out," I say. He doesn't respond, instead trying to avoid the burning wreckage with all his might. Despite having no springs, the sofa is comfortable, and I could easily drift off to sleep again, but he tugs at the arm of my t-shirt.

"You alright?" I ask him.

"Sorry if I was a bit of a dick."

"When?"

"When I met you. And on the way up to Manchester. And last night."

"I assumed you wanted some space. It's fine. I had fun with Richard."

He twists his body until he's on his stomach, and he places his chin on my leg. It digs into my muscle, and I tense to stop it cutting off the blood to my foot.

As he stares into the distance, I pick bits of ash from his hair. "I've a vague memory of Richard telling me last night that he used to work for the CIA."

Jack lets out a laugh, natural this time. "He worked at C&A, you were just pissed."

"My mum used to work at C&A," I reply. "She was in charge of the back-to-school range when I was in primary. Good discount but those jumpers itched like hell."

He tilts his head at me. "Did it take long to settle when you were adopted?"

I shrug. "I got used to it. It was nice knowing that home would be permanent. Having Daria helped as she's always been naturally good at looking after people, even when she was young herself. We used to do everything together."

I have forgotten to call her back. It's becoming a habit. I'll have to be one of those people who writes their messages on their hands in marker before long if I become any more unreliable.

"We aren't that different, y'know," Jack says. It takes me by surprise. Not that he's speaking to me normally, but because we *are* different. Very different. His family are sat in their giant house, likely eating picky bits from Marks and Spencer's (and not just the yellow-stickered items I get 'as a treat'). I let his comment hang, knowing one word out of place may cause him to storm off and return to his silent treatment.

He twists his body more until his head is level with my chest. "Can I kiss you?"

Okay, now I must be hearing things. Or maybe I've fallen asleep and my mind has decided to fuck with me good and proper. Did Richard slip something into my tea? Or are the fumes from the now dangerously tall fire causing me an inconvenience?

"You don't have to say yes," Jack says. "But I was wrong. You're alright really." No conspiracy theory. He really did say he wanted to kiss me. "We're gonna be huddled up in the tent together tonight anyway, so we were likely to get close. And you called me fit last night." Shit, did I? At least the darkness will stop my blushing from showing. "And you're attractive too, in your own way."

I pinch his cheek, like some 1940s gentleman catching up with a rascal. It isn't my finest come on, but I try my best to make it appear sensual. "You *are* fit."

He smiles and moves closer.

"And interesting. And talented. And —"

He presses a finger to my lips to shut me up, leaving an ash taste on my mouth. Propped on his elbows, he's less than six inches away. There are no fireworks as he leans in, no shooting stars or fanfares, but this doesn't make it anticlimactic.

His lips are soft, but his body firm when I pull him into my arms. He releases first, falling back horizontal on the sofa, his head on my lap, his eyes staring up at me.

I take hold of his hand and squeeze it gently. "I guess you're alright really, too."

9.

Would You Like a Sucky Sweet?

Jack and I didn't sleep in each other's arms. Even just lying next to him was troublesome enough. After five minutes, his bony elbows and relentless hiccups almost caused me to have a meltdown. It wasn't as romantic as I was hoping.

My alarm buzzed at 9am. Ten minutes later and I am yet to pull myself from the sleeping bag. I am alone, wearing yesterday's clothes, and the weather is being a twat. I pull the stiff zip and poke my head into the rain. Outside the canvas prison, last night's bonfire is nothing more than a pile of twisted, whitened wood, damped by the heavy patter of rain from the charcoal clouds. The historic, offending t-shirts now long released into the atmosphere, ready to puncture a new hole in the ozone layer.

"You ready?" calls Jack as he drops three empty wine bottles into a metal dustbin. The crash echoes across the farmland. His cheekbones are glowing, his hair perfect. I feel like a lottery winner. "We're leaving in five."

I clamber out and remove the pegs from the ground, dragging the tent into the sanctuary of the hallway. "Where are we off today?" I ask, taking a bin liner from Jack and forcing my sleeping quarters inside. Water is trickling down my spine and into my underwear.

"Portsmouth," says Richard, scrolling through his phone with one hand, his other waving in the air. "The land where all your hopes and dreams die."

"Well, we have to go there sometime," Jack replies flatly as he pulls on his yellow mac.

We dash across the garden and dive into The Duchess, me dragging Richard's heavy suitcase across the dirty drive. I take a hard-boiled sweet from the tin glued to the dashboard and crash onto the passenger seat. A new pool of water has formed in the footwell, and it instantly penetrates my shoes, our fix on the roof not holding up. "Who's down south?" My memory is still in no state to recall anything pre-cocktails at The Coaching House.

"Adebowale, my African queen." Richard snaps his fingers twice. "I hope they are still as fierce as they were back in Soho. Always the first on the dancefloor, always the last off. The one at the front with the megaphone at any protest march. Portrait of them in the Tate, would you believe."

"Which Tate? I'm meant to be at the Modern next weekend with a friend."

"Is there more than one?" Richard asks.

I gloss over his lack of art knowledge, Jack doing the same as he eyes him in the rear-view mirror.

"What was Adebowale's drag name?" I ask tentatively.

"Boo," says Jack.

I nod, thankful it's tame for a change.

"Boo Karky," adds Richard with a cackle.

"Of course it is," I sigh.

"He is a solicitor now, believe it or not. Well, last I heard anyway." Richard sits up as he applies citrus hand cream. "In the eighties, LGBTQ+ folk were seen as dirty, sneered at, and abused by the suited hacks of Fleet Street, yet every night they were in the front row. Hypocrites, all of them. I could give you the names of a hundred prominent and influential homophobes who have seen more arseholes than a toilet seat."

"Sounds like some people I know in Soho," says Jack.

Richard lets out a laugh. "Nothing like it was, my dear boy. These days, the gays are more forthcoming to discuss poppers and porn than they are to discuss their professional side. If you asked me for my friend's entire sexual history I can rattle them off in chronological order. If you asked me where they worked, not a clue."

The traffic inches forward and we crawl to the outskirts of Birmingham, according to the signs. I had presumed we were still up in Lancashire. Jack blasts the horn as a National Express to Merseyside cuts across our lane. We wouldn't stand a chance in our rust machine. The impact of the noise and the lights of the coach forces someone else into my thoughts.

"Isn't there a queen in Liverpool?" I question. My inability to spell Birkenhead on the envelope has made them stick in the memory. "Surely it makes sense to go there first."

Richard lets out a faux expression of shock. "I assume you mean Westward Hoe. I will help you, but I need to build the courage to see *her*."

"We can't complete this if you don't all agree to get on," I reply.

"Leave it, Harri, okay?" snaps Jack, keeping his eyes fixed firmly on a red traffic light through the dirty windscreen.

I place my hand on his knee, but he brushes it off. I've never known anyone to switch between moods so frequently, and I wonder if our kiss really did happen.

"Liverpool will have to come last," says Richard. "Westward Hoe and I were thick as thieves. She was never the most reliable, but then she started missing rehearsals, missing shows."

"Why didn't you say something?" I ask.

"I did. After it broke down we reconciled, but our mock insults never landed the same. She went off to Jersey after that."

"Must've been serious for her to move that far away from you."

"Nah. Was only for a week to be an extra in *Bergerac*. Thought they were the Dame of Soho after that. On her return she tried writing a play for us all to star in and prioritised it over everything we'd built. It wasn't long before the drugs came and she became a total knobhead. The last thing I did was to tell her to stick the script up her rectum and go back to the Channel Isles. And did she? No."

"Are you sure you don't want to go to Liverpool?" asks Jack.

"No thank you. We even dated briefly. She wanted us to get a house together at one point."

"Why didn't you?" I ask.

Richard sticks his head between the front seats. "I wouldn't trust her to buy a copy of the TV Times. She's about as much use as a fart in a colander. If we leave her till last, there's less chance of us messing up."

"When did you lose touch?"

Richard shrugs and sinks into the back seat. "We used to call each other every day. Then days became weeks, weeks became months."

I gaze at him in the mirror, but he is slumped, head flat on his suitcase. Westward Hoe is likely staring from her flat, my letter in hand, wondering if she should call, day-dreaming the same dreams as Richard, the pair's thoughts connecting unknown somewhere high above the north-south divide.

As we hurtle down the M3, Stonemouth is emblazoned on an overhead sign. "Left here," I call to Jack. I'm halfway through my clean clothes, and my locker at work, or ex-work, needs clearing. I'm not leaving Craig my loose change and emergency deodorant.

"My phone says straight on," Jack replies, eyes fixed on the middle lane.

"I live near here. I'll be quick, I promise."

"Not everything is about you." Jack mutters the words under his breath as the junction towards home passes on our left. It's petty, and I shouldn't react, but frustration and tiredness are not a good mix.

I turn the radio off and face him. "You're being a dick again and you've barely spoken all journey. What's up?"

"I'm fine," he replies.

The traffic slows almost to a standstill, the motorway reducing from three lanes to one. "Would you like a sucky sweet?" I ask, trying all methods to re-break the ice.

"You can have mine. It might shut you up."

I fold my arms tight across my body and sit back as he turns the stereo back on, the sound of *Duran Duran* cutting off any chance of a conversation.

The situation remains the same until we negotiate a

tricky Asda multi-storey car park thirty miles later. The backfire from The Duchess echoes across the open space louder than the guns lining the deck of The Victory.

"Lunch?" says Richard, his first word for a while. "Mummy will pay."

I google the nearest Wetherspoons, hoping a hash brown each will help thaw the frozen atmosphere built up during the drive. I drag Richard's suitcase into the boot, before chasing him halfway across the car park. Pain fires in my shins as I try keeping pace, Jack overtaking and storming off in front. The new build flats surrounding the shops soon give way to a relaxed harbour, the rippled water reflecting the struggling sun onto us all.

"Adebowale lives near here," says Jack. "It was Park Road I think?"

"We passed there a second ago," Richard replies. "Shall we go play knock down ginger?"

"It's not the 1940s," Jack says.

"Boring."

I pull Eric's notebook from my bag and flick through the pages but no Boo Karky is mentioned. "How did you know they lived in Portsmouth?" Jack bites his cheek and sits on a nearby bench. His left foot bounces on his toes and he picks at his nails. "Jack, what's going on?"

He stares at the ground, running a foot through the gravel. "Before he died, Eric heard back from Boo. They were arranging to meet, but Eric got cold feet. He couldn't bring himself to see the photos that Boo apparently kept from when they were younger."

"I bet Boo's are better than mine. Was I in any of them?" asks Richard.

"Your name was mentioned, yeah."

I stand right in front of Jack, trying to tower over him. "Didn't this occur to you to be an important thing to tell me, no?"

"It's not that deep," he mumbles.

"You knew I was going to write to them all. Why wouldn't you tell me?"

"I thought I could do it alone, that's all. I expected to do it alone."

"But even when Gloria forced us together, you wanted

to keep me in the cold. Three days we've spent together now. We're meant to be a team. Did you bring the letters?"

"No. They're in my bedsit. I just have a notebook."

"Pass it here."

"No. It's in the Duchess."

"Give me the keys," I say, holding out my hand. "If you want to find the queens, then we have to work together. No more secrets, understand?"

Jack scoffs, but slides the car keys from his pocket and throws them near my shoes. I storm back to the car, my remaining energy depleting with each stride.

"Do you want us to come?" Richard calls.

I turn on my heels, pacing back towards them, the anger warming my blood. "When were you going to tell me Eric and Boo had been in contact?"

"Eventually." Jack's confidence slowly ebbs away. He brings his knees to his chest, his whole body becoming smaller, as if he is a child hiding himself away in a corner.

"Sure," I reply. "You know how important this is to me. I've spent most of my life trying to find out who I am. You don't know what it's like being passed from foster parent to foster parent. I'm so close to finding out the truth and I won't have anybody else lie to me. I've had a lifetime of that."

"Sorry," Jack says.

"Not everyone grows up in a massive house with rich parents y'know. Some of us had to fight to get to your level."

"It's not like that," Jack replies, louder now.

"Bullshit. You've got the money so you think you can call the shots, buy your way to the top. That might've worked for your dad but it doesn't work on me, okay? I wouldn't be surprised if that's how you get the slots at the art shows and I don't."

I tuck my arms into the sleeves of my jumper and pace around in circles. I want to continue my rant, but Jack is rocking back and forth, his face buried from view. Richard catches my eye and gives me a nod suggesting I drop it. For now he is right, but the warning is there.

I sit in the back seat of The Duchess and pull open the

carrier bags in the footwell. My phone vibrates, Daria's name on the screen. I swipe to answer and place the phone against the interior door handle.

"Hi," I say as I strain to open a bag.

"You sound pissed off. What are you doing?"

I sit back and sigh. "Jack took Uncle Eric's notebook and forgot to tell me."

"I thought you had the notebook?" she says, tilting her head.

"Yeah, but there's two. Mine was incomplete. How's New York?" She doesn't answer, and when I catch her face, she is crying. "What's wrong?"

"Happy tears, happy tears," she says, flapping her hands dramatically in front of her eyes, trying to force them back into her ducts.

I throw the carrier bags to the floor and grab the phone so my face fills the small screen. I sit with my feet along the seats, glad the tension outside the vehicle is being kept at bay. "C'mon, what is it?"

She rubs her hands together. "Before I flew out, I applied for various internships."

"Yeah, I know. You got me to write them."

"Well, do you recall there was a company called Grainger & Grainger?"

"I do." I don't.

"When I turned them down, they said they'd keep my file on record. Turns out they were true to their word. They called Sunday morning offering me a full-time modelling contract."

We stare at each other for a few seconds and then both jump around in delight, which is difficult when you are in the back of a small car, my energetic bouncing causing further material to float from the roof. This reaction is the same we've had for all the important moments in our lives: passing our GCSEs, getting into college, being accepted onto an internship in the US. When we stop moving, tears are rolling down my cheeks too.

"Do you start as soon as you're home?"

She smiles again. "They want me there next week."

"Seriously?!"

"I know!"

"So what are you going to do?"
"Get the first flight back."
We jump around again. This past month has been the longest we've been apart and I never knew how much I'd miss being able to dump all my problems on her, and vice versa. Now though, we get to bask in some good news for once.
"How's your little road trip going?" she asks.
I bring her up to speed, and she can't wait to meet Richard. I leave out the other arguments with Jack, instead telling her how amazing he is based on how amazing I wish he was.
"When you're home, you can visit me in London and I'll introduce you to them. There might be more too. We're off to meet someone called Adebowale today. If they are as good as Richard, we can move things on quickly."
"I'm proud of you," she tells me.
"Likewise."
She props me on the counter whilst she grabs a coffee from Starbucks. It's still strange seeing her live like a real New Yorker, far away from the days of us sitting under a duvet watching reruns of *Friends*. I thought her internship was the best thing to happen to either of us this year, but an actual modelling contract? We've both come a long way against all odds.
"Sorry about that," she says, taking a slurp of iced coffee. "Have you spoken to Michelle?"
"She phoned earlier. I'm not in her good books."
"I messaged saying she needs to give you some slack. You've got more important things than the coffee shop."
"I'd have been sacked sooner or later anyway," I reply, and she chuckles. "I'm surprised I lasted as long as I did to be honest."
"Me too. What's next for you then?"
I pull at the carrier bags again, tipping their contents onto the seats. "I'm in Portsmouth to speak to another queen, like I said. I think Jack took a letter this queen sent to Eric recently."
"You look like you're living rough."
I grab the phone and wave it around the car. "This is

The Duchess, Eric's old VW. Death trap on wheels. Ah, here it is." This notebook is identical to the one Gloria gave me, but the pages inside are tattier. Each page has scrawls of Jack's handwriting, adding additional information throughout, none of which he has furnished me with. Even Richard's hotel is there, circled in red. Google, my arse. I talk Daria through the first few notes, flicking quickly between them as she laughs at the names of the Queens.

"Maybe you could become a designer of drag queen dresses," I say.

"No thanks."

"Fair."

I turn the page and my heart stops. There's no queen on this page, but another name entirely. Harrison Forrester. Underneath is one word in capitals.

Maplewood.

"Daria, can I call you back?"

"Sure, you okay?"

I nod and end the call. Now I've seen it written down, the memories flood back. The minibus journey with the other care kids. The stranger danger video with Tabitha. The playground and the orchard. It's amazing how powerful one word can be. The loneliness of my formative years kicks me out of nowhere.

When was Harri there?

Who did Harri know?

Would Harri want to go back?

I don't know what Jack is playing at, but our mission is to find the queens, not to dig into each other's background, especially my trips to Maplewood Hall. And what is with his questions? Maplewood belongs in the past for me, and not even Jack can prise that information from me.

I remove the page from the book and push it inside the ripped material of the passenger seat. Is he planning to try to fix me? Maybe that's what last night was about. If he thinks he can be an emotional prostitute then he can think again. I laugh at the fact I thought there could be something real, something more than friendship, between us.

If I had bothered passing my test, I'd jump in the front and drive off and leave them to it and head back home. Gloria would know what to do.

It is a ten-minute walk back to the bench, but my anger means it only takes seven. Jack is still in a ball on the seat, but Richard is next to him stroking his knee.

"Jack," I say forcefully as I get close, but Richard holds up a hand to stop me. "Keep out of this Richard."

"Gloria called," Richard says firmly. He shimmies down the bench, leaving a gap next to Jack.

"Is she okay?"

When I sit, Jack leans his head onto my shoulder. "Eric's funeral is next Tuesday."

My rage momentarily disintegrates. "Where?"

"West London Crem. There will be a wake too, in Soho of course."

He squeezes my knee, guilt firing through me at not realising how close Jack was to Eric. He may be my uncle, but I wasn't there, sharing drinks and stories after dark. Even Richard's face is plain, the joyful emotion greying away.

"Do you want to head back to London now?" I ask.

Jack pushes himself up and wipes away his tears. "I've not driven all this way to drive back home again. Let's find Boo. Did you find what you wanted?"

More than you'll ever know. I hand over the book hoping he skips past the missing page. He compares the address to Google Maps, and we are thankfully only two streets away.

10.

"Goodbye, former queen"

Adebowale's front garden is a long way from the stage lights of Central London, both geographically and in star quality. Weeds grow from cracks in the garden path, and the gate hangs by one hinge after coming loose in Jack's hand.

The inside of this queen's residence may be better maintained, but I cannot see past Adebowale's rotund frame. He and Richard are no longer performers in this moment, instead resorting to a stare-off across the fraying welcome mat, the words *Go Away!* emblazoned across the top beneath streaks of dry mud. At least Adebowale has his sense of humour intact.

I bury my hands in my pockets and breathe in the roast beef dancing to me from the oven, then look to Jack whilst we wait for the two old friends to reconnect. The longer the queens watch each other, the higher the tension rises. I should say something, anything. It hasn't reached the full unbearable level, but it's becoming increasingly awkward as they stand frozen.

Finally, Adebowale's booming voice pierces the air like a jet breaking the sound barrier. "Thigh-Ana. My G-O-D!" he says slowly. His face remains emotionless, but his hands clutch the jewellery around his neck. The gravy jug he was stirring falls to the cement steps, smashing against a plant pot containing three weedy sunflowers. The thick brown contents fire across the face of a red-cheeked gnome fishing in thin air nearby, his face now resembling the fallout of a dirty protest.

"Hey Boo," Richard says as he opens his arms wide, but Adebowale stands firm. Richard displays faux outrage, mock pain on his face. "Darling, I did say I'd come back."

As he adjusts the sleeves of his outfit, Adebowale's face relaxes. Not smiling, but less stern than before. "After twenty-five fucking years, the doubts had crept in." He walks towards Richard, studying his face closely, pulling his drag partner's skin-tight with a pinch on the back of his neck. "You're turning into the old tart you swore you'd never become."

"Much like yourself," Richard replies as Adebowale holds him tightly, "Although I'll always have six-month grace on you."

"Are these your boys?" he asks, looking to us.

"Friends. Harri and Jack."

"Adebowale but call me Boo. Nice to meet you both."

Spotting Boo is barefoot, I bend to clear the broken pieces of jug, tossing the shards into a cracked recycling box full to the brim with wine bottles. Sharp pain shoots across my index finger, claret blood running down my palm towards my wrist. I hold my arm high to stop gravity forcing thick droplets along my skin.

"Here, take this," says Boo, handing me an elephant-themed tea towel from the waistband of his plastic apron. "Leave the glass, I'll sweep it later. You'll only end up running your hands through fox shit."

We follow Boo indoors, passing through a cluttered porch. Coats pile high on both sides, acting as stage curtains to the many shoes on the broken rack beneath. My eyes are immediately drawn to the sparkling blue Doc Martins that make my plain black ones look generic and dull.

I let Jack pass through and he gives me a small nod before sitting on the stairs. He hasn't said a word since arriving, but after the elasticated tension between the two of us on the car ride south, I'm reluctant to engage him in conversation.

The wallpaper of the hall is luminous orange, a constant sunrise so bright I fumble for my shades.

"Won't be a moment." Boo opens a cupboard, a stack

of possessions spilling out onto the tiles like the end of Jenga. I look to Jack, but my eyes are drawn to the walls above his head. Every framed photo a snapshot of Boo's past life.

They're all immaculately clean, the centrepiece of the house. There's Boo, on stage at the Lord Nelson, dressed as a chicken with legs wide and mouth open. Next are all five of The Dragnificent Seven together, smiling on the front of the *East London Advertiser*, proudly holding a large cheque for over three thousand pounds for an AIDS charity. Richard and Boo have aged well. They may be slightly thinner, with additional wrinkles across their brows, but the same glint remains in their eyes.

Front and centre is Eric, the crown I inherited perched at an angle on his head. Despite the image's graininess, the background of Old Compton Street is instantly recognisable. I'd give anything to experience the day in that photograph. You can tell they loved each other, comfortable being their true selves in broad daylight. Where did it all go wrong?

"Is this all of them?" asks Jack as he silently joins me, causing me to jump slightly.

"Um, I assume so, considering there's five." My finger is throbbing as I hold the towel tight.

Jack stares closely at the newspaper article, his face slowly becoming concerned as he snaps a photo on his phone whilst reading the caption.

"What have you seen?"

He clenches his fists and punches at his thigh. Two punches, then three. "Nothing, it's just, nah it's nothing. I'm going through some family stuff."

I take my turn to stare closer at the article, but nothing of concern stands out. "Are you sure you're okay?"

"It's not that. I'll be fine. Sometimes I need space. A lot playing on my mind." He squats near the hall radiator, head in hands.

Further down the hall, posters for The Dragnificent Seven entice people to venues across the capital: The Coleherne, Brompton's, Subway. Some of the many stages long since turned into wine bars, Euro minimarts, and estate agents. Although the London gay scene is thriving, the days when underground venues stretched from Stratford to Shepherd's Bush are over.

"Good times, them," says Boo as he stands next to me, a Winnie the Pooh plaster and a bandage thrust in my direction. His multiple gold bracelets jangle like windchimes. "Want me to check out your gash?" he asks, winking.

"It's a scratch," I reply, rolling my eyes. I'll have enough double entendres to write a guidebook by the end of our journey.

Boo snaps on blue latex gloves and holds my cut closed. My fingers clench as the plaster is tightened, and I become lightheaded as the bandage is wrapped to stop the flow. Boo clutches my arm before I topple forward into the cat litter and sits me on the bottom step.

"Head between the legs, darling," he says, forcing my face between my knees.

Folded double, I try and take my mind off the pain, focussing on the reason I'm in this house. "You kept all your posters."

Boo nudges me with his shoulder. "Oh those old things. They aren't mine."

"But you were in The Dragnificent Seven." I raise my head, but Boo shoves it back between my legs.

"Of course I was, but these were collected by Vincent. He always was a bit of a hoarder, wasn't he Richard?"

"Vincent?" Richard turns his head from the mirror, a fake eyelash stuck to the end of an index finger. "As in *Vincent* Vincent?"

Boo smiles and passes a photo from the sideboard, sliding it into my viewpoint. Another queen is dressed in a yellow outfit with a skirt which must be ten feet in circumference. On their head, a variety of fruit rests on a tall headdress. "Havana Banana."

"I've not heard of her," I reply.

"She wasn't part of the group, Harri," says Richard. "Just a friend from the scene."

Boo points at Havana's picture. "Mm-hmm. This was during the phase where they would cover the audience with whipped cream, do you remember, Richard?"

He nods and smiles. "It was all fun and games until a

patron slipped over one night down The White Swan and dislocated their hip."

"He didn't get invited back after that," laughs Boo. "Whole venues used to stink of curdled milk by midnight. Thank God he wasn't part of our troupe. We'd have been barred from the City in no time. Took a lot to get banned from the clubs in those days as well."

"Must've been fun," I say.

Boo takes in a breath. "Well, I'll put the kettle on and we can have a chat."

I want Jack to be here, instead his mind is elsewhere as he slumps on the couch in the next room, biting his bottom lip, and tapping away on his phone. Whatever his family have said has had one hell of an effect. Maybe his parents aren't much different to Mum after all.

"Vincent and I used to date," says Richard.

"So did Eric and Vincent," calls Boo from down the hall.

Richard raises his eyebrows. "Life was quite incestuous at one time or another. Vincent was trying to get round the whole of Soho."

"That's not true and you know it," says Boo.

"It is," Richard whispers to me.

Boo gives a tight-lipped smile and fills the kettle, talking over the running water. "We all had our problems, I'm the first to admit that, and Vincent might've had a temper, but nothing he did was worse than anything our Eric did. Once he got sober he became a dream."

"What did Eric do?" I steadily make my way down the hall, holding onto the radiator for balance. Richard gives me a wide stare to force me into silence, but it's of no use.

Boo settles four decorative porcelain teacups onto the glass coffee table. "Vincent was given an opportunity to be in panto at the Palladium. 1997. Him, Clary, Dennis, Dench."

"He was sleeping with the director," adds Richard for context. "Brought a whole new meaning to the phrase *he's behind you."*

Boo slaps him on the arm. "Regardless, it was an opportunity that could've seen him break free of the toilet venues. Sugar?"

"No thanks."

"One for me, darling," says Richard. "The panto would've been brilliant, Harri. Vincent had real star quality. All was well until Eric stopped it."

"Until Eric stopped it," confirms Boo.

Richard looks at me and forces a smile. "Eric wanted what was best for us all."

"Didn't work though, did it? He did what was best for *him.* We should've spotted it long before."

"Did it cause you to split?" I ask.

Boo lets out a long sigh. "Yes and no. It was the beginning of the end. It'd likely have happened regardless. During the final three years the fractures within the drag community grew. Everyone wanted top dollar. Many of us fought on, but we started to drift. We were all getting on a bit then, too."

"Would you ever want to reconnect with everyone from those days?" I ask, the question loaded.

Boo stirs his drink slowly, the teaspoon chiming on the rim of the cup, before emptying a sleeve of Jaffa cakes onto a plate. He remains silent throughout. Perhaps he thought he'd never have the opportunity to relive his youth.

Despite avoiding the question, I get a sense Boo will soon be the next to agree to give his past a chance. If he's happy displaying the memories so brazenly, surely he'd be willing to bury any hatchets.

"I'm going to get my slippers," says Boo, smiling and scuttling up the stairs.

Like Gloria's flat, there's a lot of clutter in the front room, yet it all fits together. A strong elephant theme floods throughout, with tables, lamps, and paintings all depicting the animals. Behind the television, a black and white image hangs. A young Adebowale sits in between an older couple, possibly parents. They're flanked by more youngsters as they sit on suitcases outside an airport terminal, the name Lagos standing tall across the top of the building. The wide smiles of the older pair show pride in the man sitting between them.

"Lot of elephants," says Richard as he sits on the stool in front of the piano, tapping an off-key rendition of *Chopsticks.*

Ashen-faced Victorian dolls line up along the back of the sofa like an audience in a haunted theatre. Their ceramic eyes catch the sun as it blazes through the stained-glass ornaments hanging from the curtain rail, pupils glowing red like laser beams ready to destroy the hopes of anyone who's unfortunate enough to cross their path.

It's a stark contrast to the hallway. The drag scene is a separate world to this space. This is heritage, all Adebowale and no Boo. I take a seat next to Jack, his position unchanged. He scratches at his scar, eyes focussed on his shoes.

"Are you alright?" I ask again.

He shrugs gently. I move slightly closer, my hand hovering above his knee before I come to my senses and place it on my own. He breathes out. "Family things." Goosebumps prickle the skin of his arms. "Mum and Dad are taking my sisters off on a ski holiday and they want me to go with them."

"You've said yes, haven't you?"

His top lip curls. "My sisters sat their final exams last week so they're taking a trip to Val-d'Isère to celebrate."

"I'll go if you don't," I joke, but he doesn't laugh.

"They never took me anywhere to celebrate mine." He raises his head and pushes his palms to his eyes once more. "I told Dad about the funeral and he said I could fly out the following day if I wanted. The pictures of the chalet he's booked looks amazing. All views of slopes and mountains, but I don't belong there."

"Maybe it'd do you good to get away from London?"

He makes rare eye contact and frowns. "You'd want me to leave London?"

"No, of course not. I meant it's an opportunity to have a refresh. You've been busy with the art show and all this driving."

He folds his arms tightly around his torso. "I guess, but I like this life. I enjoy being part of the scene. I don't want to be the rich kid, not after escaping that image a few years ago. I should stay for Gloria, she needs me."

"I can be about for her."

"Yeah but you've your own life in Stonemouth to deal

with. This life and your home life are two separate entities."

He's right. London has the lights, the people. It has Jack. He still has that magnetic hold over me I can't shake. I can live with his quiet moments, his random desires to disappear, if it means eventually we can remain as close as we were by the bonfire on the farm. I can picture Michelle telling me not to make a bad decision, but he mesmerises me, hypnotises me, even when he acts like I don't truly exist.

London is an oasis in a desert of indifference, Stonemouth a rope binding me, wrapping tighter and tighter, restricting my lungs. Gloria's offer to use Eric's room is too good to pass and I pull out my phone.

Michelle. I'm moving to London. Come to my flat tomorrow x

Clarity, that's what it is. I know I promised to take my time, not to jump into anything, but Michelle was the one who told me to take my opportunities. If she's angry at me jumping from a sinking ship, then she should blame herself too for being the one who helped put a hole in the hull.

"Would anyone like Battenberg?" asks Boo, returning and pouring more tea.

"I'm good thanks," I reply, Richard and Jack declining with me.

Boo flicks the TV on, the four o'clock news leading with the grieving mother of the missing boy, William Bosnich. The same photo of him from the report I saw at Gloria's earlier in the week is in the top corner.

His mum is huddled behind a tree of microphones, clutching a small stuffed Garfield toy whilst a map is shown of his last known movements after leaving Bethnal Green Working Men's Club. Jack stares intently at the screen, his fingers digging into his palms.

"Breaks my heart," says Boo. "I pray he's found."

"Someone must know where he is," Richard says.

"We can hope." Boo switches channels, devouring a Jaffa cake whole as two couples search a flea market for antiques with a man in a natty tweed suit.

"So what brings you all down here?" Boo asks the

room, but clearly aiming each word at Richard.

His tinkling of the piano keys stops mid-bar and he stares out the window. "I've been meaning to visit, honestly. The timing was never right."

"You never even wrote," Boo replies.

"I wanted to Boo. Christ, you've no idea how much I wanted to. I've missed you, and I know deep down in your cold dead heart you feel the same, but in the back of my mind there was always something tapping away, telling me that burnt bridges can never be rebuilt."

"Between all of us maybe, but not individually."

"You didn't write to me either." Richard blows across the top of his cup and shuts the lid of the piano. He twists himself on the stool until he and Boo are facing each other.

Boo lowers his glasses halfway down his nose. "I didn't know where you lived."

"I'm easily searchable. Harri and Jack managed to find me."

"I can't lie and say I haven't tried looking you up. It's just, you and Vincent didn't part on the best of terms did you."

"He ruined The Dragnificent Seven's final performance by gate-crashing the stage. That should've been our pinnacle but his alcoholism was taking over, thinking he was Soho's main character, causing harm to too many people I loved. I didn't see him sober for the final year I knew him."

"You can't keep blaming him," says Boo. "You were hardly an angel, and as for Eric…" He tails off.

"That's the reason I'm here," says Richard. "Eric was still living at Gloria's flat, the last remnant of The Dragnificent Seven in Soho."

"I know," says Boo. "I need to reply to his letter. Admittedly, it's been eight months but I'm sure he'll let me off. Let me guess, the old bugger sent you to check up on me?"

Richard waves a hand in my direction, and Boo glares at me with his brown eyes fixed.

"I'm afraid Eric died two weeks ago, Boo. Heart attack."

"The funeral is next week," Richard adds. "We wanted to ask if you'd be there?"

Boo lifts himself from the chair, straightening out the hem of his long blue silk outfit. It matches the style of the one in the picture with his parents. Did they know who he was, or was he forced to live a double life like me? A photo of Wilma Cockburn on stage is placed on the coffee table and Boo lights a cheap tea candle, the flame glimmering back off the glass.

A piano chord chimes and Richard's voice floats over the top. He only manages to make it through the first line of an edited *Candle in the Wind* before he and Boo collapse into a fit of giggles.

"He'd have found that funny, too, Harri," Boo says, realising my shock as he wipes the tears from his eyes. "Of course I'll come to the funeral, it's only right. Can't do any harm, can it?"

"He'd want you to be there," I say.

"Harri is Eric's nephew," says Richard.

"He was taller than me, I know," I reply.

"I didn't think he had family after you know what," Boo replies, falling back onto the sofa.

"Turns out he did," I say. "Mum never spoke of him, either."

Boo's eyes flick briefly to Richard, his face changing shape. There is a beat of a pause. "Well, I'm sorry for your loss. Were you close?"

"Never met him. I only learnt about him after he died."

Boo places his cup down and sighs loudly. "Let me mention this to Vincent. I think he'd want to be there."

Richard stands up and flicks the channel over on the television. "We don't know where Vincent is."

"I know exactly where he is," says Boo.

"Where?" me and Richard reply in unison.

"Iceland."

"Why the fuck would he move there?" Richard asks. "He was always bitching about the cold weather."

"I mean the shop you idiot. I married him. This is his house. He's getting the roasties for dinner." Richard stands, but Boo waves him back to the stool. "He won't be back for a few hours yet. He likes to spend Tuesday afternoons playing Bridge down the local. Zero per cent stuff for him these days, of course."

Silence falls across the room again, the person picking the letters on *Countdown* the only movement of note. Boo picks up Eric's photo and strokes the frame. "Where's the funeral?"

"West London Crem," I reply.

"I'll make sure Vincent is there," Boo confirms. "This is purely for Eric, okay? We're both happy living down here. London was fun while it lasted, but it's a quarter of a century since I left town. Things will never be the same again."

"Thank you," I say.

"Will the rest of the gang be there?" Boo asks.

"I hope so. We're trying to contact everyone. We thought Ivana lived in Limehouse but Jack visited and they weren't there."

Jack brings his knees to his chest at the mention of Limehouse, the threats with the pool cue still having an effect.

"What about Westward Hoe?" asks Boo.

"Liverpool, apparently," says Richard. "I've told Harri to leave them 'til last."

Boo taps a finger on the arm of the sofa. "The last I heard about Westward was that they were thinking of moving to Tenerife and opening up a cabaret club."

"I've never been to Tenerife," I say. "This could be a good excuse to go."

"I'm not going abroad," Jack says. I'd forgotten he was in the room for a moment.

Boo blows out Eric's candle and slips his photo into a shoebox that he's, for some reason, keeping trapped under the sofa with a foot. "Westward may not even be there. Me and Vincent have been quite the recluses I'm afraid, so never went over to check it out. Vincent has gammy hips and my blood pressure has been through the roof so flying hasn't exactly been top of our agendas."

"At least we have two queens, so that's a start," I say. "Two and a half if we include Vincent."

"You make it sound easy," says Richard.

"Gloria told me not to build my hopes up. Said some of you wouldn't come back."

Boo passes me the Jaffa's. "Well, you have us two on

your side now. Luckily for you he kept all kinds of shite. Rest of his memorabilia is in the loft. I'll get it down for you if you like?"

"That'd be amazing, thanks. Wanna see it Jack?" I ask, trying to break him out of the internal prison he's trapped himself in.

He sits up straighter but only to tie his shoelaces. "I'm going for a walk. Need some air."

Boo smiles sympathetically as Jack passes him by, watching as he leaves. "Did he know Eric?"

"For a few years," I reply.

Boo looks out through a small gap in the corner of the curtain. I follow his gaze. Jack walks in circles, punching at his thigh. Two punches, then three.

Boo puts an arm around me. "I'll find the stuff upstairs. You do what you need to help him," he says, nodding to the garden. "He doesn't look in a good place, and I don't mean Portsmouth." He picks up another Jaffa, eating it in one. "Don't be like us, for Christ's sake. Keep the people you care for close."

11.

The Afterglow Vista

Richard is back on the piano, attempting to play God knows what, whilst Boo swears at the loft ladder from the landing. In the front garden, Jack stands, fiddling with his headphones.

He's gone into standby mode, staring into the distance as he stumbles around the overgrown lawn. By the time my shoes are on and I've opened the door, he's already out the gate and disappearing behind an unclipped hedge. I crunch over the broken glass on the path and lean the gate against the fence when it comes off in my hands. Portsmouth is bathed in warm spring sunlight, the noise of the starlings in the trees fighting over berries whistling through the air.

I run out to the road, chasing Jack down as he paces towards the town, taking my chance to grab his arm as he waits at a pelican crossing. He shrugs me off, slipping his headphones over his head and pulling out his phone.

"Jack, wait." I say, holding his wrist before he can hit play. Radiohead to match his t-shirt. He's in one of those moods, then. "I'm not sure what's upset you, but I want to help."

"You can't," he replies as he waits for a gap in the traffic.

"Let me try. It's what friends do."

"Acquaintances, not friends." His smile is borderline patronising. It's a sucker punch. We've driven half the length of the country together and kissed under the moonlight so surely I deserve a second of his time. I might not have been on my best behaviour at the hotel, admittedly, and I'm still unsure if I said anything I shouldn't have, but he's the one making this difficult. I wish I could make sense of him.

"I'm gonna move to London," I say, hoping to convince him I'm genuinely worried.

The lights turn red, and he steps across the road, his stride in rhythm with the beeps of the signals. "Where you gonna stay?"

"Gloria's."

"That's Eric's room." He's still walking, forcing the conversation to take place over his shoulder. I don't want to beg him, but he needs to thaw a little. I grab at his arm again, forcefully this time until he finally faces me. His eyes glisten with tears, mascara prints now stamped below each.

"Eric isn't coming back, Jack. I know it's hard, but you have to face that."

"Move in then. Take his place."

"I won't be taking his place. I'm doing this for me. I want to be part of your group."

"Sounds great." His tone doesn't show the same emotion as the words.

I thought he was bad enough on the journey down, but whatever has happened in his family is having a serious effect this time. If I were asked to go skiing in the Alps I'd be completely the opposite. Perhaps growing up in money changes your perspective on the other parts of your life. If our lives were swapped, would I be looking down on people too?

We walk in silence to the harbour, taking a seat on a bench with a view across the water. A large navy ship is docked, and the grinding of metal chains and the metronomic thud of hammer on rivets echo on sea wall. In the distance, the Spinnaker Tower looms large, a giant pin stabbed into the globe. A crane lifts containers onto the docks. They're stacked like a giant Lego wall, the names of eastern European countries large down their corrugated sides.

"Wonder what would happen if you tried stowing away on them," I say, pointing.

"Why don't you go and try it. I'd get some peace then at least." Jack kicks stones on the floor. His headphones are on, but I know they're still silent.

"You don't always have to act like a dick." I need a crowbar to open him up. I don't even care if we never become best friends, but for now we're stuck together. I need to ask Gloria what makes him tick cos I sure can't figure it out myself.

A group of boys, early teens, bundle in front of us, half of them eating chips, the others kicking a scuffed football against the bollards. It eventually spins off and finds its way to my feet. I take a swipe at it, only getting it as far as a TARDIS like police box. Half term always brings gangs of kids out, but at least they're harmless.

In Stonemouth they've become brazen, shouting insults as you pass, especially to people who dress like I do. I've never been one for wearing a matching grey tracksuit or talking as if I've graduated from Sixth Form at *Waterloo Road*.

Seeing the boys takes me back to my upbringing, and what it would've been like to have Eric in my life before now. He'd have advised me better than falling for the wrong boy all the time, no doubt warning me against getting hung up on Jack for starters.

It'd have been different if I'd more friends. Even during secondary school I used to hang out with Daria more than the boys, spending rainy lunches in the creative arts department, her drawing outfits, me learning to paint. At least we had something in common. By Year Ten I'd heard every joke about being adopted, and they stung each time despite me claiming they didn't. "I'm okay, honest." My standard reply. Just like Jack's.

He's on the move again, but I need to break through to him. I stand in his path, moving left and right as he tries to pass. "Can I ask you something?"

"If you must."

"Have you been looking into my past?"

He looks at me with a scrunched face. "No. All I know about you is what Eric told me."

"What about Maplewood? Did Eric tell you that?"

He stares at the ground. "No."

"So where did you hear it?"

He pushes me to one side and moves to the harbour's edge. "You brought Maplewood up outside Gloria's, you're not special. I keep notes of everything to help keep my brain in order. It doesn't work the same as everyone else's."

"Why was Maplewood the only thing you wrote down? I've got nothing to hide. If you want to know anything about me, ask. It'll save the trouble of doing your own research."

Jack leans on the blue railings and spits into the sea. The air hangs with the same saltiness as the promenade running past the Stonemouth amusement arcades. Seagulls swoop, picking at bread as it floats on the surface, tossed from the hand of a small girl with her family nearby.

Jack spits again and turns his body towards me. "My dad used to take me to Maplewood during school holidays."

"You went there? Why?"

"Dad worked there. Sort of. I thought it was a coincidence you'd been too."

I let his words hang for a moment. "I thought your dad was in education?"

"He's rich. Was part of their trustee's board or committee or summat. First took us down one summer when Mum had the flu. He paid for some of the kids to be able to go. The money was used to provide courses for people like you to give you a better outlook in life. I didn't want to mention it in case you thought my charity towards you this week was because I still felt sorry for you."

I get a shudder. Maplewood then, Portsmouth now. History repeating itself, forcing me to rely on the goodwill of the same family to escape a broken home life. Maplewood was a paradise. A grand house, symmetrical with dorms on the top floor. They gave views of endless fields and canal towpaths. I cried when it was time to come home, thinking I'd never return.

"Did you genuinely feel sorry for the care kids?" I ask.

"Yeh, of course," says Jack. "I used to play rounders in the fields with different groups. On Sundays we'd go fruit picking, and there were woods to build dens down by an old oak tree. Dinner was at six."

His voice is robotic again, no emotion behind the words, bored at having to say what's coming out of his mouth. I used to love picking fruit, but there was no oak tree. Maybe he's confusing Maplewood with another country house from his past.

I look across to him, but he turns away. "You are being honest with me, aren't you?"

"You don't trust me, do you?" he replies.

"I do, it's just, I've been burnt too many times before, Jack."

"The owner was Benedict Busby."

That's a name I've managed to keep locked deep in the vaults of my memory. He was tall, heavyset, always casting a darkness as he entered the room. The Shadow. That's what we called him. I lived with the fear he'd drag me to an office and beat me with his belt if I did anything untoward. I'd heard the stories.

"Does your dad still know Benedict?" I pray not. He represents a time too emotionally scarring.

"He died. Maplewood closed a few years ago now, too. It's a nursing home these days."

"Hang on, you said it was derelict?"

"*You* said it was derelict," he replies. "I just went along with that."

I nod and stare down at the water, timing my breathing with the waves crashing against the rocks from the wake, the gentle ripples of the harbour disturbed as an Isle of Wight ferry glides away in the distance.

"Did you really mix with kids like me?" I ask.

He rolls up his sleeve and reveals the scar under his tattoo. I still can't place that design of his. It's a band, I'm certain of it. "At Maplewood, there was a playground. Do you remember the playground, Harri?"

"Of course. It was the best bit."

"And, past the playground, towards the bottom of the grounds, between the apple trees of the orchard, there was a treehouse. Shaped like a beehive. Glass panels of orange around the outside with a small metal slide leading to the ground."

The memories flood my brain out of nowhere and I stagger to the nearest bench. I used to sit crying in the beehive, just me alone, playing with no friends, no family. My legs shake as the trauma is released, as if the past years of mental recovery never happened.

"I was sat in the beehive once, hiding from a rainstorm," Jack continues as he sits next to me, resting his head on my shoulder. "Dad said never to go in the treehouse during a storm. It's dangerous in a storm, Harri."

"Benedict Busby used to say the same to me."

He nods. "One day I rebelled. Hid whilst everyone else went in. Dad didn't notice. I was jumping in there and slipped. My arm went through a side panel. It sliced right through. It felt like I was there an age before they heard the screams. . They got the ambulance out whilst I thought I was bleeding to death. This scar is from that."

The beehive. Its panels were orange as he says, all except one. Near to the entrance, there was a hexagon missing, at odds with the sunshine glow lighting the rest of my sanctuary. It used to annoy that no one cared enough to repair it, as if it weren't as important as the other panels, just like me. Who cared if I was a bit broken? As long as, on the surface, I appeared held together.

"Now do you believe I was there?"

I give him a forced smile. "Yeh, sorry. I guess I'm a bit paranoid."

Nearby, a crow attacks a carton of chips, fighting off others as they swoop to steal his rewards. The wind whistles across the harbour and over the bench, slapping me with bitterness.

"What about your tattoo?"

He holds his forearm straight. "It's the symbol for The Afterglow Vista."

"What songs have they done?"

He shuffles away slightly. "The Afterglow Vista was a creepy place in the woods near my grandparents' estate in Surrey. A weathered stone circle where you could sit. I used to build fires in the centre, staring into the flames, watching the wood burn and buckle."

"The drawing looks familiar for some reason. Thought it might be a band."

"I liked the woods, and the fires. The flames mesmerised me, as if I was burning ties to everything troubling me. Fire always makes me calm."

The bonfire. Those flames and the cascading ash were responsible for him coming on to me. Once it had burnt to a white, tangled pile of wood, he'd moved away, not prolonging our body contact.

Jack pulls his sleeve up further and runs a finger along the outline of the tattoo. "This symbol was carved into a stone at its entrance. If you look closely there's a T, A, and a V, see?"

It's as clear as day now he's pointed it out. "Why did you have it done?"

"The symbol always stuck with me. I guess I could be myself there. I regret it sometimes. Was young when they inked me. Too young."

"What did your parents say?"

He goes quiet and draws heavy on his vape. "They didn't care. Well, Dad didn't anyway. He has a large Ozzy Osbourne on his upper thigh that he had done when sixteen. I might get some chips. My stomach is rumbling."

"There's some on the floor there," I say, pointing to the discarded portion.

"You sure about moving to London, then?"

The way he flitters between topics is enough to give a person whiplash. Even having lived by the sea for sixteen years, the expanse of water in front is not presenting a sense of longing to return to my old life. "I don't belong in Stonemouth. Maybe I never have. My sister is on her way home from New York so I really should meet her when she returns tonight. It will give me a chance to put some things right."

"What has Gloria said?"

"I haven't told her yet. I'll phone her on the way back to Stonemouth tonight."

"Are you sure you don't want to head to London first with us in The Duchess?"

I shake my head as more boats pull into view. "We both need some space."

"It's not your fault by the way, all this," he says, waving his hand around himself. "My family is exhausting, and I know I shouldn't complain, but I've learnt I need to put myself first sometimes, and if that means removing myself from a situation, then so be it. It's nothing personal."

"Understood. That's the problem with families. I spent years wishing for one, and then when I got one I still wanted more, something better, something perfect."

"There's no such thing as the perfect family," Jack says.

"I guess." I stand and brush the dirt from my jeans. "I'm gonna head back to Boo and Richard and let you get back to your depressing music. Will you be back before I go?"

Jack shrugs, burying his chin in his t-shirt.

"I'll move my things to Gloria's during the week. It'd be good to have you there. We can have a celebratory takeaway if you like."

"Maybe."

I punch him on the arm and leave him on the bench, his foot tapping on the floor as *Paranoid Android* filters from his headphones. As I cross the road, I look back, his body appearing as a fractured silhouette against the shallow ripples of the harbour. He turns his head, giving a small raise of his hand. I reply the same and make my way towards the terraces.

Boo and Richard are on the sofa as I re-enter. They don't notice me at first, instead laughing loudly as they browse through the photographs and newspaper cuttings laid across the tabletop. Eric's candle sits between empty Roses wrappers, it's flame now burnt out.

"Hey." I kick off my shoes, catching them as they quickly bury a few clippings to the bottom of the pile. "What are you two so nervous about?"

Richard looks at Boo, before standing and putting an arm around me.

"We don't have to, not yet," says Boo, but Richard takes his hand gently.

"Come and sit down," Richard tells me.

I place myself between them on the sofa. The television black, all focus on the newspapers in front of me.

"Your uncle," Richard continues. "He was a good man. Admittedly we had our differences, but he always meant well."

"And I'm genuinely sorry he's gone before we could, y'know," adds Boo. "How old are you, Harri?"

"Twenty-three."

"He was the same age when he moved to London," says Richard. "It's striking how similar you both are. Moving from a small town to find your people."

Boo hands me a pile of papers. "These are some articles he wrote for a local gay fanzine. I want you to take them."

"Are you sure?"

"Yes. It will help you understand the way he thought, the things he did. You'll learn how things were for us in the eighties, too, and all we were up against."

Richard leans back and sighs. "So many people in these photos have gone now. They fell like dominoes."

"And so many people thought we were the ones in the wrong." Boo swipes a bottle of gin from the base of a drinks globe and pours a shot into three glasses. "We lost a lot of friends."

Richard looks down at the floor as he talks. "Every week someone else from our circle was taken to hospital, never coming back out. Each morning you'd look at yourself in the mirror, a thought in the back of your head telling you you'd be next. *Has that mole always been there? Have my eyes always been that sunken? Why am I sweating in January?* Question after question."

Apart from half a documentary I once saw, I'd hate to admit I don't know enough about the subject. In my head it was the distant past, all in a place miles away from home. Now, here I am, sat between two people who were there, fought through it, survived.

"We were part of a group demanding answers," continues Richard. "After so much inaction, we teamed up with the lesbians and fought for an answer. The government didn't care for us, Thatcher and her lot treating us with utter contempt instead of doing everything they could to help.

"People we thought were friends turned their backs. Christ, some were celebrating us dying, as if we were proving their theories right. They could've stopped the game, but instead they discarded us."

"We were the ones at their bedsides," says Boo. "We were the ones making sure they weren't alone at the end. We picked up their food from the floor, dropped off by nurses too scared to even look them in the eyes. Most of their families never even visited."

Richard has anger visible in his eyes. "All of us marched to try and get answers, to try and get support. We marched alongside others in the community, we marched with the miners, we marched with the few celebrities who cared. At times it felt like we were raising our heads above the trenches for target practice."

"And the die ins," says Boo. "The *ACT UP* one outside *The Telegraph* in '88 was my first arrest."

"I thought you were bundled away in '87?" Richard cocks his head.

"They all blend into one."

Much like the photo of Eric in my new bedroom, the raw emotions of the people who were caught on film are still as powerful today. Every inch of the black and white photos releasing their power back into a modern world.

"Did Uncle Eric march with you?" I ask.

Boo and Richard look to each other and Richard hands me a copy of *Gay News,* opened on a double-page spread. "That's him in the centre with the sign."

Even without colour, blood can be seen on Uncle Eric's temple. He stands straight, *Action not Hysteria* scrawled across the cardboard placard in his hand.

"This was at a particular nasty incident in Wardour Street," Boo continues. "We were marching from *Gays the Word* to Soho, late '86, demanding the government listened to us."

"What went wrong?"

"This was normal," Boo says, pointing to the photograph. "The mainstream media were running smear campaigns against us daily. We weren't no better than the rats who caused the plague in their eyes. We got to Wardour Street and were faced with a counter protest. Bricks were thrown, spit was spat, and well, as you can see, the verbal abuse was horrendous."

"It's a powerful image which tells you more than any words could," says Richard. He slides the photograph closer. "I'm so sorry."

They fall silent as I study the image. Eric's body may be beaten, but determination and power radiate from his face, his eyes mixed with equal parts strength and fear. He looks on the verge of being defeated, but a fire burns inside.

Opposite him, a woman stands, screaming in his face with a megaphone in one hand, his banner being ripped by her other.

She may not have the perm these days, but there's no mistaking the eyes. I've seen that stare a million times before. The stare when she found out about my detentions, my truancy, another missed curfew. The stare I'll face tomorrow when I tell her I'm leaving Stonemouth for good.

12.

Once more unto the breach

There's a water stain on the ceiling of my old bedroom in the shape of Snoopy. I've spent the past four days staring at it, horizontal in bed. Jack didn't return to Boo's house before my train home. In fact, he hasn't messaged me since, not that I've been tied to my phone, waiting anxiously for him to do so.

He'll be researching the latest designer ski boots and goggles, or whatever else rich people take with them to the slopes. Having never been abroad, I wouldn't know.

Also, my constant belief he might be thinking of me can't be doing my mental health any favours whatsoever. What happened on the farm was a one-off. He was vulnerable, clearly, and I shouldn't have taken advantage.

I down a glass of water, willing my body to give me energy to shower, yet all I can do is starfish in my boxers on top of my sheets. I'm slap bang in the middle of a funk, as Michelle called it in our one text exchange this week.

I've felt like this since I set foot out of the station, not wanting to meet anyone or do anything other than sit in a blanket fort watching *Netflix*. It's amazing how well *Squid Games* can drown out the sound of Callum's porn in the neighbouring room. The walls are so thin I could use the rhythm of his masturbation as a metronome if I were of a musical persuasion.

Flu-like symptoms were the excuse I made to Daria as to why I couldn't be at her welcome home picky tea. Telling her how Mum had treated Eric and the others might break her heart, so it's easier to delay it by hiding away alone in this pit.

A month ago I'd complain consistently about Craig and his stupid café, but with that problem extinguished, I still can't shrug off the feeling I'm underachieving. I should be showing some 'up and at 'em' attitude. When I next arrive at Waterloo Station, the storm clouds will surely fade.

I slide off the bed and pull open the curtains, the sunlight illuminating my room. The summer-like weather makes the back entrances of the shops one floor down seem less grim. I'd allow some air to flow through the flat if the scent of overfull Biffa bins wouldn't be brought in on the breeze.

My bedsheets need changing but I don't have the energy. Even my wardrobe suffers the effects of my laziness, my choice of clothes diminishing rapidly. Most are bulging out the laundry basket to my right. I'll look like I've completely given up when Daria arrives, dripping in high-end fashion.

The stack of dirty plates remain balanced on the journey from my room. I turn on the hot tap and squeeze a lemon-scented jus from a non-brand bottle into the washing up bowl.

The crunching of tyre on gravel from the driveway below flicks my attention away from my static-like thoughts. I catch Mum's red Mini as she pulls the handbrake on sharply, diagonally across three spaces. She isn't meant to be here, nor do I want her to be.

I throw on the cleanest jumper from my bedroom floor and open the door, standing nonchalantly, waiting for them to exit the lift. The anger bubbles below my skin, and I bite my lip to stem the shower of verbal bile I want to spit when she comes into sight. When the lift pings, only Daria emerges.

"Alright?" she says. Her voice bounces, as if everything in the world is fine. In hers, I guess it is. She walks hunched towards me with one arm outstretched, the other dragging a suitcase. The sleeves of her expensive dress billow around the elbows, its golden colour matching her bold eyeshadow.

I take her into a hug. It's like being wrapped in a warm blanket. "Welcome home," I say. "Mum not coming in?"

Wishful thinking.

"She's getting some bits out the car. She knows about you quitting work so is half angry and half worried you're not eating properly."

"I'm not." The closest I've had to vegetables this week was when I attacked a family-size carrot cake whilst crying over *Notting Hill*. I'm such a mess. "Want a coffee?"

"Could murder one," she replies.

I pull her suitcase through to the hall and prop it next to the shoe rack. "I don't have a hot skinny latte with an extra shot from somewhere trendy in East Village, but the next best thing."

"Nescafé?"

"I'm honoured you think I could even afford that."

She follows me into the kitchen, wiping crumbs off the hob before leaning on it and staring me down. "What did you want to talk to me about?"

"I'll tell you later," I reply, checking over her shoulder to see if the car is parked up. It's not entirely in between the lines, but the driver's seat is empty.

"Harri, tell me."

"Mum hated Eric. Well, not only Eric, but everyone," I whisper. "She protested against the whole community. Like, megaphone-in-the-face protests."

Daria rubs my arm as I grab the milk from the fridge. "That's disappointing."

I glare at her around the fridge door. "Disappointing is your favourite comedian having a kid and starting a shit podcast about it, Daria. This is way beyond that. I don't even want her in my house. She'd disown me if she knew the truth."

Daria lets out a sigh. "The truth about you, or the truth about your hunt for Eric's friends?"

"Does it matter?"

"Guess not." I've a feeling she doesn't want to be involved. Listening to a family argument would be the last thing I'd want that deep into jetlag. A problem for one of us used to always be a problem for us both so I'm not letting her bail now. Anyway, it was her who first landed me into this mess.

"You haven't asked about Grainger and Grainger." Daria says slowly as she pulls the mugs down from the corner shelf, inspecting them closely in case they aren't up to her standard.

I open my eyes wide. "I've had more important things on my mind. Have you not been listening?"

"Fucking hell, Harri. This is important too."

She really doesn't get it, but it's a battle that won't be won in this kitchen. Once this is all over, I can attack again from London. "I'm pleased for you."

"Tell your face," she replies as she drops three sweeteners into her mug.

"Give me some slack, I've been bedbound all week. When do you start?"

She becomes animated, her hands clenched together. "I went to their office yesterday. They've promised me the world, but then they would say that."

"You could be the next Naomi Campbell," I say.

"And you could be the next Picasso." I admire her ambition. At least one of us has some. "They allowed me to bring some of last season's clothes back."

I grab at her cuff as she stirs her coffee, running the material between my thumb and index finger. It's expensive, as silky as caramel and no stitch out of place. It hasn't been mass-produced in a warehouse in Southern Asia like the fast fashion filling my wardrobe.

"I asked if they'd anything for men too, you know, to help with job interviews. The suitcase in the hall is yours. Word of warning, some of it's a bit, well, out there. Anything you don't want I can take back."

"Thanks. Will save me another day of washing too." It should be me giving her slack. Solitude can turn you into a selfish prick. She doesn't understand Eric like I do, but she does care. And how did I repay her? Telling her I'm leaving. "Will you visit London much?"

"You're definitely going then?"

I nod.

She holds my face in her hands. "They told me yesterday most of my photo shoots will be there. We can meet up as much as possible. Hey, we can go to The Ivy one day. Or I can get you a front-row ticket for fashion week."

"Won't you be too busy for me?" I say as I wipe my sweaty face on the tea towel.

"Never. And at least I'm not in New York." She kisses me on my forehead and steals a banana from the fruit bowl. "Maybe I can meet Gloria soon?"

"Did you want to come to the funeral on Tuesday?"

"Harrison?" Mum's voice echoes before Daria can answer. I roll my eyes and drag myself away. "You look dreadful," she says as she pushes two full Lidl carrier bags into my arms. She skitters about in her work uniform as if my flat is the next room on the hotel cleaning list. "I got you some food in. You're wasting away."

"Thanks." Ginger nut biscuits sit on top of each bag, her failing to remember my hatred for them.

"Don't take it for granted. I'm not a charity. You need to get your life sorted. You're an idiot for quitting your job. Luckily for you I spoke to the new night manager at work and he says you can have some shifts at the hotel. Cleaning the bar, polishing reception, things like that."

"I'll think about it." I put the bags in the kitchen and carry my coffee through to the hall.

"There's a trial shift next Monday night."

I'm twenty-three for fuck's sake. I shouldn't be encouraged to work graveyard shifts, especially with my mum, at a hotel less than a decade away from being torn down. It's the direct opposite of ambition. "I can't do Monday."

"Daria, talk to him, will you?" Mum calls as she heads back towards the communal stairs.

I wait until her footsteps fade and head into the front room. Daria flicks through the TV channels at pace. "You've not mentioned London to her at all?" she asks.

"Not yet. The timing hasn't been right. Gloria is excited for me to move though and says she'll help soften the blow here."

"You can't leave without saying anything."

"I know."

We sit in silence until Mum returns. Two more bags of shopping are brought in. "This was sticking out your box," she says, handing me a ruby envelope with my address written in gold. "Where are you next Monday, then?"

"I've an event at the Tate with Michelle. We're gonna stay overnight."

Mum furrows her brow. "I'm sure Michelle told me she's visiting her sister in Leeds all next week."

If I'd called Michelle back I would've known this. I'm a boat drifting away from the dock where she stands. It mirrors the queens, their lack of contact now understandable. I wish life were straightforward. I slide the envelope open and a small card falls to the floor. I have to read it twice to acknowledge what it says.

"Wedding invite?" asks mum as she runs her finger along the top of the television, wiping the dust on her tabard. "It's filthy in here."

"Better," I reply. "I've been asked to exhibit my paintings at a gallery in Camden." I flip it over, already convinced it's a hoax, but it looks genuine. "Someone saw my portfolio online and wants me to be involved. For three weeks my art will be displayed as part of an Emerging Talent show at The Potteries near Mornington Crescent."

Daria squeals and nearly strangles me. "Can I come to the opening?"

"One step at a time," replies Mum. "It might not be anything grand."

I might not be Britain's next top model, but she could at least pretend to support me as much as she does Daria. I pull out my phone and type an acceptance to the RSVP number. "This is big for me, Mum."

"But does it pay the bills?" she replies.

"It might do. I could sell some of my work."

"But you don't paint anything recognisable."

"Well it's no different to standing in some stupid clothes which no sane person wears in real life."

"Harrison, enough of that," Mum snaps. "Your sister has worked her arse off to get where she is."

"And yet all I'm good for is to work in the same hotel as you?"

"Stop it, both of you," says Daria.

I slump down on the sofa next to her. Mum pulls out the pouffe and sits opposite. "I'm sorry love, but I worry, that's all. That's what mums are meant to do."

"Parents are meant to be supportive. Ever since Dad died, all you do is mollycoddle me. I'm not a kid anymore. I'm taking them up on their offer." I hit send on the text and force a smile at mum. "If it doesn't work out, at least I've tried. The hotel will always be there, London won't be."

"Where will you stay?" she asks. "And what about this place?"

"I've some art friends in Soho. They might have a sofa for me or know someone with space."

"Soho is dangerous. And dirty."

I'm not sure if she means present-day Soho or during The Dragnificent Seven's era. I shouldn't be shocked by her opinion with her having been brainwashed during the eighties.

She takes a sip from my coffee. "Your milk is off. Look, you're still young and it isn't always safe after dark in London."

"I'm only four weeks younger than her," I say pointing at Daria. "Either way, I'm going."

"How will you afford it?" asks Daria, unhelpfully.

"I'll get a job. I'm sure there's some dead-end hotel looking for some gullible prick to polish the reception desk for a few weeks."

Mum spins her head and gives me a killer stare, but I'm over it. My phone buzzes with a reply from the art gallery.

Glad to have you on board. The spare room is ready. Gloria.

I should've known she's behind it.

"The people at the gallery have given me a place to stay. Are you happy now?"

Mum sighs and looks out the living room windows, seagulls squawking as they feast on last night's takeaway remains, her hands clasped behind her back, as if planning her next attack. I focus on the television, another new daytime quiz show on mute, but Mum's next question doesn't come. Instead, she silently heads into the kitchen, the clinking of plates being washed filtering through shortly after.

"I'll be safe, I promise," I say to Daria. "Also, I get to hang out with you when you next come up."

"Will you ever come back home?" she replies without making eye contact.

I look at the black mould climbing the walls from the skirting, and the mud stains on the carpet like the footprints of a monster. "This house is no longer a home. Gabe and Callum don't need me here, and what else do I have going for me?"

"You might meet someone you like."

"I've nearly completed Stonemouth Grindr and I'm still single," I reply, but she doesn't laugh. "Look, Daria, London has already welcomed me and I've only scratched the surface. If you were staying here then it might sway me a little, but you'll be up there too. This is what we always wanted as kids, wasn't it?"

"I said Los Angeles, personally."

"LA, London, it's the same thing. You wanted to be a model and I wanted to be an artist, and we both knew neither of those could happen here. Now both are a reality, why are you trying to dissuade me?"

"I worry about you."

"Oh change the record, you're as bad as her," I say as I stand and gesture towards the kitchen. "Gloria getting in touch and telling us about Eric was a sign."

"You know about Eric?" comes a shaking voice from behind me.

I turn and face Mum and the blood rushes to my muscles. All moisture leaves my mouth, and it feels as if my jaw is wired. Mum stands, frozen, her hands wrapped halfway through being dried on her top. Her eyes are glazed and for the first time in a long while, she looks vulnerable.

"We received an email a few weeks ago," I say. It feels wrong to confront her with the full truth, as if whipping a horse that's already down.

"We?" she says.

"Me and Daria. Someone called Gloria sent it." I look to the sofa, but my sister's eyes remain fixed forwards.

"Is this why you're going to London?" asks Mum. She walks to the small dining table and sits on the chair, coffee cup shaking in her clenched hand.

"No," says Daria. "He does have an art show."

"Would you've told us about Eric?" I say, my body refusing to move any closer.

"He's a friend I used to know when younger. Gloria too. They aren't important."

Her not being able to admit he was her brother over thirty years later tells me everything I need to know about how much she cared. I wait for her to choose the right words. When she remains silent, I go for the jugular. "He's dead, if you care."

Mum's eyes flash towards me. "Dead?"

"Harri," says Daria, but I'm on a roll.

"Had a heart attack a few weeks ago. Shame you couldn't have buried the hatchet. But as he was *just* a friend…"

"Enough, Harri," Mum snaps. "I knew you were up to no good when Dai White wrote. Why did you deny it when I questioned you?"

"He's nothing to do with me." I say with a smirk. "Never met him, never will. Same with Eric."

"You better keep away from them when you go to London. I won't have you hanging around with anybody from their group."

I hold my hands up. "I'm making no promises. Soho isn't the biggest place."

Daria flicks the television off and storms across the room, taking my hand and dragging me into my bedroom. "You've said enough," she spits. "None of this will help anyone, including you, but you couldn't help yourself, could you?"

"You should be on my side."

She holds onto my arms, her face softening. "I'm on your side Harri, but you need to learn to control your emotions."

"You've not even met these people," I reply. "I'm the one who has travelled around the country finding them, learning about their history. They're no longer names scribbled in a notebook or on the back of a polaroid."

"Attacking Mum won't solve anything."

I scoff. "You haven't seen her, Daz. Eric was stood there, bleeding, pleading for people to help, yet she did everything in her power to hurt him. It might be in the past for her, but this is my life now."

"Things are better for people now," Daria replies.

"You really believe that?" I laugh. "Wait 'til you're in Soho and see for yourself."

Daria releases her grip and slips on her shoes. "I'm going. I'll take Mum with me. This was meant to be a nice catch up. Will you be in later this week to try again?"

"Who knows? I'm going to London once I've sorted myself here. Might take two days, could be tomorrow."

She nods slowly whilst biting her lip. I've known her long enough to spot the body language showing she's thinking I'm deciding my fate too quickly, but she doesn't argue. Instead, she kisses me on the forehead. "Call me before you go."

I fall onto my bed, wishing the ground would open up and swallow me. I don't leave my room until I know for certain they've gone. The flat falls completely silent, as if a distant bugler is waiting to play The Last Post, ready to signal the end of my time in Stonemouth.

13.

Love, Potentially

The suitcases I'm hauling along the uneven pavements fracture the fresh Soho morning peace. A tumble down the escalator at Waterloo saw a wheel break free from the larger case, and it scrapes rather than glides as a result.

The strength in my arms has diminished, but I've made it, Stonemouth firmly behind me. Yeah, my old landlord might be pissed off at having to find another loser to fill that room, but that's his problem. Me in London, who would've thought. In time, Mum will understand I won't be coming home. Both she and Daria are giving me the silent treatment, not so much as a phone call in the three days since their visit.

Michelle came on Sunday to help with ironing whilst I threw my less important belongings in the wardrobe, ready for when I collect the remainder next week. All I have to my name are the two suitcases of mid- to great-clothes, and an overwhelming sense of belonging.

Gasping for caffeine, I enter Roberto's café. He leans against the counter thumbing through the latest *Time Out* listings, his Mediterranean-rooted olive skin smooth, as if the stress has been ironed out like the creases on my t-shirts.

I'm not alone this time. A customer is sat on the table in the corner. He's leant back casually, dressed immaculately in a white cotton shirt and cream chinos, tapping away at a document on a laptop. A six out of ten.

He cocks his head slightly and flashes a smile, my cheeks flushing as soon as we make eye contact. He's borderline hypnotising. A seven out of ten.

Late-twenties maybe? No older than thirty for sure. I momentarily forget Roberto as I weigh up whether approaching him is in anyone's best interests. He's sweeping me closer, a hidden river undercurrent, like he's meant to be sat in that seat at this moment. He adjusts his Airpods, continuing to give quick glances across the café floor.

Roberto kicks an empty chair out on the table behind me, the noise snapping me into reality. "Harri, good to see you. Hear someone got quite drunk in Manchester. How are you?"

"News travels fast." My chance of a Hollywood boy-meets-boy moment has been cruelly pulled from under my feet. This wouldn't happen if Richard Curtis were directing my life, that's for sure. Hugh Grant would be here too, probably.

"You seem half the world away," says Roberto, snapping his fingers to bring me back to the room. "You're looking well."

I toss my backpack to the floor. "Likewise. Have you been away?"

"Only as far as Regent's Park. How's the search for The Dragnificent Seven?" Between questions, he dips his tongue into a glass tumbler. Small bits of greenery float around the dark beige liquid inside. It looks like a forgotten pond.

"We've two queens on board, and they'll be at the funeral tomorrow. Shame the others won't make it, but we've done what we can."

"It will be lovely to see them. Where are you driving next?"

I shrug. "We know Westward Hoe is in Liverpool. Well, there or Tenerife. As for Ivana, that's a mystery. Jack tried finding them but came back empty-handed. We'll run out of options soon and I don't want to let Eric down."

"Or The Duchess will break down." He laughs, but then concern wrinkles his forehead as he lowers his voice. "How are you feeling ahead of tomorrow?"

"I'm alright. Kinda. It is what it is." I'm still yet to

grieve, and don't expect to until I've found the real Eric. With the move to London and the argument with Mum hanging over me like a pressured storm, the dust hasn't settled in any part of my life. I look across the road at my new home.

"Gloria says you might be wanting some work," says Roberto.

"I will be, yeah. I don't want to freeload. You don't have anything going do you?"

Roberto laughs. It was a stupid question when half his tables haven't been used for what looks like days. He gulps at his drink, his lips pulling back over his gums as he swallows.

"What the hell are you drinking?"

He plucks some cotton from the cuff of his white uniform and nudges the glass towards me. "Some ginger and spinach thing I saw on *Saturday Kitchen*. It's meant to work miracles for your gut. Winona Ryder allegedly swears by it."

"Yeah, she probably says it tastes like shit. It certainly looks like it." I gently move the glass back towards him. "I'll give it a miss. Any chance of a latte though?"

He heads behind the counter and wipes at the coffee machine's nozzle with a cloth as he whistles a jaunty tune.

"I wouldn't drink that either." The seven has stopped typing, a hand on the now spare chair. "Mind if I join?"

An image of Michelle's duck flashes through my mind, quacking at me to grab it by the bollocks. The way his thigh muscles test the material of his trousers aids my decision. I gesture to Roberto's empty seat, hoping he isn't planning to return. Maybe he's an eight.

"I couldn't help overhearing," he says, a slight accent revealing itself from under his fluent English. He opens his laptop and drops a sugar cube into his coffee, "Your plight sounds interesting."

Am I so chaotic that we have to resort to the word *plight*? "What plight?"

He laughs, revealing two lines of unstained teeth, and holds out a hand. "I'm Dan from Goliath PR. Samson and Goliath PR, to give their full name. Danilo de Souza to give mine. Not many care to say either in full. It's

Brazilian, before you ask. Pleasure."

His palm is soft. Even from this short distance his warm bronze skin has a golden hue, and when paired with his short, tight curls, something deep within me twitches.

"I don't think I've ever really known what PR is," I fumble. Not the greatest chat up line, admittedly, but it's more chilled than the first three that landed on my tongue.

"Everyone just thinks I go to parties all the time."

"But you don't?"

"Most nights." He laughs again. Even his laugh is hot. "They get boring after a while."

"I wouldn't know."

"You'll have to come with me to one sometime."

Is he joking? I think he's joking. It catches me off-guard so now I'm just staring like a goldfish across the table. Thankfully, he's more trained in the art of normal human conversation.

He twirls a pen around between his fingers. "I'm currently working with the council on an advertising campaign for Soho. The Dragnificent Seven name keeps cropping up and I heard Roberto mention them. Did you know them?"

I bite the inside of my cheek. "Sort of. Eric, sorry, Wilma, was my uncle. I've been looking for his friends from the old days."

"Maybe I can help." Danilo chews his pen and links his arms above his head. Now it's his biceps fighting to escape the Ben Sherman stitching. He must be doing it on purpose, but I'm not complaining. "If you wanted me to, of course."

I'd jump on him now if I could but must play it a little cooler. It's been difficult enough working around Jack's mood swings, so would adding another unknown into the mix muddy things further?

Roberto places a drink next to me and winks from behind Danilo's back. I lean towards Danilo, close enough for his sweet aftershave to fire up my senses. "What are you thinking?"

"Not decided yet. I could include them in an article. People would love to hear about the historic drag scene, I'm certain. *Gay Times* or *Attitude* could publish it. They owe me a favour."

"Will I be in it?"

"Not if you didn't want to." Danilo leans his head back, allowing sunlight to bathe him. "Hearing their story would educate people on what they experienced. The hardships, the fun parts. We're the sons of those who came before us, metaphorically, and they're as important to Soho's history as any building out there."

I'm still uncertain what PR is, but he seems good at it. His idea appears logical, but would Eric have wanted his face splashed across a national magazine? Without his permission, it seems wrong.

"There's no requirement to agree now," Danilo says. "We can meet for a drink sometime. Do you live nearby?"

"Over there," I reply, nodding across the road. "Moved up today. It's my uncle's funeral tomorrow but maybe a drink soon would be good."

He removes a small leather wallet from his shirt pocket and slides a business card across the table. "Call me anytime."

With my track record of getting not only the wrong end of the stick, but the wrong stick entirely, I try to remain calm but sweat is pouring down my back, and I haven't touched my coffee. His dark eyes glint as the card is held between our hands. I'm totally filing this in the drawer labelled 'flirting'.

"I'll let you know," I say.

"Please do."

He shakes my hand again as he stands, our palms remaining together for just slightly longer than standard. With a lace undone, he hitches his foot onto a stool, giving me a full view of his arse. It's like two watermelons in a tote bag. I come over in a hot flush as he gathers his laptop charger, giving me a wave as he exits.

As the entrance bell finishes jangling, I open Instagram and type his name. The top two accounts are both him. One professional, one personal. I click on the personal through curiosity, only to find it private. My finger hovers over the 'request' button for a few seconds but fuck it. I press send. His interest might solely be about Eric and the queens, but I need to do my research before bringing him into our circle.

To my horror, a notification crops up within seconds saying he's accepted my request. A follow from him comes straight after, and then a message. *Hey x.* He's keen.

I check to make sure he isn't lurking in the shadows, before scrolling through his grid. He likes being shirtless. Often in public too. There he is lazing by some water, which is Hampstead Heath according to the location tag. It isn't the cleanest of pools, the algae-strewn surface the same colour as Roberto's drink.

Other pictures show him at Pride, marching in a harness, and another is taken in what looks like the dark locker room of a gym. His Roman statue chiselled body my new obsession. I move my fingers across the screen to increase the picture size, close to taking a screenshot.

"Stop thirsting," says Gloria from behind. I quickly lock the phone and throw it face down on the table. "He's a nice kid. Dan summat. I've known him a while now. Did some guff for an exhibition last Christmas and managed to get my face in Vogue."

"He was flirting with me," I reply.

"It's London, babe. Flirting gets you everywhere. Except with Jack."

"I haven't been flirting with Jack," I protest, but Gloria raises her eyebrows. "Okay, maybe a little, but he's a part-time arsehole so that's done."

For once, Gloria is not in comfortable home clothes, dressed now more like a Victorian witch, her long emerald dress partly obscured by a heavy cape.

"You coming to sort your room or not?" she asks.

"In a minute." Despite how often I glance at the street, Danilo never passes. All my life I've been one hundred per cent atheist, but what are the chances of a ten out of ten being the first person I meet after moving here? It's as if he's been sent from above to prove I've done the right thing coming to London.

Gloria grabs a Kit Kat from the counter and takes the smallest of my suitcases.

"Did you get Danilo to meet me?" I ask.

"Aren't you mister suspicious?" she laughs. "He's one of Roberto's regulars."

"Only regular," Roberto calls from somewhere underneath the counter.

"Give him a call, that's all I'll say. Now, are you gonna come with me or sit here like a spare prick at a wedding?"

I down my latte and grab the rest of my belongings. "See ya later, Roberto."

Gloria looks up and gives me a beaming smile. "Welcome home." She hangs her cape over her arm and pulls two gold keys from her dress pocket. "Big one is for this door, small one is for upstairs."

Both look identical. I try the wrong one first, almost jamming it in the rusting lock. The brass zero is missing completely now, replaced by a simple matt white circle.

"There's a pot of coffee on the side. Should still be warm. If there's enough, pour one for me and Jack will ya?"

He's still alive then. "What time's he arriving?"

"He's in the shower now."

I nod my head. "I haven't spoken to him since Portsmouth and didn't know if he was alright. I didn't want to message in case it caused problems."

"He can be off sometimes, I know. What you have to remember is Jack always comes home. Sometimes he needs his space, like you."

"He was worried about his family stuff."

"What family stuff?" asks Gloria, looking concerned.

I wave her away and push open the front door with my shoulder. "It's nothing I expect, they were stressing him out a bit, but whose family doesn't?"

My suitcases clunk heavily on each stair. A voice yells from the first-floor flat telling me to shut up. I shout an apology but continue pulling them noisily up the remaining twenty steps. The windows to my new home are wide open, allowing the stale cigarette smell in the air to dampen. I empty the ash trays into the food waste bin on the fire escape and pour the coffee from the percolator into three mugs, heaping sugar into Gloria's.

Cirrus clouds cool the sunshine as it beams over the rooftops. I lean on the outside railings, taking a deep breath as I stare at the mews below. From this height it resembles a Lego village, all narrow passages and dark overhangs, but this move will be right provided I stick to three main principles; Progress with my artwork, don't give up on Eric's legacy, and, most importantly, don't fall in love with Jack.

"Hey."

Jack is in the doorway, shirtless, wet hair hanging over his face, a small towel not even reaching mid-toned-thigh length. That's my third principle absolutely fucked already. Great start Harri.

"You alright?" he asks.

"I'm good." My hands fumble as I lift my cup, splashing liquid onto the lino. "Fancy getting some lunch?"

"You not coming to Camden?"

I frown. "Camden? No, why?"

"Forget I asked." He downs half his drink and tops it up with the dregs from the pot.

"What have you been up to?" I ask. "All okay with the family?" He grabs a biscuit from the jar and takes it whole in his mouth, before extending them in my direction. "Still want you to go skiing?"

"Meh," he mumbles, crumbs spitting into the air. "I'll get through the funeral tomorrow and then decide. It's the first time it's been properly hot here for ages so it's pointless going somewhere cold. I'd rather go to the villa in summer."

"You have a villa?"

"Somewhere outside Valencia. It's nothing fancy."

I fail to hold in my exasperated laugh. We've quite different views on what fancy is. Fancy to me was being allowed *Vienetta* for pudding on a Sunday. "Sounds grander than the caravan in Skegness where me and my sister got dragged to for eight years straight."

Jack swallows another biscuit. "Speaking of sisters, one of mine is about tomorrow for a job interview."

"How has she managed that considering she's just finished her GCSEs?"

"She's always been precocious. Also, having a dad who's minted helps get your foot in the door. Unless you're me, anyway."

"She not skiing either then?"

Jack looks to the floor. "Oh, no, they're flying out in the evening. Her interview is around the corner. Some music bollocks on Denmark Street. Said I'd meet her for lunch. If you see us, don't mention I've been driving The Duchess. My family worry I'm doing dangerous things."

I mimic zipping my mouth shut. "Your secret is safe. You're not gonna miss the wake, are you?"

"Do you always ask so many questions?" He turns on the cold tap and rinses his cup, the bath towel holding itself around his waist by a thread. His scar is more prominent in the sunshine.

"Hot water for washing," says Gloria as she passes through the plastic strips and slaps his bicep. "And you, get yourself unpacked. There's some of Eric's clothes left in the wardrobe. Dump 'em in the bin bag in the hall and we can take them down the chazza."

"Can't it wait? I'm knackered."

"Richard is coming," says Jack.

"Our Richard?"

"Do you know any others?" Gloria pulls her underwear off the makeshift clothesline hanging between a shelf and the curtain rail, gives them a sniff, and then stuffs them in her pocket. "He's messaged saying he's somewhere near Dunstable. Had booked some place near the British Museum, but the reviews on *TripAdvisor* said it's only suitable for rat lovers. I'm going up Camden with 'im in a second so he can stay at Magento's place."

"I hate rats," says Jack, his body shivering.

"Isn't Magento the creepy guy I met?"

"Magento is the one who's given you your art show," says Gloria. "You get used to his advances. Usually trying to be kind but not understanding personal boundaries. Just tell 'im to piss off. Anyway, drink up. We've stuff to do."

Richard stands a foot away from Jack's latest artworks on the mantelpiece, his thumb and index finger rubbing at his chin. Occasionally he'll go to speak, before remaining quiet. "How much did you say they were?"

"I dunno. A grand?" says Jack. He's crouched on the floor picking at a hangnail.

"Each?" I reply. Richard stares at Jack with mock shock.

"Just buy one," says Gloria, laying on our new leather sofa in a facemask, left hand raised and dropping chunks of Bakewell Tart into her mouth.

"They'd look good in the hotel," I say.

Jack's art has become less protest-based this month, and although the Pop Art primary colour backgrounds remain, there are no words, just a large black elephant in the centre of each. Jack stands and holds one at arm's length. "They were inspired by Boo."

"I'll check my budgets." Richard flops into an armchair.

"As you wish," says Jack, wetting his finger and removing a fleck of dirt from the edge of a frame. He takes them from the mantelpiece and leans them against the radiator. The Barbie death count is now at sixteen. Above there is a large clay chicken, painted green, teetering on the edge of the shelf.

"Do I want to know why you have this?" I ask. It's surprisingly weighty.

Gloria removes one slice of cucumber and side-eyes me. "They misunderstood when I prayed for a twelve-inch cock." I wasn't expecting a sensible answer. "Saw it down Portobello last week. Thought it'd look good with the rest of the junk."

"How many are we expecting tomorrow, Glo?" Richard asks, taking a swig out of a non-labelled medicine bottle.

"Don't ask me. Could be ten, could be hundreds. Hopefully enough to eat the buffet or you fuckers'll be living off sausage rolls for a month."

"Maybe I could entice more to the Nelson with a performance," Richard says. "The return of Princess Thigh-Ana."

"I'd pay to see that," I say.

"Maybe your new fancy man can write an article on it," Gloria says.

Jack looks at me sharply and I come over all hot. No words form in my mouth, air trapped in my lungs. The silence is unbearable but I don't know why I'm feeling guilty. Six Instagram messages from Danilo remain unanswered, burning a hole in my pocket. I've remained professional, but the flirtations in his texts have increased each time and I can't bring myself to agree to that drink he keeps requesting. Michelle would tell me to pull myself together and go to see Danilo now. I'll see him next weekend.

Richard leans forward, his head resting on his hands. "That's not a bad idea."

Did he read my mind?

"You don't have your outfits with you," says Gloria.

Princess Thigh-Ana. Not me. Phew.

"I don't need an outfit, and anyway, I wasn't talking about tomorrow, but in the future. It'd be a fitting way to remember Eric. What better way to keep a memory alive than by reliving it." He points in my direction. "If he's banging someone who can do an article, then it's win-win, isn't it?"

"I'm not banging anyone," I reply sternly. I look to Jack, his face tight and brow furrowed. "I'm not, I promise."

Richard rises from his seat, taking Gloria's cape and swirling it with both arms around his head, the ends almost whipping me in the face. "Ladies and gentlemen, he's, she's, gays and theys, please welcome to the stage, The Dragnificent Seven!"

"There's only two of you," says Gloria, flatly.

Richard stops mid-twirl and looks down his nose. "Worked out alright for Bucks Fizz didn't it? Picture it, Gloria. Friday night, on stage under the bright lights. How iconic would that be? Boo has already hinted to it, and if he does it, Vincent can step in too."

"It wouldn't be the same," says Gloria.

I run the idea through my head, and it makes more sense with every second. "It could work." All three stare at me. Why hadn't I thought of this before? I bound around the room, punching my thigh at not having spotted the obvious until now. "All the young gays would come for sure. And it'll bring back those who loved you at the end of the last century."

"Don't call it the last century you little shit," snaps Gloria.

"You make us sound ninety," adds Richard as he throws a Kipling at me.

"Jack, back me up."

Jack shrugs, but a smile fires across Richard's face. "Gloria, fancy one more shot at being our manager?"

She moves from her horizontal position and opens her eyes, staring out at us through the green facemask like a papier mâché alien. "It's all of us, or none of us."

"Ivana won't be there," says Jack, now sat in the corner and hugging his knees near his chest. "We don't know where they are, and I doubt they'd want to be involved if we did."

"You don't know that Jack," I say. "We can't assume."

"Gut feeling," he replies.

I turn away from him, putting a boundary up to his negativity.

Richard grabs me and spins me around the room. "The Dragnificent Seven: The Reunion. It's on. Let's spread the word."

I laugh, happy at finally finding my place in the world. "I'll call Danilo after the funeral tomorrow."

"Danilo?" says Jack.

"He's just someone I met this morning," I reply.

He scoffs. "I wondered how long it'd take him to move on to some fresh meat."

"He seemed nice."

"Everyone seems nice if they want to get with you."

"I told him that," says Gloria. "Look, Richard, let's not get too far ahead of ourselves. I need to see Mark down the Nelson this afternoon, so can ask if he could let us have the place for a night. Mates' rates and all that."

Jack jumps up and throws his backpack on. "I'll see you all tomorrow," he says flatly as he trudges across the room and heads down the stairs.

I whack my coffee cup on the table and bound down after him, two stairs at a time. I throw my hand against the front door, stopping him from opening it fully. "What's up with you?"

"Nothing."

"There obviously is. Is it family stuff?"

He smacks my arm away from the door and heads into the sunshine. "Harri, I'm fine."

Does he not want to succeed in getting the drag

queens back together? Maybe this was the reason why he was pissed off in Manchester. "Please Jack, I promise the reunion will work."

"I'm sure it will."

Just when I thought I'd figured this boy out, I realise I'm nowhere near. "Is it Danilo? I only spoke to him for like, five minutes? Ten at most. He only wants to help."

"So you're ditching us for him, is that it?"

"Us? There never was an us. What happened at the bonfire was a one-off, or that's how you've made it seem. I tried Jack, Christ I tried, but you moved on before Portsmouth."

"It's cool, honestly."

"Jack, you don't understand how much I wanted there to be an 'us'. I was stupid believing there could've even been an 'us'. Danilo is just a friend, but let me get over you the way you've gotten over me, okay?"

Given the choice between Jack and Danilo, I'd choose Jack every time, but I can't repair someone who refuses to be fixed. Jack pulls his coat tight around his body and walks towards Wardour Street. I keep pace beside him as we push past the tourists.

"Did you want me to come to Camden with you?" I ask.

He nudges me with his shoulder. "I'll see you tomorrow, okay. I'm driving up in The Duchess. I'll pick you and Gloria up from here at ten. And *don't* bring Danilo."

I lean against the wall of The Breakfast Club and let him walk away. Again. The hipsters in the queue for pancakes look at me sympathetically. Jack was correct from the start. We're only acquaintances, like we always have been, more like brothers in a disjointed family than lovers destined to find one another.

I don't have the mental capacity to deal with his reluctance to engage, and everything I do seems to be wrong. Money may not buy happiness, but it buys the belief that you should always get your way. The sooner he realises that, the better he'll be. As for 'us'? No. I deserve someone who wants me.

My eyes remain fixed until he disappears around the corner. I pull out my phone and go straight to Instagram. I don't read the fresh messages from Danilo, instead typing two words in response. "Free tonight?"

14.

Kenneth Williams' Offcuts

My head pounds with every bump of Shaftesbury Avenue and I try not to vomit into the footwell each time a red light forces a stop. I should be thankful to Danilo for driving me to Soho, especially as he could easily have let me get the early morning tube from Clapham.

Coffee Tequila was again the protagonist in my downfall. The hangover anxiety is strong. Although I slept, waking up face down on his sofa an hour before I was due to be collected for the funeral was not the smartest move.

"Are you ready for today?" Danilo asks as he takes a left onto Dean Street.

I fold my arms across my body. "You should've sent me home before I got so pissed." I know it isn't his fault, but I need a scapegoat. I don't care if his toned thighs are on show in his short shorts, I'm blaming him.

"You were the one who insisted on shots." He grabs my right knee and gives it a squeeze, my body tensing. "It was a nice evening though."

I wish I could remember it.

"Mind if I drop you here?" he says, pulling onto the pavement. Ahead, a small Tesco lorry is blocking the narrow road, its orange hazard lights blinking through the drizzle.

The five-minute walk to home in the rain might wake me up. I open the car door, clattering it into a pile of green bin bags. "I'll message."

He reaches to the back seat and grabs my rucksack, smiling as he throws it out to me. "I'll give you a call if I hear from my BBC contact."

Hopefully, as I sober up, details of this contact will seep back into my memory. I hope I haven't agreed to do anything stupid but with my track record, who knows.

The eyes of the public are on me as I stagger to the flat, each pupil judging as I down a scotch egg to soak up the alcohol in my stomach. The buildings on either side appear to fold onto me as the sky turns from steel to smoke. My breathing short, I toss the food to the gutter and falter towards the safety of my new bedroom.

I tumble into our building and pull myself up the stairs, collapsing onto the landing. The dirt embeds on to my cheek as I hold my knees, hoping the anxiety attack fades. I'm curled like a child, back in a new home. If I hold my breath, will there be a social worker discussing my behavioural issues from a neighbouring room?

The flat door opens, a pair of sports socks inches from my eyes. "You're late."

"Leave me for a minute," I croak.

"Gloria won't be happy if you don't get a move on," Jack says as he walks back inside.

"You aren't my parents," I call after him. Flashbacks. My go-to line whenever I was preparing for conflict. I'm not an infant anymore, so why is my brain putting me back there. The loneliness, the abandonment issues, all flooding over me.

The footsteps return, but this time softer. My rocking stops and pink slippers appear. Gloria lets out a grunt as she lowers herself down to my level, taking my head gently and stroking my greasy hair.

"It's okay, Harri, take a moment."

"Sorry," I mumble, causing the stroking to intensify.

Soft music plays in the background, the tone rising and falling. Jack crouches behind Gloria with his phone out, a meditation on YouTube.

"Breathe in time with the sounds," says Gloria, laying my head on my outstretched arm. "I'll get the water running for you."

"Did you have a good night?" asks Jack once Gloria has gone.

"We didn't sleep together," I whisper.

"I believe you," he responds.

I don't know if that's a lie. Even if me and Danilo had slept together, why should he care?

"Sorry if I've messed you about," I say.

"Sorry I was a dick." He moves to the stairs leading to the top floor. I push myself until I'm on my elbows and look in his eyes. They immediately flicker to the side, and he punches his thigh. Two punches, then three. His words are directed at me but spoken to the wall. "I told my family I didn't want to go skiing yesterday. Dad was angry and Mum was upset."

I lay myself back down, staring into space. "Is life always this difficult?"

"Seems it."

"I don't think you're a dick, by the way. Not all the time anyway. Difficult, yeah, but not a dick."

He shrugs. "I can be, especially when my head takes charge. I wanted to find the queens, but I'm gutted they won't be at the funeral. And then last night, you and Richard, you know."

"What?"

He bites his thumbnail. "You planned the reunion together. And Danilo too. I'm being replaced."

"Don't be stupid. No one will replace you." In all aspects of my life, I hope one day I can prove that.

"You best get ready," he says.

I drag myself inside the flat, tossing my damp shoes into a corner. The TV is showing a mock fireplace, the flames flickering across the screen. Jack falls into the chair in front of it as Gloria shoves a cereal bar into my hand. Both are ready to leave, looking smart in bright clothing. Jack's blazer is tailored, fitting perfectly against his body, the buckles on the shoes he's pulling on catching the pale light forcing itself through the clouds.

My head spins as I stand in the shower, the steam fogging the room. I throw up into the plughole, my mouth filling with acidic coffee flavours as I force the chunks down with my big toe. Eric best be amused, wherever he is.

With my stomach continuing to try to turn itself inside out, I dry and pull clothes out of my still unpacked suitcases on the bedroom floor. I slide on a new blazer from

Grainger & Grainger and grab my wallet and a bottle of Lucozade from the dresser. Wilma Cockburn stares out.

I remove their picture and kiss the glossy surface. "We won't let you down." I slide it into my inside pocket, throw in some chewing gum, and head to the waiting car.

The wind rustles the high branches towering over the crematorium. The imposing structure is brutalist in appearance, symmetrical but windowless. In the centre, pillars rise from the floor to the roof, so high the cloud movement causes an imbalance when you look up.

In a different setting, the crem would be a wonderful example of architecture, much like the Tate Britain, but the dark clouds that swirl, both metaphorical and literal, give an impending sense of doom.

Richard taps my arm, holding out a pack of cigarettes, his eyes bright against dark eyeshadow, toned down to match the occasion. The bags under his eyes have doubled in size since our first meeting. "Want one?"

I wave him away but he removes two, putting one between his lips. "I hate funerals. They're always so fucking depressing."

Jack takes the second cigarette and slides it into the top pocket of his shirt. "They aren't meant to be fun."

"This is the first one I've been too," I reply.

The three of us are away from the entrance, hiding behind the large stone cross of an old grave. It's not because we don't want anyone to spot us, more that Gloria will be jealous she can't have a smoke. The thirty minutes without tobacco since she climbed out The Duchess must be a new record.

"Good turnout," says Richard, taking a long drag and blowing smoke into the air.

"Will everyone fit inside?" asks Jack. He looks around nervously, his feet bouncing slightly as he talks, as if preparing to do a runner.

"Standing room only, probably," I reply. "It's a fitting way to see old Eric off."

More taxi's pull onto the driveway. Jack sits like a hawk, studying each guest as they arrive. He pulls his cigarette out and fumbles with the lighter. He draws deep on the nicotine, and then crouches into a squat exhaling the smoke out in a column. "I'm not sure I can do this."

I put my arm around him, but he shrugs me off.

"I'll look after you," says Richard.

"I don't need looking after," Jack snaps, throwing his half-smoked cigarette onto the gravel and walking away. I want to follow him, but nothing I can say will help. Everything here is a symbol of death. Why does everything have to be so stereotypical in these places?

There's no reason why they can't brighten the place up. Not everyone wants to leave this mortal coil surrounded by morbidity. But no matter how you dress it up, there will always be a body in a box. Sentiments, however they're portrayed, are just the icing covering the fact that someone you love has gone. Or should've loved if you were given the chance.

For Eric, people are trying, but the sooner we're back in Soho, the better. Minimal black was the only stipulation in the messages Gloria sent out. As a result, the front lawn resembles the opening night of a West End show. Many arrive in ballgowns, air kissing as they meet. Compared to the other mourners, I'm the only one who hasn't stuck to the dress code. The issue is all my smart clothes are black. In fact, aside from the *I heart Stonemouth* t-shirt I've been sleeping in recently, all the clothes I brought to London are black.

I straighten out the material of the new blazer. I've no idea how much it'd cost on the high street, but the lining's silkiness easily puts it outside my normal price range. Jet black, not greying like my other clothes, the subtle silver stitching acting as trenches in a sombre battlefield, giving a touch of glamour. I'm sure Eric would've appreciated it. The blazer would look incredible with Chelsea boots and tailored trousers, but for now my Docs and skinny jeans will have to do.

"Can you see the man down there?" says Richard. I follow his finger to the lone figure on a bench next to the war memorial. "That's Vincent. Met him and Boo for a G & T last night after you'd slinked off with your fancy man."

"Danilo is a friend." Another default answer.

"Sure. Anyway, want me to introduce you?"

"Later." Even though I've been in their house, seeing Vincent in the flesh is another step towards our goal. He turns in our direction and nods, and Richard gives a salute. Where Richard and Boo have been bundles of energy, Vincent moves more steadily, his cane holding his weight as he limps towards the car park where Boo is punching the ticket machine.

Behind Boo, more mourners emerge. The car park is so full now that those arriving this late may well be part of the congregation, but they're dropped off at a distance where they could be mistaken for an observer. A veil hangs over the faces of many. Whoever they are, someone in the group has Jack transfixed. He leans forward on the bench between the yew trees, glaring at the assembled crowd, his eyes refusing to blink, the punches striking his thigh. Two punches, then three.

"I'll be back in a minute," I tell Richard and pace across the lawn in his direction.

"Here, Harri," calls Gloria, forcing a bunch of red carnations into my hands.

"One second," I reply, but she grabs my arm.

"Eric is on his way. The front pew has been reserved for us so make sure no one's stolen it."

I sigh. "I'll get Jack."

"Leave him." Her eyes show determination, and her stare is a web stopping me from moving forward. "Just go in."

Jack seems hollow, sat alone as if waiting in the playground to be picked up by someone who will never come. I should know, I've been that boy. He draws a diamond in the gravel with his right foot whilst the punching intensifies. I've been too harsh on him, not supporting him today like I should've. I'm Eric's nephew in name only, but Jack was a nephew in person, more than I could've ever been.

Soft music plays as I move down the aisle, fresh lilies standing proud in tall vases at the front. The curtain is open, a cold surface waiting for the coffin's arrival. I focus on the flowers as the eyes of all in attendance follow me to the front pew. I'm an imposter, not deserving of my front row seat at Wilma Cockburn's final show.

Jack enters shortly after, shuffling to the far end of the row. He cracks his knuckles methodically, left hand and then right. His glare is glazed, a trance, only breaking as Gloria joins me. Her eyes are bloodshot and the tissue in her hand is slowly disintegrating. I heard her sobbing this morning as I dragged myself out the bathroom, yet still she put me first. She must be running out of tears left to cry. I don't know what I've done to deserve her.

I rub her arm gently as *Nessun Dorma* plays from the speakers, the hinges of the entrance creaking as Eric is brought in. She keeps her eyes fixed forward, as if ignoring the six pallbearers will stop this from being real.

As Pavarotti's voice swells, Eric's royal blue coffin is laid on the conveyor belt. Rainbow-coloured flowers spelling out Wilma sit on top, alongside a photo of Eric in his heyday. Gloria turns her head to me, smiling.

"Are you okay?" I ask as we retake our seats.

She leans her head close to mine. "Eric said being on a crem conveyor belt would make him feel like a cucumber at the supermarket."

"He's better than a cucumber."

She shrugs. "Both have probably been stuck in holes at one point or another." Our giggles are stopped as the celebrant coughs to signal the start of the service. "Eric wrote his own eulogy," says Gloria, holding my hand. "Buckle up."

Twenty minutes of innuendo. Either the funeral staff didn't get the jokes, or they were too professional to laugh. It was less funeral and more a collection of Kenneth Williams outtakes. The curtains surrounded Eric to *Goodbye* by The Spice Girls. When he left our view, my body became a shell.

There was no mention of family in the eulogy. Nothing about the niece and nephew he was longing to meet. I guess he thought me being present could never be a reality. My anger towards Mum fired through me again.

Gloria, on the other hand, blossomed once we were back in the fresh air. As she chained three cigarettes in a row, even the pallbearers were invited to the pub.

The Lord Nelson is packed as Gloria climbs onto a chair at the bar, quivering as she reaches full height. One false move and she will topple through the buffet tables. They're stacked with a bizarre collection of food brought via convoy, arranged by another of her mysterious contacts. It's the first time I've ever seen a cheeseboard with only Hob Nobs and Dairylea Triangles.

She'd asked me last night if she should get some MDMA in "just to be safe", which I thought strange, until I realised she must've never said the word 'edamame' out loud before. A plate with too many of the green beans balances at the edge of the table, next to a tower of Party Rings, Gloria's shadow cast over them.

One hundred shots of whisky have been poured, and everyone present clutches their small plastic cup tight. I stand with mine raised in the air, Jack to one side, Richard to the other.

"Right, you lot," Gloria shouts as her legs wobble. The bartender holds the chair steady. "Let's do this properly. As we all know, Eric loved a stiff one. To Eric!"

The sound of non-whisky drinkers retching flows through the pub like a diseased Mexican wave. My eyes close up and saliva fills my mouth as I swallow the burning liquid.

"Vile," says Jack as he spits into a pot plant. "I'm gonna get something decent. Want one?"

"An IPA if they have one," I reply.

"How pathetically straight," says Richard, before he nudges me with his elbow. "Look who's here."

. No sooner has Jack made a move to the bar, Danilo enters. A linen shirt pulls tight around his toned pectorals and my heart flips as he smiles at me and pushes through the crowd. He sits in Jack's place and kisses me on the cheek, his left thigh pushed against mine.

Jack stares from across the room, occasionally glancing outside, but nothing is untoward on Old Compton Street. He aborts his place in the queue and strides past. "I'm going for a smoke."

"What are we drinking, then?" asks Danilo. "IPA for you Harri?"

"Please."

"And for your friend?"

"Sorry, this is Richard," I say. "He was in The Dragnificent Seven. We met in Manchester."

Danilo leans forward. "Lovely to meet you."

"He hosts a drag quiz," I say.

Richard winks. "*World famous* drag quiz."

"If the world ended on the boundaries of Greater Manchester," I reply.

"You can't even remember it. Anyway, big star or not, I'll have a Bacardi and coke please, darling."

"Can you grab a white wine for Jack?"

Danilo nods. He moves to the bar, leaning over it. Both me and Richard stare as he bends forward.

"That arse could crack walnuts," says Richard.

"He's one of those gym gays," I reply. Falling for him might not be in my best interests, but he's hypnotising.

"One Bacardi and coke," Danilo says, placing a glass down in front of Richard. "It's a double. They're changing the barrel for yours."

I note there's no wine. Jack is now on the opposite side of the road. He's walking in circles, grabbing at his hair. It's as if a ghostly figure is haunting him, but it can't only be Danilo's arrival.

I excuse myself from the table and head onto the street. I keep my distance, waiting for Jack's next move. He's looking around, but seemingly not taking in his surroundings, punching at his thighs. Two punches, then three.

"Jack?" I call across the road, but he turns and departs, almost breaking into a run. I chase after him but when I turn the corner onto Dean Street, he's blending himself into the crowd. By the time I've reached Chinatown, he's nowhere to be seen. I pull out my phone and call him. Voicemail. I try again, same result.

"Jack, it's me. Let me know what's wrong. I can meet you alone if you need."

. I stand on the corner waiting for him to come back past, but I know my efforts are in vain.

"Hello you," comes a voice from my right. Boo is stood in a formal suit with a salmon shirt, carrying a small paper bag. He holds it up. "Got some spring rolls for Vincent. Why aren't you in the pub?"

"I was trying to find Jack," I say, my eyes still scanning the busy streets. "*Jack always comes home*." Those were Gloria's words. It doesn't make his latest disappearance any easier to deal with.

Boo puts his arm around me and strokes my back. "I've got a quick errand to run, why don't you go and get me a gin ready?"

I saunter back to Old Compton Street, helpless, as if it's my fault. I need Jack to know I care.

Although the pub is full, I'm disconnected from other punters. The conversations could be in a foreign language, but I try to nod and say yes in the right places. Danilo clutches my phone as I once again make a call.

"Sorry." I tuck it into my pocket, willing it to vibrate.

"Well, what do you say?" he asks.

"About what?"

Richard swigs at his Bacardi. "You've been zoned out for five minutes now."

"I guess I'm tired."

"Not a lot of sleep last night from what I heard," Richard says with a smile.

"I told him how we were up until four this morning talking," says Danilo, squeezing my thigh. "*The One Show*, are you in?"

"*The One Show*?"

Danilo looks at me with astonishment. "Blimey, you're really out of it. How much have you had to drink?"

"This is my first," I say as I sip my fresh pint. It tastes bitter, ready to cloud my judgement.

Richard slides his chair closer. "Danilo has spoken to his contacts and they were interested in hearing more about The Dragnificent Seven."

"They've asked you both on to talk about it," says Danilo proudly.

"On the television?" I must be mishearing, unable to understand over the sound of Cher blasting from the speakers above.

"It might help you find Ivana and Westward." Danilo says.

"What if they don't want to be found?" I ask.

"Did you say that about me?" asks Richard.

"Not everyone is you. When do they want to put us on?"

Danilo and Richard give each other a stare. "Tonight."

"Tonight?" I shout, causing everyone nearby to stare in our direction. I move my voice back to a whisper. "Why tonight?"

"They have a slot as the British Hedgehog Project launch has been pushed back to Thursday after all the allegations," says Danilo. "It's a sign."

I lean my chin on my closed fists, closing my eyes to think. "We might've just been lucky so far. I'm worried the next person we ask will say no."

Richard waves a hand at me. "Nonsense. I bet you five pound the next person will say yes." He nods towards the bar.

Vincent is making his way towards us. His skin is tanned, his teeth white and his hair short. His diamante encrusted cane clinks onto the wooden floor with each stride, his body limping to the left like a veteran returning home.

"Here he is, the decrepit tripod," says Richard as he embraces Vincent.

"Oh shut up, you," he replies. "Good to see you, Richard."

"Likewise. Where's Boo?"

"Getting the next round. He might get it sorted before Eric's embers burn out."

Richard gives him a nudge but I know his comments weren't meant to harm. "Vincent, this is Harri."

Vincent smiles widely and offers his hand, gold rings on each finger reflecting the spotlights. "Pleasure. Sorry for your loss."

"Thanks. I've heard everything about you," I reply.

"Hopefully not everything," Vincent says.

"Nothing will shock him," says Richard. "He's moved in with Gloria."

Boo arrives, clutching three glasses in triangulated fingers. He raises his eyebrows and nods. "She's a good woman."

"It's only temporary," I say, hoping that it's anything but.

A conga has started somewhere near the stage. Gloria is swept up into the centre but I push myself into my seat. It snakes around the venue, knocking tables, sending plastic glasses to the floor. Danilo stands as it approaches, throwing the door wide, and it heads onto the street, with many joining the back.

We all breathe out, the venue allowing us some space finally. "Has this changed much since your day?" I ask.

Boo scans the walls. "Not as much as you'd expect."

"The stage is better," says Richard. "It used to be higher."

"You'd catch your wig on the lights," says Boo. "All your clothes stank of burning plastic the following morning."

Vincent nods along. "I broke my ankle one night falling from it. They were good days though. Boo tells me Eric wanted to get the gang back together. Is that true?"

"Richard told me," Boo says, raising his hands. "Don't think it's my idea. I never thought I'd be back in here with you all again. It's made the trip up worthwhile."

"That and the funeral, I hope," I say.

"And you got to visit your new niece in Stratford," adds Vincent.

"Yes, but babies all look the same and the little shits vomit almost stained my cashmere. I'm glad to be away from it all. Being back here is making me feel twenty years younger."

Vincent taps his cane. "Shame we all look so old."

Richard picks a vape off the table and breathes it in. The bartender throws a pack of peanuts in his direction and he waves a hand apologetically. "Speak for yourself. I still look thirty."

"I can't do my high kicks anymore," says Boo.

"You never could," Vincent replies.

"He could if you offered him a fiver," says Richard. "You should see what he does with a ping pong ball for a tenner."

It's like they've never been apart, poking each other's buttons, cackling between themselves. They pull out chairs and the five of us cramp around the small table. Danilo takes my hand out of sight, and I give his fingers a squeeze. The conga is nowhere to be seen.

"So, Harri, what brought you to London?" asks Vincent.

"Eric. But I've also moved to try and breakthrough with my art."

"He's good," says Richard. I appreciate him bigging me up even though I've never shown him any of my own work.

Boo reaches into his pocket and throws a greasy bag onto the table and Vincent's eyes light up.

"Ah, my spring rolls. You remembered. I do miss Mr Wu's food. How are things up north, Richard?"

"Steady. A bit slower these days."

"Still performing?"

"Every weekend. The crowds are less gay though."

"You said you'd stop if you became a novelty act," Boo says. "Portsmouth is much the same. I let the younger people go out front now, I just pull the strings. No one wants to see me strutting about. I'm lucky if I can tie my own shoelaces most days."

"Don't you all miss it?" I ask. "Performing together, I mean."

Vincent side-eyes me. "My hips aren't what they were."

"You don't have to lie on your back or do the banana trick," says Richard. "Be like me, propping yourself up and lip-syncing to whatever crap kids listen to these days."

"Boo misses it," I say.

Vincent laughs. "Every day is a performance for him. He'd wear suspenders to Costco given half the chance."

"Be better than those slacks he had on last night," says Richard.

"They're my driving trousers," Boo protests.

Richard slams a hand on the table and screeches. "Driving trousers! What has happened to us?"

I get a warm glow seeing them talk about the old days. We're so close to honouring Eric in the best way possible. I lean my head onto Danilo's shoulders. His hand grips mine and he kisses me on the top of my head.

"Anyway, I do have a proposition for you girls," says Richard as he leans across the table.

"For the last time, I'm a married man," says Vincent. "

Richard takes a spring roll from the bag, using it to point at the other queens. "The Dragnificent Seven. One final performance. For Eric. What do you think?"

Vincent puts his drink down and leans back in the chair, staring at the others.

"You're thinking about it, aren't you," says Richard. "I can tell what you're thinking, even after all these years. Wouldn't it be fitting to get the whole band back together?"

"Two of you, anyway." I say.

Richard holds up his hand. "Three including Vincent. He's an honorary member. And it's four including Eric." I guess he'll be there in spirit.

A smile crosses Boo's face, so contagious it spreads to the others. "I'm in."

Vincent sips his drink, swilling it in his mouth before swallowing. A sparkle is visible in his eyes and his mouth widens into a determined grin. "Let's do it."

15.

Ghost in the Shell Suit

I fumble the key in the door lock. A few pints could've steadied my nerves, but the only thing worse than making your debut television appearance would be making your debut television appearance drunk.

"Let me have a go," says Danilo as he shoulders me to the side. It opens first time. I follow him to the flat, Richard, Boo, Gloria, and Vincent a few stairs behind. How has this escalated so quickly? I head to the bedroom and remove my top which is trying its best to stick itself to my skin.

Danilo jumps onto the bed and lies back on my pillows. "You need something striking to wear."

"As long as it's comfortable." I kneel and pull clothes from a suitcase.

"You're welcome, by the way."

"What for?" I ask.

"For getting you on *The One Show*."

I sit back on my legs. One day I'll learn gratitude. His smile draws me in and I pull myself onto the bed next to him, leaning my head onto his chest. The rhythm of his heart pulses against my temple. "Thank you."

He kisses me and wraps an arm around my body. A chance meeting in a coffee shop. Maybe Richard Curtis was watching over me after all. I could lie here for hours, the bird song drifting over us as we melt into each other.

It'd be so easy to spend the afternoon like this if there weren't three drag queens waiting for us on the other side of the wall. For five minutes, however, I'll allow myself to enjoy it.

"Did you want me to come tonight?" he asks.

"Yes please. He's your contact so would make things less awkward."

Danilo continues to stroke my arm. "I'll ask him to meet us when we arrive so it isn't intimidating when he interviews you."

"Your contact does the interviews?"

"Well, he *is* the presenter."

"You aren't saying Dexter Buchanen is your contact?" I've spent many hours in front of *The One Show* with my microwave meal for one, drooling at the screen.

Danilo gives me a flash of his straight smile. "I did his PR when he cycled the length of Britain for *Children in Need*. Why are you looking so worried?"

"You could've mentioned that!" I jump off the bed and pull open the suitcase of clothes from Daria. "Dexter is iconic! Like, *actually* iconic."

"He's lovely, don't worry."

I've had a serious man-crush on Dexter for about ten years. I'd get Mum to record every episode of his nature programme when I was young. When I was fourteen my focus shifted, his short shorts piquing my interest more than the animals he was chasing around the forests and wetlands.

"His Olympic programmes were amazing," I say.

"I was behind some of those pieces."

"I'm proper jealous." I've watched Dexter's swimming episode so much I'm worried I've worn out the YouTube servers. "That footage of him in his speedos should've been flagged as X-rated."

Danilo joins me on the floor and picks each item of clothing up as if doing an inspection at border control. "How about this?"

"Green silk? Are you insane?"

He holds the disgusting-looking shirt up to my head. "The colour brings out your eyes."

"I'd look like a pimp. It needs to be subtle, something smart but flirtatious."

"He's twice your age."

"So?"

"And married."

I push Danilo to the floor and sit on him until he can't move. "Stop trying to ruin my dreams."

"Maybe I don't want him to fancy you," he says giving me a wink.

Everything stops. Forget Jack, forget Stonemouth. In fact, forget everything. All I need is right in front of me. I lean forward and kiss Danilo hard, his arms locking behind my back as we roll on the carpet.

"How long have we got?" he asks.

I press my forehead to his. "Not long enough." I don't want to be ungrateful, but I wish the queens had taken an extra couple of hours to reform. "We will finish this later."

I kiss him again, allowing my hands to run under his shirt so I know what I have to look forward to. His chest is cool against my palm as I slide it across his toned pecs.

"Have you got anything planned for later tonight?" he asks.

I roll off, crossing my legs as I face him. The voices in the flat filter through from the front room. "I should be here for Gloria. She'll need me after today."

"Can't Jack do that?"

Fuck, I still haven't seen him. "Urgh, I'm sorry. It won't always be like this."

Danilo takes my hands in his, rubbing the backs with his thumbs. "I understand. I know what he's like. Don't start relying on him. He'll only bring you down with him. I've waited twenty-seven years to meet you though, so another day won't matter. That's if you did want to take this further?"

I'd run through a pack of wild dogs, jump out of a burning building and swim the Nile twice to have Danilo rip my trousers off right here, right now. "I'm sure another day of waiting will be fine. How about dinner tomorrow?"

"Where do you fancy?"

"The Ivy?"

It was a joke, but Danilo kisses me again. "I've a contact there too."

Two minutes later, my new bedroom floor is covered in tens of outfits. "*Nothing chequered. Nothing too bright. No ripped jeans. No logos. Nothing grey in case you sweat.*" Who knew there were so many rules for a five-minute early evening slot? In the end I settle for a blue shirt with a white collar and cuffs, dark chinos, and a silver collar chain. Even the shirt's scent is expensive.

As I apply a new layer of mascara to my lashes, raised voices bounce down the hallway. I catch Danilo in the mirror, his head pressed against the door.

"It's kicking off," he says, looking sympathetic.

I throw the make-up into the dresser drawer and run to the front room. Vincent and Richard are stood face to face, screaming. I force myself into the middle and push Richard back while Danilo holds Vincent, one hand on his cane to stop him from swinging it and catching me on the head in the crossfire. Richard is feisty, and despite him being a good half foot taller than me, he's easy to calm.

"I shouldn't have come back," says Vincent. "I knew it was a mistake the moment I set foot off the bus at Victoria. I could've been a star if it wasn't for you."

Boo slumps to the sofa, his body sinking deep into the cushions, and points in my direction. "Eric was the one who ruined your dream and you know it."

"You took his side though," Vincent replies.

Boo sighs. "What were my other choices? Our group were the only people I knew. My family had moved home by then and the last thing I wanted was to go back to Nigeria."

"Still nearly ended up there, didn't you?" says Gloria.

"Don't you start," I say. "It's painful enough listening to these two go at it."

Gloria pulls out the coffee table and sits, the glass top creaking. "Vince, are you happy?"

Vincent looks at Boo. "I am." His answer is tinged with an element of defeat, unconvinced he believes it himself.

"Do you remember our show at Hackney Empire?" says Richard, rising to full height.

"We never played it," says Vincent.

"I know. That's my point. We had the booking. We even had the outfits. And what happened? We let our bickering ruin it."

"Eric was pushing too hard, too soon," says Boo.

"He wanted us to do it, for all of us." Richard paces around the room. "Eric may have been many things, but selfish wasn't one of them. We started this together and we should've finished it together."

"He's got a point," says Gloria, behind her shades and cigarette smoke. "It's too late to change the past, but we can change the future. Either you're all in, or you're all out. What you gonna pick?"

Danilo stands behind me and holds my waist. We're no more than a fly on a dressing room wall of a dark 1980s Soho club. Gloria is the puppeteer, and no number of years will prevent her from controlling the queens with a sharp wake-up call.

"I'm in," says Richard.

"Me too," says Boo. "And so is Vincent."

He nods slowly. "I'm in."

Gloria stares them out as she stalks the room, everyone in the palm of her hand. "Once we have Westward Hoe and Ivana back, we'll be full strength." She nods in my direction. "Plus we've got these two lovebirds."

"And Jack," I add.

"Precisely." Gloria walks between us like an army officer inspecting their troops. "1987. Side by side we stood against every bastard who tried to tear us down. Governments, licensees, skin heads. They hated us, thought we were dirty, said we were scum."

"Like his mum," says Vincent in my direction.

"I'm *not* my mother," I snap.

"If it wasn't for her, Eric may still be alive," he replies. Each syllable is singed with venom.

Silence. Danilo wraps his arm around me and I grab his hand to stop myself from getting angrier.

Gloria pours herself a large gin and collapses into a chair. "We can't blame his mum. In fact, blaming anyone won't bring our Eric back. But we can save ourselves. We may have more grey hairs and a few more curves but it don't mean our minds ain't sharp. We've still got our fighting spirit, but we can't use that on each other. In my house that won't wash."

"The past is the past," says Richard. "We did all we could."

"Wrong," says Gloria, taking a large gulp and pointing her glass at him. "We ain't only fighting for ourselves no more. There's hundreds of kids out there who need us. You've seen the news unless Manchester has been cut off from the world for the last decade. Even now with that poor kid who's missing. Christ knows who took him. They fucking need us more than ever. There's still fight in us old dogs. The next time someone comes for our community, we'll take to the streets. Like we always did."

The coffee is rich and dark but I'm too nervous to drink. Richard is in front of a full-length mirror in the green room, doing squats 'to tone the thighs', as Danilo remains deep in conversation with Dexter. What I'd pay to be the meat in that double-D sandwich. The famous green sofa is only metres away. I check for fire escapes. If one is close enough, I can still duck out.

"Are we keeping you up?" I ask Richard as he lets out a lengthy yawn.

"Slept like shite. I'm certain Magento's place is haunted by a Victorian child. The door kept rattling."

"It's a new build," replies Gloria.

"We don't know what was there before it. Could be a plague pit or an orphanage. Swear I saw an apparition behind me in the mirror this morning."

"It used to be Camden Leisure Centre," says Gloria. "Was only built in eighty-two. Hardly summat for Derek Acorah is it?"

"Was the ghost wearing a shell suit?" I ask. Richard mouths at me to piss off but lets out a chuckle.

"Positions in five," says a girl with a clipboard as she dashes past, her finger pressed to a navy earpiece. "And no smoking indoors."

"Spoilsport," says Gloria next to me, the unlit cigarette sticking to her red lips. "Now you two, remember, all you have to do is tell them your story, and put a call out for the remaining queens."

Despite going through the main points in the taxi from Soho, I'll forget everything as soon as the director shouts action. "What if he asks a question I'm not expecting."

"Like what?"

"I dunno."

"You're worrying for no reason. Just sit there and smile. Tits and teeth."

I lean back in the chair and allow the make-up artist to add a third layer of dull powder to my shiny, sweaty forehead. "Have you heard from Jack this afternoon?"

"He's probably at a gallery," Gloria replies.

"You didn't see the way he left. He was skittish, as if being stalked. Remember at the crem? He was like that." The three messages I sent remain unanswered, however many times I open the app to check. This is unlike his other periods of silence.

Gloria leans forward, waving the make-up artists away as she attempts to touch up her face. "Jack sometimes needs his space."

"You've said that before."

"Because it's true. We've a meeting tomorrow morning with the gallery in Camden so I'll check in with him then."

"Did you need me there?" There's only two weeks before my work is displayed, and everything I have is still back in Stonemouth.

"This is to discuss the financial parts. You can come if you want but I'll warn you, it's boring. Loads of blokes in suits talking about targets. You're better off staying home and looking for a job or summat."

We haven't agreed on how much rent I'll pay, but I don't want to take Gloria's hospitality for granted. Bar work would be easy to find, but do I need the late nights? There's no way I'd be a Monday to Friday office monkey, yet retail is also off the table.

"Hey," says Danilo. "This is Dexter."

"Lovely to meet you," says Dexter, his voice as smooth as melted chocolate, his eyes pulling me in like whirlpools. Flecks of grey pepper his temples, his skin as unblemished in real life as it is on the screen. An eleven out of ten. If he knew how many times I've paused his videos to help get myself started, I'd not be allowed within twenty miles of these studios. "You and Richard are on after the VT about squirrels."

"You won't ask me anything weird will you?" My voice is stuttering and my palms are sweaty on the wooden chair.

"Such as?"

I go blank. He'll ask about the drag queens, why would he ask anything else?

"You'll be great, kid," he says. He gives me a gentle punch on the arm. I might never wash again. I lose the ability to speak. Dexter jumps onto the set and shuffles his papers, giving me a smile when he catches my glance.

More people with clipboards enter the studio, camera operators taking their positions. Richard is still squatting, much to the chagrin of runners who dodge him with polystyrene cups in each hand. I stand tall, and Danilo brushes white flecks from my shirt.

"You're going to be great," he says, before kissing me quickly on the lips.

Gloria slaps a nicotine patch onto her upper arm and stands against a long dark curtain behind the cameras. I take a deep breath and run through my key points, but there's not enough time to finish.

The theme music leaks through the crew headphones, and soon the countdown is on. "Five, four, three…"

Dexter Buchanen leans over me as I lay horizontal on the black floor, studio lights hanging above me like stalactites. "You were excellent."

The last thirty minutes were a blur but I'll take his word for it. I spoke about Eric and how I wish I knew him, but anything specific has already washed itself from my mind.

Richard is relaxing on the green sofa, chatting with the twinky boyband who are glistening after performing their latest painful single. They're encapsulated with his every word as they each sign the poster he's pulled from the green room wall.

"Everyone off set," calls the director.

Dexter reaches down, taking my hand and lifting me

to my feet, my legs buckling as I stagger towards the disabled toilet. My phone buzzes against my thigh and I virtually crawl into the loo, locking it firmly and laying on the worryingly damp floor.

"Michelle?" I say, my breathing heavy.

"Why the actual fuck have you just been on my telly?" she says, her voice echoey with plates scraping in the background.

"It was all last minute or I'd have given you a heads up. Was I okay?"

"I doubt BAFTA will come calling, but it could've been worse. Good job Richard is such a natural."

I don't plan on rewatching. I can barely stand seeing myself in photographs. "How's work?"

"Same as always. It's boring without you here. Why haven't you called?"

"You know how it is."

"Do I?" She laughs, but it's fake. "I don't know you at all now."

I run the tap and splash icy water on my face. "I'm sorry, it's been crazy, what with the funeral today and then this. I'll make it up to you."

She sighs. "Will I get to meet your boyfriend?"

My mouth goes dry. "My what?"

"You said you're dating someone who finally understands you for you."

"On the phone or on the telly?"

"In between dribbling over Dexter."

My thoughts flash to Danilo. He's probably waiting outside this cubicle now, ear pressed against the door. "Can I call you back?"

She laughs genuinely this time. "Make sure you do."

"I will."

"Pinky promise?"

She'll be sat crossed legged with puppy-dog eyes, downturned lips, and flaring nostrils. "We ain't ten, Michelle."

"Pinky. Promise."

I sigh. "Pinky promise."

I flush the chain and wave my hands under the dryer, giving myself one final check in the mirror. Richard is stood outside, arm around Danilo. He releases when he sees me, and grabs my head in his hands, kissing me firmly on the forehead.

"Get off," I tell him.

"It's worked," says Danilo, smiling.

"What has?"

"Everything," says Richard. "Westward Hoe has called the show. She wants to meet."

16.

Now I'm Sixty-Four

Eric's bedroom is a pigsty. Not bad after me only being here for four nights. I'm forever destined to be chaotic.

"Wakey, wakey," comes Richard's voice from the other side of my door, milliseconds before it flings open, smashing into the shelves. Eric's unread books slide horizontal, a couple falling to the floor near Richard's slippered feet. "Don't know my own strength sometimes."

Danilo groans and turns over beside me. He pulls the duvet half off the bed leaving me more exposed than I'd wish to be at whatever time it is.

"Alexa, what's the time?" I call out of habit, forgetting my digital companion is sat alone in my old bedroom.

"It's five thirty," Richard replies. Another groan from Danilo.

"Why're you here so early?" I ask, squinting at him through the bright sunlight piercing the blinds. A white dressing gown barely kisses Richard's knees, his forehead obscured by a peach towel. Fresh gold eye patches sit atop each cheek.

He places a coffee on my bedside table with a thunk and slaps my legs. I shimmy towards Danilo to allow him space to perch, hoping he doesn't sit on the lube stains on my pale blue fitted sheet. I was hoping my first time with Danilo would be more special than a Tequila Rosé fuelled handjob. The early wake-up call by someone resembling an uncooked pork sausage wrapped in a napkin doesn't add much romance.

"Whilst you two were drinking your way through the cabinet last night, I was in my Magento's hot tub speaking to Westward Hoe."

I prop myself on an elbow and blow across the top of my drink, the first sip sending a lightning bolt through my body. "How is he?"

"She," Richard says. "Cynthia is doing well. Off the drugs, into yoga. She's got a lovely little flat overlooking Stanley Park and works for a charity in Birkenhead."

"So she stayed up North after all?"

"We were thirty miles away from each other. Nothing at all, is it? Luckily, she's still as catty as ever."

"And no animosity between you?"

Richard shrugs. "We both had a good cry. I apologised for any past behaviour if you can believe that."

"Did she accept it?" I ask.

He takes two pills from his pocket and downs them with the aid of my coffee. "She said she forgave me years ago but couldn't remember what for. She'd been reluctant to reach out."

"Until last night?"

"Until last night. Now, get yourself showered."

"Can you give me half an hour?" I ask, nodding my head towards Danilo, who's facing the wall and snoring gently behind me.

Richard grabs the duvet and pulls it onto the floor. "You have fifteen minutes to be downstairs and in The Duchess."

I throw on a hoodie, hope pulsing through my veins. "Is Jack here to drive?"

Richard rubs my shoulder. "Gloria will take care of him." Someone needs to. It's been sixteen hours since last contact. "What I do have," continues Richard, "is a set of keys and a full tank of petrol. Liverpool awaits."

He takes my empty cup and pulls the door closed. I flop back on the bed, my eyes glazed as I make shapes out of the Artex on the ceiling. All I need is for Jack to message back. Nothing will ever make his silences comfortable. Danilo turns over again and I bury myself into his body.

"You need to stop worrying about Jack," he mumbles.

"I'm concerned about him, that's all."

He pulls me in closer until our bodies are locked. "You've got me now. Focus on the people who care, it's what you deserve."

"I still care about him, regardless."

But perhaps he's right. Portsmouth Harbour flashes through my mind, a vision of Jack looking out to sea, struggling with the demands from his family and his want to be alone. I guess his sister convinced him to go skiing after all, but what if he hasn't? What if he's running away from everything – his dad, Soho, me? I need to know.

I stare at Danilo, running my hand through his tangled hair. "Do you wanna come to Liverpool?"

He doesn't answer, instead pulling my head back into his chest. Lying here won't solve anything, so I force myself away and pull on some trousers. "Wait here. I'll be back in a min."

I leave him in bed and head to the front room. Gloria is on the sofa, flicking through a magazine, her hair damp with dark dye. I open a window to release the ammonia cloud.

"Where does Jack live?" I ask.

She looks up instantly. "Why?"

"I need to see him."

"We've got a long drive," says Richard, entering from the kitchen with a custard-coloured smoothie in a tall glass.

"I won't be long, I promise."

Gloria stands and takes my hand. "I'll see him at the gallery soon."

"I know, but I need to see him myself. He hasn't answered my messages and his phone is ringing out."

"Harri, I'll sort him."

"Gloria, please let me do this."

She sighs and falls back onto the sofa. "There's a kebab shop around the corner, next to a stationery shop on Dean Street. He lives above there. Flat four, top floor. Don't buzz flat two, whatever you do."

"Massage parlour, right?"

"Correct."

I grab my Converse from the hall and give Gloria a kiss. "I'll be ten minutes, I promise."

It's less than a five-minute walk. Similar to my first visit to Soho, I stand outside a black door of a tall townhouse, its polluted brickwork towering into the sky. Someone smoking from the second-floor spits down onto the street before eyeballing me. I take a deep breath and press the bell.

"Yeh?" comes a male voice on the intercom after the third ring.

"Is Jack in?" I ask.

The door clicks and opens slightly. Inside, junk mail and takeaway menus are stacked on the stairs. The walls are dirty, the only clean space being where a fire extinguisher once hung. Towards the first floor, the naked brickwork is exposed behind peeling plaster.

As I climb, the heat intensifies, the air inside stifling. The entrance to the massage parlour is open, revealing a small kitchen full of dirty plates, lingerie hanging from picture hooks, smoke from joss sticks giving the air some spice. Shouting comes from above, but I can't turn round, not now.

I tap on the door to Flat Four, and it's answered by a man, not much older than myself. He licks the edge of a Rizla and tightens his joint.

"Jack's in there," he says, nodding to a room at the end of a dim corridor, the lightbulb flickering like a strobe. I wait until his flatmate is out of sight and press my ear to Jack's bedroom.

"Jack?" I whisper, crossing my fingers hoping for an answer, but only silence is returned. I kick the door gently, revealing the dishevelled room inside. The bed is unmade, McDonald's packaging amongst empty Coke cans resting underneath, tossed from the only place he can sit. I wouldn't even call it a bedsit. A small stove, stained from spilled grease, is in the corner above a mini fridge, a *Beano* mug with oil-slicked tea resting to its side. I open the fridge and wretch at the tub of yoghurt, mould forming a field over its surface.

Jack's suitcase and backpack are present yet sit empty.

A phone charger is plugged into a broken socket and a set of keys lay on his pillow. I grab a carrier bag and clear some of the rubbish strewn across his floor. He might kick off knowing I've been here, but I want to give him somewhere nice to return to, from wherever it is he may be. As I sweep old tissues from the bedside table, a small notebook falls to the floor.

The book is a window into his mind, all he's told me laid bare on the pages, including detailed notes of a ski resort beneath a picture cut from a magazine of a happy family on the slopes. On the following page is a picture of a large house, his family home no doubt. It isn't a photograph, but an estate agent advert. £1.8million. He never mentioned his family was selling.

Below, the names of his family are written over and over. Kenneth and Deborah, his parents. Maggie and Lisa in ink below, their age, sixteen, in brackets. The twin sisters.

The same information is on the next page, as if he's trying not to forget where he came from, testing himself on his siblings and their interests. Other pages are covered in ideas for his artworks, sketch after sketch of slogans, some crossed out, some circled in red pen.

I flick through quickly with my thumb, stopping dead on the final completed page. Harri. My name is in bold and underlined six times. There's the name Maplewood again, followed by questions: *When was he there? Does he remember the Beehive? Did he play rounders in the field? Who brought him there?*

All questions he relayed when on the south coast. I slam the book shut and throw it in a drawer. He's been researching me after all. I should be angry at his lies, but him not being here disturbs me too much.

"You his boyfriend?" asks the flatmate, blowing a cloud of weed into the room.

I take the keys and exit the room, locking the door behind me. If he's in trouble, I don't want anyone to be able to access his room as easily as I have. "I'm a friend," I say as I push past. "When did you last see him?"

"Jack? He was here yesterday afternoon."

"What time?" My question is met with a shrug. "What time?" I ask again.

"About five? I dunno, I'm not his mother."

I nod and walk back to the stairs. "If you see him, ask him to call Harri."

As I stride up Dean Street, my phone rings and I grab it out of my pocket, disappointed it's only Danilo. "Hey."

"Where are you?"

"Was seeing if Jack was home."

There's a short silence. "I have to get home and get ready for work. I'll call you later, yeh?"

"I'll be back in a second."

"Good. Richard is waiting." The line goes dead.

I break into a jog, dodging between the traffic until our flat is in sight. Richard is stood talking to Gloria and Danilo, leaning on The Duchess as her engine ticks over. They both glare as I approach.

"You need to get going or you'll get stuck for hours," says Gloria.

"Jack wasn't there."

She raises her eyebrows. "Probably at The Gallery already."

"It's not even six, Gloria. His room looks like he's got up quickly and gone. Everything's been left behind."

"Harri, he's fine," says Danilo as he holds me.

"Shut up Danilo," I snap, before taking a breath. "Sorry, I'm concerned."

"He'll come home," says Gloria. She takes my hand and pulls me into our doorway. "You go with Richard and I'll call you when I see him, okay?"

I want to believe her. I need to believe her. She kisses me on my forehead and I run up the stairs to grab a change of clothes and an overnight bag. When I arrive back to The Duchess, Danilo is gone.

Earlsfield Services is one place where I never imagined myself being trapped. The Duchess did well for two hundred miles, but she let us down short, like a racehorse falling at the final fence at nearby Aintree.

Our conversation has been stilted, Richard failing to take my mind from Jack. Every time my phone vibrates I pray it's Jack or Gloria, but all fifteen times it's been Danilo.

The one downside of The Duchess, apart from the steam filtering from under her bonnet and the new pool of water gathering in my footwell, is her lack of a decent music system. It doesn't even have a CD player, meaning we had to rely on the one cassette in the glove box to soundtrack our journey. As nothing good has been released on tape for thirty years, Richard forced *The Best of Phil Collins* on me until I tossed it onto a hard shoulder somewhere west of Stoke-on-Trent.

Richard sits behind the wheel, eating a Curly Wurly with the driver's seat reclined, repeating directions to Westward Hoe over speakerphone as she navigates the car park somewhere unknown nearby. Her calm voice is broken by sharp expletives aimed at other motorists in her barbed scouse accent.

With neither of us mechanics, nor wanting to be sat here for hours, we're leaving The Duchess parked up to recover for a day. My palms are sore and my fingers red from pushing her across to the long stay.

"Can you see the Starbucks?" says Richard. He's now standing on the edge of the car doorframe, waving his hand in the air.

"What does it look like?" replies Westward.

"A big wooden building with Starbucks on."

"I can see ya, I can see ya," she screams down the line. "This is like *Challenge Anneka*."

"She means *Treasure Hunt*," says Richard as he hangs up.

My phone rings again, another call from Danilo. I cancel it and get out the car. Westward Hoe is in a red power suit, striding across the tarmac on a mission, her hair bouffant high, her eyeliner millimetre perfect, filtering to sharp catlike angles near her temple.

When close, she stops and glares at Richard from head to toe. "Well, well, well, look what the cat dragged in." She flicks open a pack of Tic Tacs and pours them into her mouth.

"The rest of the trash was already here," Richard replies.

"It's good to see you, you little bitch." She glances at me as she hugs him. "Harri, right?"

"Hey, Westward."

"Call me Cynthia love, please." She holds my shoulders and studies me. "I know you're young but to someone my age you're practically a foetus."

"Everyone looks young to people our age," says Richard.

"Even so. You're different from our Eric."

"He was taller and better looking," I say.

Her mouth drops open. "Nonsense. If I were forty years younger I'd ravage you like a hyena." She slaps my arm and lets out a laugh, also somehow in scouse. "I can't believe The Duchess is still going."

"Well, not technically," I say, hoping the clicking under her bonnet isn't a sign she's reached the end of the road. "We're lucky we got this far."

Richard taps her roof. "The M6 was an experience, that's for sure. Driving The Duchess is like giving gin to a twink. It's all fine for an hour or so, but you know at some point it'll break down."

"Well, I'm glad she's here with you," says Cynthia, grabbing my hand and nudging me towards Starbucks. "If I don't have a coffee in the next sixty seconds fists will fly at the next driver who pisses me off. Shall we?"

Westward talks non-stop until I squeeze myself out from between the cardboard boxes in the back seat of her Ford Fiesta. Her apartment is in a tall, modern block. The glass balconies are unstained, the exterior paint still white. We stand like sardines in the small lift as it takes us to the fifth floor.

"'Scuse the mess inside, got a job on tomorrow," she says as we fall into the hall.

"Drag?" I ask.

"Kid's party. I'm the Claude Monet of the Bootle face-painting scene. Can't wait to be screamed at by all the little scrotes telling me I've got the wrong shade of yellow for their Pikachu. Fuck 'em, that's my motto." Her snarled contempt for her clients is given more impact by the guttural sound she makes with the letter C.

"Thanks again for rescuing us," I say. "I hope we didn't interrupt anything."

The door opens without a creak. She removes her silk scarf and kicks off her heels, waving my gratitude away, flashing her manicured nails in my direction. "I was halfway through a bikini wax when Richard called last night. Will have to go back for an emergency appointment tomorrow morning now. I can't risk anyone seeing me when my labia have a mullet."

The hall is bright and the air floral from the Selfridges reed diffuser tucked into a pair of dusty heels.

"I can't believe you saw us on the telly," says Richard.

"I always have that shite on when I'm cooking." Cynthia punches his arm and laughs again. "You should've seen my face when I saw you. Had a face like a nun at an orgy. There I stood, mobile in one hand, blowtorch in the other. Despite all you put me through, I knew I had to call. And I have missed you, genuinely. It was worth burning the crème brûlée for. Cuppa?"

Richard takes a seat on a sixties-style egg chair, flicks on the television, and spins slowly as he files his nails. Posters from modern artists adorn three walls. They're vibrant in the light flooding the room from the floor to ceiling balcony windows. The panoramic view of Liverpool they frame is as stunning as the Hockney behind me. In the distance, the Mersey flows past the docks, the Liver Building showing its face between high new builds.

Cynthia enters and turns the television back off. "Have you seen the news about that kid from down your way?"

"William Bosnich?" I ask. "Please tell me they've found him."

She shakes her head. "Not good news I'm afraid. Broke my heart this morning, it did. His poor parents. They must be going through hell. Found him in some woodland."

It's as if my body deflates. I lean against the wall and stare toward the outside world. A light aircraft flies over the nearby Anfield Stadium, a sound taking me back to lying in the long grass at Maplewood. I used to watch as they flew overhead, guessing where they were going. It'd always be an exotic land I'd never be lucky enough to visit.

"Those planes get on your nerves after a while," says

Cynthia. She places an overflowing cafetiere onto a table between three burnt-orange Le Creuset mugs.

"I'd love a go in one someday," I reply, taking a seat on the sofa.

Cynthia pours a coffee and passes it to me. "You should add it to your bucket list."

"I don't have one."

"Oh, you should. Or at least forty things to do before you're forty."

I blow across the steaming liquid. "I've got time."

"How old are you now?"

"Twenty-three."

"There you go see." She takes a seat opposite and folds one leg over the other. "You're over halfway there already. You'll soon learn time passes you by, don't it, Rich?"

He nods. "Too bloody fast if anything."

"Our Eric would've loved another twenty years I bet," she says. "I can't believe he stayed in London."

"He had a good life there," I reply.

"Him and Gloria were probably waiting for the other to make the first move away. Let me guess, they're still in the flat above the AIDS Centre?"

"It's a tattoo shop now," says Richard.

"Surprised it ain't a vape shop. That's all we have popping up round our way. Rent probably got too high for her to keep it going."

I sit forward. "Gloria ran the centre?"

"She should be a dame for the work she did, la." Cynthia struts to a modern cabinet, before rummaging through its top drawer. "That woman was shaking hands with people years before Diana did. The number of people she allowed to pass with dignity when their families had given up on them must've reached triple figures."

"And the boys too," says Richard.

"The boys?" I ask.

Cynthia blows the dust from a photo frame and hands it across. "Our community was like a broken vase, kicked apart by people who thought we deserved to die, said we were the victims in our own downfall. Gloria though, not her. She were the glue. If there was someone without a home, she took them into the flat."

"Must've given a bed to over fifty of them," adds Richard.

Gloria is instantly recognisable in the photo, her face unchanged today as it was when she was captured in black and white. She's smoking at the window of a bistro, the fast-paced life of Soho reflected off the glass behind the photographer's silhouette.

"Kenny snapped this," says Cynthia, her voice full of melancholy, her eyes singed with anger. "One of the last pictures he took before his body couldn't fight anymore."

Richard moves across to join us, as Cynthia hands more photos across to me.

"August eighty-five, February eighty-six, Christmas Day eighty-eight."

Even though forty years have passed, Richard and Cynthia have the dates their friends passed carved into their memories. Well over half the faces in my hands belong to those who didn't see the nineties, people I'll never be lucky enough to meet, people who deserved better.

"I'm sorry," I say. The bare minimum I can offer. It's evident how much pain from this period of history remains. I think of the photo Boo showed me down south. Eric, stood staunch, as my mother, his *sister*, told him he was deserving of everything coming his way. He was not estranged from our family, but cut off, thrown aside as if he were worthless. That ends today. I may be too late for him, but these stories are worth more than to be hidden away on a bookshelf on Merseyside.

"Can I borrow these, please?" I ask.

"Sure, love." Cynthia gathers them into a pile and hands them across. "Would love to digitalise if you know anyone who could do that? I had a go but this old bird doesn't understand technology."

Cynthia pulls a dark-filtered, slimline cigarette from a metal box and stands on the balcony, flicking ash down to the car park. I join her with Richard and stand in silence as a group of kids kick a luminous ball around the park, four BMXs acting as goalposts. On a bench nearby, two teenage boys sit close, their hands entwined, the blonder of the two resting his head on the other's shoulder.

"I hope those lads have it better," says Cynthia. She doesn't need to add anything more. The blonde catches us looking, but instead of pushing his boyfriend away, he waves. "That's our Adrian. His mam works in the bakery on the corner." She takes a long drag of her cigarette. "Good kid."

"I was thinking," says Richard.

"Always dangerous," replies Cynthia.

Richard laughs and rests on the metal table against the wall. "It's a good idea this time. I was thinking we should do one more show."

Cynthia rests her smoking arm on the other folded across her stomach.

"None of us are getting younger, despite the Botox," he says, waving a finger towards Cynthia's smooth forehead. "Now with Eric gone, it may be our last chance."

She chews her lip. "You didn't mention that little nugget on the television, did you love? What have the others said?"

"Boo has said yes."

"Vincent too," I add.

"And Ivana?"

Richard screws his face. "We don't know where Ivana is."

Ivana is irrelevant. Four will be enough to make the show work.

"One night in Soho, that's all I'm asking," says Richard. "One final chance to finish what we started. We could use it to raise money for charity."

Cynthia turns so she's facing us, arms outstretched to her sides, holding the balcony rail for balance. "As long as it isn't for Comic Relief. I'd pay fifty quid *not* to see the cast of EastEnders dancing to *Thriller*."

"Gloria still has contacts," Richard says.

Cynthia takes a long drag of her cigarette. "A few months back I did a show for a local youth group. Some young 'uns there hadn't any hope. Can you believe some bastards are still kicking their own flesh and blood onto the streets?" She looks back to the two boys embraced on the bench. "It'd be wrong if we didn't step in. Let's give the kids a chance."

"You're in?" I ask.

"I'm in."

After a walk around Stanley Park and a hearty lunch in a rundown pub, a bottle of prosecco is popped as the morning's sunshine gives way for mid-afternoon drizzle. Cynthia pours a third of a bottle into three beakers. "I don't have posh glasses I'm afraid."

Richard raises his high. "To us,"

"To The Dragnificent Seven," replies Cynthia as our cups thud softly together.

They down theirs in two, but the fizz doesn't sit well for me. As she tries to work the remote control for her CD player, my phone buzzes. *Not now, Danilo.* I remove it from my jacket pocket, but when I see Gloria's name on the screen I dash onto the balcony, sliding the door closed behind.

"Hey."

"Harri, it's Gloria." Her voice is monotone and shaky.

"Are you okay?"

The silence lasts for far too long to be comfortable. "Harri listen, I'm at the police station. Jack didn't show at the gallery today. Can you come home?"

17.

Easy Lover

The streets of Soho are full of drinkers who had gone out for a quick pint after work four hours ago. They stumble into me as I walk against the tide. I stand strong and bounce them aside, desperate to see Gloria. I message Danilo seeing if he's nearby, hopeful his PR event will be wrapping soon.

With my battery on three per cent and my charger stuck in the stranded Duchess' boot, I make the stupid mistake of searching the internet for Jack's name. No results. I then try 'missing gay man London'. I can't help myself, despite knowing it would only bring pain. Jack doesn't show, thankfully, but there's a report of another boy. Joao. Nineteen. Student. Three days ago he left Heaven and no one has seen him since. UCL have flooded social media with his face, but it's taken this long for it to hit mainstream. The CCTV image of him departing Heaven with an unknown older man hits hard. That could easily have been me. Now, it could be Jack.

The press conferences for William before his death were even worse. His boyfriend breaking down as he pleaded for him to be safe, his face strobed with a dozen flashes as journalists prey on him for column inches.

I can picture myself being in that chair, thrust into the limelight sat begging Jack to call whilst true crime fans eat it up. They'll blame me, like they have for the boyfriend. "*He knows where he is*" – the go to phrase for the Instagram armchair detectives wanting their content to go viral. According to the article, the police aren't treating them as linked. But if Jack makes three? Then what?

The front door of 50 D'Arblay Street is opened before I can take the key from my pocket. Gloria is make-up free, her eyes hollow. Broken. I pull her in close and rest my chin on her head.

"He'll come home," she says as the tears start. Her body trembles in my arms and I guide her up the stairs. She collapses into the armchair and glares into space, whilst I flick the kettle on. One spoon of coffee, three heaped sugars.

"Here, drink this," I say as I hand her the cup. She smiles, but her light remains extinguished. "Have you eaten?"

"Ain't felt hungry."

I brush some dust from the mantlepiece before falling onto the sofa. My brain has been in standby mode since Cynthia dropped me at Liverpool Lime Street to board the quickest train south. "Has he done this before?"

"Once," she says softly as she takes a small sip from her mug. "We had an argument over something stupid. Can't even remember what for. Only time we've had a crossed word in the six years I've known him. Walked out one night but was back the following lunchtime. This is different though."

"How so?"

Her eyes are focused on the outside world, as if sending a signal to him. "He left his art satchel here for starters. At the funeral, his coping mechanisms were more evident, the solitude, the punching of his legs. Usually it's subtle, hard to notice." Two punches, then three. Our first meeting in Soho, in the car to Manchester, the harbour talking about his family. At the wake. "It took me a while to spot it too," she says, reading my mind. "But at the crem, the punching was harder, as if unable to control it. I tried calming him, but the new environment, the unfamiliar faces, they clouded him and I hate myself for not being there like I should've."

"It's not your fault," I say. "You had to look after yourself too."

Gloria pulls out a fresh pack of Sterling Duals and lights one with a trembling hand. I pass her the ashtray, remaining crouched next to her seat. "All we can do is wait," she says.

"I'm scared."

"Fear won't solve anything." She takes my hand, stroking the back with a thumb. "You've seen a sunset, ain't you?"

I furrow my brow. "Of course."

"Do you have a photo of one in your phone?"

I unplug my device from the wall, fifteen per cent, and perch on the arm next to her as I open the photo app trying to find the picture I took from the train as I passed Stevenage.

"I don't need to see it," she says, waving me away. "I wanted to prove a point. Sunsets are like life, y'see. When you see a sunset, you take a photo, everyone does because part of you, however deep inside, believes it will be the last light you'll see. The purples and yellows illuminating the clouds, changing colour until the sky fades to black. The next day, another sunrise comes along and the process starts over."

Her eyes sparkle with tears, her words aimed as much at herself as they are at me. "Life is full of moments Harri, and you must never assume a sunset is the end. We all live under the same sky, even if we may have been born on a different cloud. Whenever you feel you're at the blackest moment, you need hope. Wherever you are, you have to remember that the sun will rise." She takes a long drag of her cigarette and blows the smoke towards the light. "Always believe in the sunrise, Harri."

I wake up to the doorbell. After the half bottle of medicinal whisky, I managed to get Gloria back into her room, before spending at least four hours staring at the ceiling from my bed. I throw on a dressing gown and bound down the stairs two at a time. "Please be Jack, please be Jack," I tell myself as I grab at the latch.

"Hey," says Danilo. No work clothes today, instead a short-sleeved t-shirt and tailored chino shorts, the laces of his boat shoes dragging on the tiles. He doesn't wait for an invite to come in, instead wrapping his arms around me and kissing me on the neck in the hall. "I was already in bed last night sorry. Any news?"

"Not yet," I mumble.

"Have you tried his flat?"

"The police will have. I told Gloria about my last trip there and what I saw." Jack's keys. They're still sat amongst the mess in my top drawer. "We should go back this morning."

"Don't interfere," Danilo says, pulling me up to the flat.

In the front room Gloria is dressed and piling old magazines and ash into bin bags to keep her mind occupied. The television is off, unplugged from the wall so there's no chance of us stumbling over the latest news conferences with wrongly accused boyfriends.

"Morning boys," she says, before taking a large swig of coffee. "Richard's driving back today. He's gonna kip on the sofa for a while to look after me."

"I can look after you," I say.

Danilo takes my hand. "You need to take care of yourself."

"He's right," Gloria concurs. "We need to keep sharp. There's breakfast in the kitchen. Fill yourselves up and then we can come up with a plan."

"Have the police called?" Danilo asks. The silence answers his question. "What if they're linked? Jack and the other kids."

"William and Joao," I reply. They deserve to still have their names.

"We'll leave it for the police," Gloria says. "Speculating won't help find him. I've asked Roberto to print off some posters, and the Evening Standard will have him in this evening's issue."

I take the bin bag from Gloria and toss it onto the landing, before running a cloth over the leather cushions of the sofa. "Has anyone been to Wimbledon?"

"Wimbledon?" asks Gloria.

"His family are there, although they might be on the ski trip now."

"Yes, of course. I'll—leave it to me, okay?"

"Richard could drive you over there when he's back," Danilo says.

"I said leave his parents to me." I take a step back at her raised voice. "Sorry, I mean, leave me to look into that."

"Is Cynthia coming with Richard?"

"Who knows. An extra brain is good but too many cooks and all that bollocks." She pulls out a feather duster from beside the bookcase and hums the chorus of *Chim Chim Cher-ee* to herself as she drags it across the mantelpiece. The electricity that fires through her nerve endings is disconcerting by its absence.

Jack's satchel is on the cluttered desk, and after Danilo asks her two questions which she appears not to hear, I take it from behind her back and head to the bedroom.

"You've an amazing taste in films," Danilo says as he jumps onto my unmade bed.

I look to the walls via the dresser mirror, my make-up sprawled out on the surface in front of me. "They're Eric's posters. Not seen any of them myself."

"How have you've never seen *Priscilla*?"

"It wasn't on Mum's approved list." I remove my gown and run a wet wipe over my face, a layer of dirt smudging across it from last night's travel. Danilo slides to the left side of the bed and I drop down next to him, cocooning myself into his arms, giving my body a chance to rest.

"Who's Daria?" he asks, spotting her name on the screen as I check my phone for the first time this minute.

"My sister."

"Heya. Not heard from you for a while. Call me urgently xx"

"Unless it's about Jack, I don't care." I say and lay back into Danilo without replying.

"He'll come home you know, regardless of how much you worry."

"You don't know that."

He kisses my ear, his right hand stroking my torso. My skin prickles with each pocket of breath he releases onto me. Minty, with an underlying element of tobacco. They were right, I do need looking after. Thank God I've someone to do that. I twist my body until we're face to face, Danilo running his hand down my body, feeling the outline of each abdominal muscle. His kisses move from my mouth and down to my neck, slowly heading to my chest. When he reaches my waistband, I push him away.

"I can't do this, not now." I sit up and he rolls onto his back, letting out a deep sigh. I hate to disappoint, but it's not right when Gloria is in the next room worried sick. I don't care if Danilo is annoyed at me refusing his advances again. I didn't want to back out, far from it, but Jack needs me more.

He runs a finger along the frame of the nearest poster. "I'll go and pick us up some decent coffees. Latte?"

"Wait." I take Jack's satchel and empty its contents across my bedroom floor. His whole life is laid bare. Sketchbooks, notebooks. His passport. "He hasn't gone with his family."

"Put it away, Harri. You're not doing yourself any favours rummaging through his shit."

I ignore his demands, putting the passport to one side and opening up the first notebook. Does he need this with him? More family photos, details on the queens, Maplewood. If this is the key for his brain to retain information, what will he forget without it?

His address?

His friends?

Me?

This book only covers January to June. All he's told me is contained within the covers. I toss it to the side and flick through the newspaper cuttings that had been bound together by an elastic band like a bundle of banknotes. I haven't seen Maplewood Hall anywhere aside from my memories for seventeen years. Until now.

Eight years ago, according to the date stamped on the Oxford Mail pages, Maplewood Hall's west wing burnt down. The wing that was my summer bedroom during my days in care. Our first steps on the road trip. I told him it burnt down, so why hasn't he shown me these before? The feelings of abandonment and guilt flood back. I can't do it. Not now. I fold them tightly and bury them back inside the bag.

"Let's go get coffee," says Danilo.

"Just give me five more minutes."

Danilo moves next to me and puts his arm around my shoulder. "Please stop, Harri."

I shrug him off and open the small sketchbook, the last remaining hope of finding out where he may be. The pages are blank, but as I flick through, a set of Polaroids falls to the floor, face up. My heart stops, my world crashing. I'm a ship in a storm, the photos the sirens singing me to shipwreck.

Jack looks natural, happy even, in the four snapshots. Why wouldn't he when he has Danilo pulling him against his body tightly. Danilo is a shadow now, hugging his knees with his back to my bed.

"You and Jack?" I say, the words stumbling across my tongue.

"It was a long time ago."

"How long?"

He shrugs. "A year?"

"I can't fucking do this." I throw the belongings back into the satchel and pull some joggers on. "What else are you keeping from me?"

"Nothing, I swear." Danilo follows me out of the room as I thump down the stairs. "Harri, stay, please."

I turn to him, pointing a finger into his face. "No wonder you tried to keep me away from him. You know damn well how much I care for you, and for Jack too, and all this time you're both doing your best to fuck me over. You ain't still hooking up, are you?"

"Obviously not. Look, I think he's a dick but I want him found just as much as you do. You're not the main character in this story, so stop overreacting. It's all in the past. He's the one holding onto those memories, not me. Come and get a coffee and I'll explain."

I can't stand the sight of him, but what are my choices? Me going off on my own will pour more shame and worry onto Gloria. I tie my laces tight and head onto Berwick Street, Danilo three steps back. The pace is sending bullets of pain through my shins, but the adrenaline keeps me going.

"Harri, listen for a second," Danilo calls, but he's cut off by an unexpected source.

Phil Collins. *Easy Lover*. Full volume. Too loud even the length of Noel Street away. The Duchess is parked outside O'Neill's, Richard and Cynthia leaning on the bonnet smoking, remonstrating with a traffic warden.

"Alright, la," says Cynthia as I reach the vehicle. "Fancy seeing you here. Any news?"

"I thought I got rid of this album?" I say.

"Well I bought another at a charity shop," says Richard, leaning into the car and turning it down a notch. "Knock him all you like, but his body of work is not to be messed with."

"Harri's right," Cynthia says, pointing her cigarette at him. "The only good thing he's done is the *Tarzan* soundtrack."

As much as I'd love to debate the pros and cons of Phil Collins' back catalogue, other matters must take precedence. Richard sits between me and Danilo on the bonnet, barely a word said between us for five minutes. I know it was over before I arrived on the scene, but one of them mentioning the relationship would've been nice.

Cynthia takes a seat, her newly heated panini from the neighbouring Starbucks sending a tuna stench into the frosty atmosphere. "Gloria says you need to go home."

"I've just been home," I reply.

"Well you need to go back again. Said it's urgent." She takes a deep bite of her breakfast and nods towards the flat. "Wanna lift, love?"

My legs, however much they shake, are more reliable than Eric's car, even on a thirty second journey. Danilo decided to stay back, probably for the best. I hope to God that when I get to the front room Jack is on the sofa. I put my coffee on the floor, but as I reach for the handle , the door swings open.

"Daria?" She holds a finger to her lips. Her nails are fresh and her skirt suit tailored flawlessly to her body. "What the hell are you doing here?" I whisper as she blocks the entrance.

"I tried to warn you. You should learn to use your phone once in a while."

"Warn me about what?" I brush past her and into the front room, kicking my shoes off and slinging them into the wicker basket. There she is, in Gloria's chair. For once out of her cleaning uniform.

"You've got some explaining to do," Mum spits.

"I don't have to explain anything to you. Why are you even here?"

"Helping your sister. Unlike some she tells me what she's up to."

"You can't be here," I say, picking up her handbag and throwing it on her lap. "How did you even get in?"

"Gloria let us in."

"Not like you gave me any choice," Gloria says, entering from the kitchen. "You're the last person I wanna see, believe me."

"He's my son," says Mum.

Gloria studies her with a look of contempt. "You don't own him. He's happy here."

Mum turns to face me. "Sit. Now!"

I place myself at the end of the sofa, as far away as possible. "I'm happy, Mum. Sorry for not calling."

"Don't apologise," Gloria says.

"He needs to come home," Mum snaps.

"This is my home."

"I saw your little episode on the television the other day." Mum stands and circles the room, screwing her face at the artworks on the wall. Her fingers jab in Gloria's direction. "This is why I told you to stay away from people like her. They corrupt you."

Gloria stands behind her, a mushroom-coated frying pan in hand, and I can tell she wants to swing. I don't blame her. Part of me wants to do the same.

"I can't go back to Stonemouth, I'm sorry."

"Don't apologise to her," reiterates Gloria.

"Mum, everything I need is here."

"I'm tired of your lies," Mum says.

"He didn't lie about the art show," says Daria.

"And I have a place to stay." I add.

"This shithole?" Mum replies with an exasperated laugh, her eyes scanning the room. "Please come home and we can start again."

"This *is* starting again."

"We miss you. The job offer is still there. You can get

yourself a nice little flat, rejoin the art college."

I clench my fists. "What can't you understand? I don't want to come back. And you only want me to so you can deny the truth. I'm happy for the first time in my life, happy to be in London, and happy with my boyfriend." Whether that status exists between me and Danilo currently is neither here nor there. "I know you're scared to admit the boy you rescued has grown into the last person you wanted him to be, but that's not my problem to solve."

"It isn't that," she protests.

"Bollocks. You let Eric down and then blamed him. I've seen the pictures, I've heard the stories. You've already thrown your own brother under the bus and you expect me to believe you wouldn't do the same to me?" She approaches me but I back away. "Don't even try it."

"He'll be safe here," says Gloria as she blows smoke in her direction. "You should take your own saviour complex to where it's wanted."

"Why don't you move in with Daria? She's a lovely place down the road with none of…none of this," she says gesturing to the decapitated Barbies nailed near her head.

"You've moved to London?" I say to Daria.

She nods. "Got a stunning place on Shaftesbury Avenue."

"That would've been nice, wouldn't it?" says Mum, her voice as soft as if relaying a nursery rhyme.

"I only have two bedrooms," says Daria. "And I'll have a flatmate from the agency soon."

"I don't want to live with you," I reply. "No offence, but I'm staying here."

"At least come round for lunch."

A telephone rings from the end of the flat, the old-school trilling of the landline stalling our conversation. Gloria stubs her cigarette into the yucca and glares at Mum as she goes to answer.

"Things are good here, I promise," I say to Mum. God knows why I'm trying to convince her. I'm twenty-three, not ten. I don't need her permission.

Mum raises her eyebrows. "Don't come crawling when it all goes wrong."

Behind us, footsteps rise up the stairwell. Cynthia's lavender perfume enters the room before she does. She stands at the doorway, raising her shoulders and standing tall, dabbing the leftover tuna from the side of her mouth with a beige napkin.

"I was always told to wipe my feet so I didn't bring shit into the house," Cynthia says in her Scouse drawl, her eyes narrowing towards Mum. "Come to take us down again have yer?"

At first, Mum looks puzzled, but the penny dropping is almost audible. "Jonathan?"

"It's Cynthia." She takes a step forward, towering over Mum with an extra foot of height. "I always knew you'd come back begging eventually. Shame you couldn't do it before Eric kicked the bucket."

"Don't put it like that," Mum replies.

"As if you care." Cynthia's spine is up, her claws out, ready for violence. "Harri knows all about your little escapades. All the stuff you put me and the girls through. Well we ain't letting you do the same to our Harri as well."

One wrong movement and Mum will be snapped in two, eaten, and spat back onto the street. She looks at Cynthia from head to toe. "At least you got what you wanted."

An unlit cigarette hangs from Cynthia's mouth, her top lip curled, snarling. "Got what I wanted? You don't know the first thing, love."

"You've had the ops ain't you?" Mum replies, shaking her head.

"That's none of your business. Never was and never will be. You never did understand me or our Eric or any of us. You never listened to our protests, preferring to believe the homophobia in the rags over your own brother. Shame on you and shame on me for not stopping you."

"So what's today's protest about?" says Mum.

"The same as it always was." Cynthia leans close. "I might be doing alright but if I, or any of us, don't keep fighting, others will go through the same. Christ, others *are* going through the same. You must've seen the boys on the news, unless you've been living under a fucking rock. Either we're all safe or none of us are. You coming here won't make us retreat. You ain't half got some fucking nerve, Julia."

"Oh calm down," says Mum, but Cynthia doesn't back down.

"You haven't seen the last of me," she says, spitting each word forward. "I'm gonna fight for every gay kid out there, every trans kid. Letting them down will be letting myself down. They need protecting from pricks like you."

"I can protect my own son," says Mum.

"I don't need protecting," I reply, the blood pulsing through my veins. "I'll visit Daria, but I'm not coming back to Stonemouth."

"But your flat, darling."

"I'll collect my belongings and then I'm gone."

I pick up the cups Cynthia has knocked over with her heels. Mum moves to the window, hands clasped behind her back, knuckles white as her nails dig into her palms as she works out her next line of attack. Before a verbal assault can happen, Richard enters, putting an arm around my shoulder and pulling me into the hall.

Gloria is sat on the top step picking at her nails, her face as white as a sheet. She slowly turns her head. "That were the police on the blower. The body of a young man has been pulled from the Thames."

18.

Beef Teriyaki and a Strawberry Daquiri

I won't miss the mould. It's creeping up from the old iron radiators and into the cracked plaster of my walls like ivy on a forgotten factory worker's terrace. Gloria's flat may have its issues, but at least Eric's bedroom is warm and dry.

The drive back to Stonemouth was a blur. Did Mum and Daria leave before Danilo bundled me into the passenger seat of his Subaru? I'll never know. I wanted to stay, but with a stocky Detective Constable arriving to speak to Gloria, the our second-floor flat became overcrowded. There is a fine line between helping and interfering, and despite the knowledge of Danilo's past with Jack, returning to Stonemouth with him was my only option.

I throw open my curtains and release the stale air. A flock of pigeons on the rooftop opposite scatter and shards of paint fall from my walls as the first breeze of the day flows over them, damp brickwork revealing itself further.

I promise I'll make a start I told Danilo as he kissed me on the forehead before heading to get my caffeine fix, but the cardboard boxes which tower in the corner of my bedroom remain empty. We've planned to escape back to London before sunset, but my body has shut down. I've no appetite, not even for the posh chocolates we picked up somewhere on the journey. Danilo has been gone for over an hour, though I'm not certain what time he left.

The flat is silent with the television off. I can't allow

myself to stumble across more reports on the body. Seeing intrusive footage of divers on the banks makes it all too real, but Jack is still alive. If I believe he is, believe in the sunrise, the more likely it is to be true.

Calling his phone will be of no use, the battery depleted. Straight to voicemail. I'll try again in ten.

I take the newspaper cuttings I removed from Jack's bag and lay them on the bed. Why didn't he show me them? It could've started the healing I need. Gloria said he can be obsessive but telling him about my childhood was a fleeting comment to open conversation, not an invitation to research my biography.

"What you got there?" Michelle leans casually, smiling when I look up with red eyes. Coffee stains run down her Disney jumper, her hair frayed despite the tight scrunchie.

"What are you doing here?" She sits on the edge of the bed and gives me a sympathetic look. Head tilted and a flat grin. The last thing I need is Therapy Michelle. "I'm doing okay before you ask."

"I haven't come to pry. I've taken the afternoon off so I don't forget what you look like. Gabe let me in."

"Gabe?" Perhaps he was behind the pile of pizza boxes building up in the unvacuumed hall.

"Arson, eh?" she says, taking the cutting from my hands. It displays the charred remains of the dormitories, the wooden roof blackened and twisted, masonry lying across the car park and water dripping from contorted brickwork.

Other clippings detail events which took place before the fire: Scout fundraisers, Christmas pantomimes, a party for WWII veterans. They show the main hall in all its glory, bunting and balloons. In one, a door is circled in red pen. The chokey. We named it that after a group reading of *Matilda*. It was creepy as fuck in real life, and quite small when you were put in there for time out. It emanates haunted vibes even in print.

"Research for something?" asks Michelle.

"I found these in Jack's bag. I was curious."

"Maybe he likes the drama," she says, tossing it back onto the pile. "No different to me and my murder docs."

"He keeps notes, Michelle. Of everything. Says his brain is wired differently. These are about me and *that* place."

"Maplewood?"

I hate hearing its name. "Why's he obsessed with my time there? I get he might want to know more about me, but why all the pieces on it burning down?"

"Could be an art piece?" Michelle pulls some canvas from under my bed and starts coddling them in bubble wrap. "He does protest Pop Art."

She takes some snippets from the bed and her eyes scan the words, before pulling out her phone, studying the articles as she Googles. "Has Jack ever spoken about Charlie Baker?"

"Who?"

She turns her screen to me, an Oxford Mail article. "Says he was responsible for the fire. Was sent to a young offender's. Maybe he was a friend of Jack's."

"That'd be too coincidental. Anyway, Jack doesn't have friends." I pick at the fluff on my socks. Even his name brings a bolt of pain to my chest. "Only acquaintances."

Michelle crawls across the bed and puts her arm around my neck. "I know you're hurting but I'll be here whenever you need me."

I squeeze her hand. "I'm going to London."

"Now?" She sits straight.

"This evening. Danilo bought me home to pack last night. Me and Mum had a row. Soho is home now."

She removes her jumper and tosses it onto the pile of two-week-old laundry in the corner of my room. Legs crossed, she leans her head on her closed fists. "You're giving it a go then?"

I offer an apologetic smile. "I have to, Michelle. Danilo says it's for the best."

"But is that what *you* want?" She blinks back the tears and guilt floods my veins. "Are you doing this for Danilo or are you doing this for you?"

"Me, I guess. Look, I'd take you with me if I could. You know I would. This town sucks the life from you and I have to be there for Gloria, be there to find Jack. He could be anywhere and the thought of him being alone and scared, or worse, is pushing me to breaking point."

"I know." She stands from the bed and grabs some of my brushes, tossing them into a box. "Does he have family in London?"

"Wimbledon, but they're in the Alps or somewhere on a ski trip. Jack didn't go cos I found his passport, but at Eric's funeral he was acting all weird, all erratic."

"He'll come home," she says.

I wish people would stop saying that when they've no proof it could be true. I open my phone and flick to the gallery. "This is him." He hated the photo I snapped of him driving The Duchess, demanding me to delete it. To me he was new, exciting, and I couldn't bring myself to do it. Now I'm glad of my stubbornness.

"He's cute."

She reaches for the phone but I pull it away as I side-eye her. "He can be an arsehole, and anyway, I'm with Danilo now so it's immaterial."

"Did you think you could change him?"

I shrug. "I guess so, but Jack isn't like that. He has his own way of doing things, likes his space. We kissed once. On this farm up north. Nothing came of it, which is for the best as it would've complicated things further. Him and Danilo used to date as well. Me and Jack, we're from completely different worlds. Whilst I was shipped to Maplewood, his family funded it."

Michelle points a paintbrush at me. "Maybe that's why he kept the articles. If you had links to somewhere, you'd keep them too. In fact you have done," she says, picking one up and waving it near my face. "I get you hate Maplewood, but it shaped who you are. Look at you now, on the verge of your first exhibition."

"Maplewood didn't get me into art. Anyway, I'm not sure I'll do the exhibition."

Michelle throws a book into the box hard and grabs a canvas from the side of my wardrobe. "Art is what you're about." She thrusts it into my hands as I throw myself flat on the bed.

I discard it to one side. "Aside from you, no one else has ever cared about my art."

"Miss Kennedy did," she replies.

"She was an art teacher. She was paid to care."

Michelle bites her lip. "There are many Miss Kennedys out there, Harri."

I frown at her. "Like Mr Ritzman?"

"I don't mean our art teachers specifically. If Miss Kennedy enjoyed your art, other people will too."

I pick the artwork back up. My testicles crawl halfway into my body at the sight of my scribble on the back panel. *The Unbearable Loneliness of Being*. God, I can be such a pretentious prick.

As I twist the art, the sun catches the bumps of my thick paint strokes. A messy swirl of greys form the background like a storm overhead, subtle reds firing gently from the black cumulonimbus metaphors of frustration.

This was one in a productive series of ten I created the afternoon my ex Adam moved up to Glasgow. Whilst he was at fresher's fairs and sleeping around with other students, I was alone on this floor, angrily dabbing paint onto canvas.

I lay back and press my palms onto my eyes. "Am I doing the right thing?"

"In what way?"

"Leaving my family behind."

Michelle crawls and leans on her stomach opposite. "Yes. And anyway, families are meant to be fluid. You don't have to be blood related, well, adopted in your case. They're the friends you make along the way."

"You're sounding like a Hallmark movie," I laugh.

"Well, you get my point. If you stay in one place the world will move on regardless. If you let it pass then that's your fault. You knew as soon as you heard about Eric it was something with potential."

"See. I told you it was life-changing."

"I'm not getting into that again. But from what you've told me about Gloria and Richard, they seem to care, not only about you, but for Eric too, and you've never had a better opportunity to push yourself."

I stand and grab my collection of Converse from the shoe rack, tossing them into a cardboard box. "You'll come and visit, won't you?"

"Hell yeah," she replies. "I'll be there for your exhibition as long as you get your act together and keep painting." She folds the clothes I threw onto the floor this morning. "Are you sure you wanna take this?"

I stare at my old barista t-shirt as she holds it high. "I'd rather burn it."

"Speaking of which, what are the plans for Eric's ashes?" It's a brutal segue, but something which hasn't crossed my mind. He didn't sound the type to have wanted them scattered over a rose garden or poured on the centre circle of Wembley. "How about turning him into a tree?" she asks.

I twist my head and narrow my eyes. "What are you on about?"

"I saw an advert on Instagram," she says. "A company takes ashes and mixes them into the soil with an acorn. You plant it in the garden and your loved one regrows. How amazing would it be to become an oak tree?"

I put my fingers down my throat and mock vomit. It's far too twee for the thunderous presence of Wilma Cockburn.

Michelle whips me with my favourite blue cardigan. "I'd love to be an oak tree."

"Have you been drinking?"

"It was only an idea."

"Gloria lives in a second-floor flat. Even if he came back as a buttercup we'd be pushed for space."

Michelle pulls off squares of bubble wrap and lines the remaining boxes whilst I clear my reading shelf. My to-be-read pile has been neglected of late. The only book with a cracked spine is *Moby Dick*, and only because I used to hide my condoms in it when living with Mum.

"Did you want your posters?"

I look at the album covers on my wall and the Oasis one jumps out. "Morning Glory! I knew I recognised Berwick Street from somewhere." I stand in front of it and jam my finger on the bottom left corner. "My new flat is just here."

"It's destiny, see?"

Michelle is the oxygen being brought into my suffocating existence. My head no longer aches from the pressures building inside and the reflex action of checking for messages has increased from seconds to minutes.

For the next hour we have the radio on, some sports channel covering the cricket, and before the players break for lunch, most of my belongings are sellotaped inside cardboard cages, ready to be shipped.

We sit on the white rug in the centre of my now bare room. Michelle inhales deeply on her vape and fills the air with a strawberry daquiri haze, wafting her hand at the newly formed cloud. “Sorry. Habit from smoking in bed.”

“I don’t care, I won’t be here in a few hours.”

She pokes out her bottom lip and takes another drag. I pull it from her hand and breathe it in deeply, spluttering the sweet vapour back in her face. “These can’t be healthy.”

“It’s chemicals and a battery, course they aren’t, but I’m making the most before my stocks run out. Only got four boxes left from when the minimart had to clear their supply. Surprised you ain’t smoking with Gloria chaining them so much.”

“I prefer to stick to caffeine.” I stand on a chair and check the top of the wardrobe, dust from the top falling onto my face as I sweep my arm along in search of hidden belongings. All I find is a forgotten Stone Cold Steve Austin action figure. Daria had said to take my toys to the charity shop when I moved in here, but the innocence of keeping them balances out my wilder moments.

Michelle changes the radio station, and Crowded House are telling us not to dream it’s over when my phone buzzes on the bedside table.

“Grab that can you?” I ask her.

“It says it’s Danilo.” She brings it across and holds it up like the Statue of Liberty’s flame. “It’s on speakerphone.”

“Heya Dan, where are you?”

“I’m outside.” His voice is muffled. “Your buzzer doesn’t work.”

“Ooh, do I get to meet your mystery man?” mocks Michelle as I cancel the call before she embarrasses me.

“Jack isn’t a mystery man,” I reply firmly.

“Jack?”

"Shit. Danilo. He's Danilo de Souza and he's my boyfriend. No mystery, no intrigue."

"If you say so." She jabs me in the ribs. "Made a nice change to see someone on your phone who doesn't have the surname Grindr."

I give her a shove but set a mental reminder to clear out all the boys I've had the displeasure to wake up to. I can't recall the faces of at least three-quarters of them and some of the ones I can still picture should be cast into the depths of hell. I lead Michelle down the hallway, jamming the button to release the foyer doors.

"I can't believe you've fallen for two boys in London already," she says. "You used to be so picky with actual date-worthy boys here."

"Everyone here knows each other," I reply. "Half of them are probably related. It's hardly a blossoming metropolis of gay culture is it? We could fit our pride parade in a Sainsbury's Local."

Michelle sits and rethreads the laces on her Docs. "What about the one who worked in Shoezone?"

I let out a snort. "His name was Norbert. I couldn't date a Norbert. I'd sound like a war widow."

"Beggars can't be choosers."

"Oh, says Claudia Schiffer down there."

A couple of gentle thuds strike the door. I push my eye to the peephole. Danilo is on the other side with a tray of coffee, a bag of pastries between his teeth as he knocks with his forehead.

"Is Claudia your most up-to-date reference?" says Michelle.

I pull the door wide and Danilo hands me a latte. I wince at the Smile Café logo on the recyclable cup. "You took your time."

"Come to the bedroom with me, quickly," he says.

"Does he demand that a lot?" Michelle whispers.

I grab her from the floor and drag her along. Now's not the time for jokes.

In the bedroom, Danilo stares as we enter. "Have you had the news on?"

"Obviously not," says Michelle as she sits on a two-stack of boxes, gesturing to the empty room.

"Danilo, Michelle. Michelle, Danilo."

"It isn't Jack," Danilo says.

I freeze. Getting his name wrong once is bad enough, but to his face is never going to go well. Danilo walks across and holds my cheeks, squishing them together. "Harri, do you hear me? It isn't Jack. The boy in the Thames isn't Jack."

I'm worried there's been a mistake. "Are you sure?"

Danilo nods. "Confirmed about ten minutes ago. Sky News."

I fall to the floor as tears flow down my cheeks, releasing their saltiness onto my lips, my body a balloon slowly releasing air. The pressure recedes and my vision becomes technicolour again.

"Was it that other kid?" asks Michelle.

"Joao," I say.

Danilo doesn't need to confirm. Of course it is. Even with Jack still out there somewhere, my heart can't be full knowing another member of our community will never get the chance to come home. The permanently online parasites will already have his name trending.

I grab my phone and Gloria answers within seconds.

"I've found him," she says immediately.

"Where?"

"I'll explain later. Are you at the flat?"

"I'm in Stonemouth. Will be back tonight."

A click of a lighter and the soft crackle of fresh burning tobacco floats down the line. "When you get here, there's a fold out bed in the glory hole. Can you set that up?"

"Sure. Is it for Jack?"

"Hopefully. Won't be for a few days. He's recovering with a friend of mine. Look, I gotta go, but I'll be back to Soho after the weekend. Plenty of food in the fridge. The girls have set up a rehearsal Monday evening at Roberto's. I'll see you there."

After I hang up, Danilo opens the BBC News app. The top story is the body. He turns the volume up on the live feed. Joao only went out to watch a drag show. The reporter repeats this fact as CCTV from the night he disappeared plays on loop, his dignity less important than a scoop for viewers.

"The poor kid," says Michelle.

"It could've been any of us," I add solemnly. To the news channels he's just another statistic. Social media will be full of speculation and abuse. I bet the same was said about Jack these last twenty-four hours. It's easy these days to hide anonymously on social media thinking words don't have consequences. It wasn't like the eighties where homophobes had to make the effort to find you before they abused you. It never mattered if the antagonists were a stranger or your own sister.

Eric and the queens went through hell, and nothing has changed, not for them, not for William or Joao or all the others who will never get to graduate, never get to fall in love, never get to grow old.

Only my possessions for travelling remain unpacked, the last link between my old life and new. I collect up the takeaway trays, my stomach full of teriyaki beef noodles from the Thai opposite. It's my first decent meal in God knows when.

Danilo downs his tea and offers me a prawn cracker. I wave it aside, nauseous at the thought of more food. "We should get going."

I've been dreading this moment. "Do you wanna come, Michelle?"

"I'd be getting in the way."

"Maybe I should stay home for one more night."

I hold Danilo's hand, and he pulls me in close. He kisses my neck and leans until his mouth is centimetres from my ear. "This isn't your home."

Michelle sits on my bed. I join her as she sits staring, tapping the back of her head against the wall. The noise echoes around the empty shell of my room. The moment we separate has come too quickly and the realisation I won't be able to call her round with a second's notice is a torpedo.

She wipes the tears from my eyes and hugs me. "Don't make this more difficult than it is."

"You will come for the reunion show, won't you?"

"Like I wouldn't be there anyway. It will be nice to meet these London people."

"You should move with me."

"Maybe one day," she says.

Danilo lifts the top box from the stack, his cheeks puffing at the weight. "I'll start loading the car."

"It won't all fit," I say, still holding Michelle. "We can pop back Monday and get the rest, maybe?"

"No need. I've called in the troops." He winks at me as he heads out of the flat.

Michelle releases me and puffs her vape hard, her face a picture of defeat, reflected in my own expression. "What's that noise?" she asks as music rattles the windowpanes.

A tsunami of warmth and love floods over me. "I think you'll find that's Phil Collins."

My shelves are empty, the wardrobe bare. All my possessions, everything I've gathered over twenty-three years, all taped up in stupid coffee cup boxes from the shithole café. It isn't much to show for a life, but now's the time to build a new one.

19.

Now That's What I Call Music

I sit in Roberto's café, pleased to be out the flat. It's been a lonely forty-eight hours and I'm sick of eating lasagne. Danilo went to work when we arrived back on Friday, and last I heard he was in Richmond working on a press pack for *Netflix*. Our relationship has stagnated a little now Jack is back on the scene, Danilo not understanding I can care for both him and Jack simultaneously, even if in different ways.

My artworks for the exhibition are complete, drying on the mantelpiece. They're pretentious, but unmistakably mine. Alone and suffocating has always been when I've worked best, the only break taken this weekend was to visit the nearby garage to hear the latest troubles with The Duchess. Richard says she broke down twice on the A40 and is now one hubcap lighter after he gave her a stern kick.

I cling onto my latte as a bizarre scene unfolds in the space ahead. Monday the twenty-sixth of May. The day The Dragnificent Seven returned. The four queens face off across the makeshift rehearsal room, shimmer curtains gaffa-taped across the windows to keep prying eyes at bay. Roberto's small office at the rear has been transformed into a cramped dressing room, his apron hooks now home to a rainbow of synthetic wigs.

"They were always like this." Roberto has a pen in mouth, finger lingering over the play button on Gloria's old CD player. He lets out a long, frustrated sigh and looks at me forlorn.

"I was saying the chorus needed more oomph, that's all," complains Cynthia as she waves her sequinned cape around her shoulders.

Roberto throws a curtain over the counter. "If any of you get glitter on my hotplate you'll be getting the bill."

Richard points to the other queens with his cigarette holder. "Cynth, my love, the kids have moved on from Donna Summer and Gloria Gaynor."

"They're the classics," Boo responds.

Vincent screws up his heavily made-up face. "It might be nice to freshen things up a bit, darling."

"See," snaps Richard.

"You're meant to be on my side," Boo replies, raising her middle finger to Vincent.

"When did I agree to that?"

"On our wedding day." Boo pulls out a chair and sits down with difficulty, the large wire hem on his hot-pink skirt hiding his face completely. "Has the Lord Nelson upgraded from their cassette player yet?"

"They had CDs on at the wake," says Richard.

"I bet the new stage is as shit as the old," says Cynthia. "My heel will sink through those rotten floorboards before I hit a chorus. The only proper new thing in that place is a higher price for a double. Over ten quid they charged me for a large voddy."

"Have you tried sobriety?" asks Vincent. "It's done me wonders."

Cynthia looks over the top of her absurdly large shades. "For three weeks. Anyway, I only drink socially now."

"You were on the G&Ts before nine this morning," Richard says.

"I was being social."

Boo clutches Cynthia and Richard's arms and drags them to the centre. "We only have a couple of weeks to get this together, and I don't know about you girls, but I want to go out with a bang."

"That's what Eric used to say," says Roberto. "He treated every performance like his last."

"Then that's how we'll approach this," says Boo.

Cynthia leans back against the counter. "I guess we

didn't get the chance to the first time around."

"We've a reputation to uphold, especially if his boy comes good with press contacts," says Richard, pointing at me. "I hope he chooses a good photo."

"Hopefully, you're kept out of shot," says Cynthia, chucking a sugar cube at him.

Every member is pulling in a different direction, all having their own conversations. As the volume continues to rise, I can't help but laugh thinking what Eric would make of them being together. I can see why he loved the scene. If they can turn a drab, tired café into a vibrant stage, the reunion gig is sure to be a hit.

Boo strides towards the group, rifling through a pile of CDs from a nearby charity shop. He holds up a copy of *Now That's What I Call Music Vol. 8* "What about Kim Wilde?"

"Let Harri choose," says Cynthia. "We need a youthful eye, not your rose-tinted crap."

I look up from my coffee, all queens staring at me. "I guess the old music will make the reunion like the glory days."

"I agree," Boo says.

"But," I add, "some modern songs would go down well. Entertain the younger ones, especially for the solos."

"I was going to do a lip-sync to Bananarama," says Vincent. "Havana Bananarama."

"Let's focus on the group number first," Roberto says. "I've got to close up in an hour to get my daughter from the airport." He presses play and the marching intro drumbeat of Tiffany's *I Think We're Alone Now* echoes off the tiled surfaces as the queens reluctantly get themselves in order.

It's amazing how four people can be at each other's throats one second, and the next strutting across a café floor with synchronicity. They manage to get halfway through the second verse before it judders to a halt. Richard's blouse buttons finally lose their battle against his chest, slightly expanded since the last time he squeezed into this particular handmade outfit, and ping across the floor.

Cynthia rolls her eyes at Vincent. "That's the fourth time you've missed your cue."

"That was Eric's line," he protests. "We need someone to take his place."

The lightbulb above Cynthia's head is almost visible, and her head slowly turns to me. She stares with puppy-dog eyes.

"Not. A. Chance," I say.

Her shoulders drop and she throws on a sad face like an overacting clown, leaning her elbows on the table. "How wonderful would it be for you to honour your uncle by becoming the embodiment of Wilma. Forget those hologram shows, you could be the real deal."

"There's no way you're getting me in his outfits," I reiterate. "I'll honour him with my art."

Vincent claps his hands together. "Five-minute break and we'll try again. We *will* get this right even if it kills us, no offence Harri."

Roberto busies himself making a fresh batch of coffees, whilst Vincent lays next to the window preparing for his twice daily hip exercises. Cynthia stares, straw in mouth, as Vincent bends his body double against the glass. "I can do that."

"Anyone on the street would see what he'd had for breakfast if those curtains weren't up," Richard replies, taking a seat.

"You're only jealous his hips are supple."

Vincent moves on to stretching his spine, letting out a grunt when his right leg passes ninety degrees.

"He looks like one of your wrestling figures," says Richard. "Which reminds me, your boxes are still in The Duchess."

"I'll grab them later, sorry. I need to pay the repair bill after I'm done here. Thanks again for coming down."

Richard looks at me as he gets a nudge in the ribs from Cynthia. "Harri, we weren't entirely honest about our time in Stonemouth."

Cynthia's face twists. "We went to see that mother of yours. Gloria made us. I'd much preferred to have been pulling my toenails out with a pair of rusty pliers."

"That can be arranged," Richard replies.

I roll my eyes. “How is she?”

“Not happy as you can imagine,” says Cynthia. “But when faced with the two of us and no escape route, she had to listen.”

“She still wants you to stay in Stonemouth,” says Richard. He crouches beside me as Boo drops a plate of cakes between us, running his finger through the cream of an éclair.

“I can’t go back there,” I mumble.

“That’s what I told her,” says Richard

“Maybe I should call her.” When I take out my phone, Richard grabs it from my hand.

“Don’t put yourself through it. She needs some time for it to sink in.”

“Is she angry?”

“Disappointed,” says Cynthia.

Richard nods in agreement. “But then she always was. We took her some posters and photos of Eric.”

“Also articles about the activism we did, the news reports from the die-ins and the marches. One day she’ll learn she let our Eric down,” says Cynthia.

Richard takes my hand. “And we won’t let her do the same to you.”

I doubt Mum will ever care for Eric, too stubborn even four decades later. “Was Daria there?”

“She’s already in London, love,” says Cynthia.

My sister has offered a whole tree of olive branches since my return to the capital, but I need time. The plaster is fresh, but we will heal. We always do. I can picture her walking past now, staring as we sit here. She’ll have a suitcase of clothes to smooth things over, no doubt.

God I miss her.

She’s sat less than a mile away in her new flat, planning outfits for the shoots, the runways, the networking dinners, turning the plus one I sent for my exhibition’s opening night in her hands, deciding if she should accept.

“You were right about one thing,” Cynthia says. “Stonemouth is a shithole.”

Vincent grabs the shoulder pads of Cynthia and Richard and pulls them towards the practice space. “We have to get back to it. How about some Kylie?”

"A bit stereotypical," laughs Cynthia.

"Any Chappell Roan?" I ask.

"Who?" says Richard.

"Let's stick with Tiffany," Cynthia says. She stands on tiptoes and pulls her leggings tight.

Richard slaps her hands. "Pull them any higher love and your pubes will give you a moustache."

"Children, behave." There's an immediate silence as our eyes turn to the door. It's slammed shut with a swift kick of a fluffy slipper. "You lot never change. It's like I've walked back into Brompton's in eighty-eight." Gloria walks across to my table and throws a purple ring binder in front of me. "These lot wouldn't agree if you told them snow were white and the Thames flows into the sea."

"Where have you been?" I ask.

"Oxford."

She lights a cigarette, ignoring Roberto as he points to the no smoking sign, and stands in the middle of the queens. "Richard, your eyeliner's on the wonk. Boo, looking gorgeous. Nothing a bottle of hair dye won't fix anyway. Cynthia, you ain't wearing leggings on stage. You were the glam one so act like it. I've gotta go to Camden. My flat is full of canvas and I've a pile of washing coming out my arsehole. Thought I'd swing by and see what you've done without me. Not that I'm expecting anything."

"What about me?" asks Vincent. He gives her a flash of the bright blue lining inside his ringmaster-style blazer.

Gloria takes a long drag and studies him up and down. "As they say, you can't polish a turd but you can roll it in glitter. As long as you don't smell of actual shite you'll be fine. Roberto, hit play."

Gloria's cigarette fizzes as it extinguishes in my coffee. She drags out a chair and relights another, tapping her foot on the floor as the intro kicks in. The Dragnificent Seven make it to the final chorus this time before the CD skips. The queens hold their position and stare at Gloria expectantly.

"Well?" says Richard.

Gloria glares at them, eyes wide. "Apart from you all clearly being about a hundred years old, it ain't bad.

Richard, you need to sharpen your turns, and Vincent, your squats look like you're having bowel issues in the woods."

"It's my dodgy hip," he protests.

"Have you done your stretches?" Gloria asks.

"We had to witness them," I say.

"Good. Now, keep at it. When's the next rehearsal?"

"Sunday," says Boo.

"Practice your solos. We ain't even got two weeks." She pours the rest of her coffee into a pot plant and lobs the cup to Roberto. "Right, I'm off. Harri, bring the binder, will ya?"

She's out before I've got my bag on. I wave at the queens and follow her onto the street.

"Did you want a lift? I can collect The Duchess," Richard calls after us.

"I don't trust her to make it," Gloria replies, before turning to me. "Only good place for that old thing is the scrapheap, much like them."

A taxi stops short of hitting Gloria as she stands in the middle of Berwick Street, arm raised. "Camden, please driver."

"Am I coming with you?"

"Nah, no need. I've packed your artworks. I'll be back for last orders. Now get yourself upstairs. There's a fresh lasagne in the oven and someone who wants to see you in the front room."

She's gone in a haze of exhaust fumes. I wish she'd involve me with the gallery set up. I need to plan where to hang everything. There's a skill to it. At least Jack's back. My palms are sweaty and my mouth dries as I close in on our front door, a million questions running through my head. Where has he been? Was he safe? Was it my fault?

I hope he hasn't seen the newspaper clippings I stole from his bedsit. My key lingers by the latch as the sound of footsteps float from inside. I take a deep breath, put on my best caring smile, and enter.

"Hey!" Danilo is stood in the centre with a handful of sultanas. My shoulders sink. "I thought you'd need a dinner date. It isn't much, some sushi, and a can of fake coke but it's the thought that counts. When you heading to Camden?"

I drop my bag onto the floor and sit on the arm of the sofa as he wraps his arms around my torso. "I'm not going to Camden today."

"What's wrong?" he asks.

"Nothing."

He lets go and sits away from me. "You were expecting Jack, weren't you?"

I let out a sigh. "It was the way Gloria said someone was waiting for me."

"Well, I'm sorry to disappoint." He stands up and takes one tray of sushi. "I can eat in the office."

I grab his wrist. "No, please stay. I'm happy to see you."

"Tell your face that."

"I said I'm sorry."

He frowns. "No you didn't, but don't worry. I'm sure you'll get to see the golden boy soon."

"Is he coming round?"

Danilo balls his right fist and flicks on the news, not bothering to change channels when another report about Joao starts. It's his family being used for views now, filmed from down the street as they hold onto each other, laying flowers in the arches behind Charing Cross. Joao's boyfriend's eyes are raw, bags heavy under each as he's supported by friends carrying helium balloons.

"You need to stop obsessing over Jack," Danilo says as the news changes to sport.

"I'm not obsessed with him," I snap.

Danilo laughs and looks away. "He's all you talk about."

"He's a friend who went missing, what do you expect me to talk about?"

He goes into the kitchen and slams a cup down on the counter. It's like being a teenager again, how Mum used to show her anger through actions not words. I storm through the curtain and he stands with his back to me.

"You realise he doesn't care about you?" he says.

"He needs some space now and then."

He pulls out a chair and falls into it. "I spoke to him, Harri."

"When?"

He shrugs. "Day before the funeral. I was helping put a portfolio together for him to send to *ArtReview*. Get him some exposure."

"Exposure? He's minted. He can pay for whatever exposure he wants. I'm the one who needs that." I flick the kettle on and spoon coffee into a mug. He may be unreliable, but me and Jack are in this together.

"I'm sorry Harri, I was given little choice. My client at the magazine wanted a submission from an artist urgently. I was sworn to secrecy."

"I'm an artist too, remember? We could've worked together on it."

"Me and you, or you and Jack?"

"Here we go again." I march to my bedroom and throw open a drawer, grabbing a fresh set of clothes. It isn't long before Danilo appears in the doorway. I sink back onto my knees, staring at the floor, breath shallow. "I'm going to Camden."

"You said you weren't needed,"

"Well I've changed my mind." I pick up my reserve artworks and stack them into a secure box. "I know in your world art doesn't seem like a real job, but it is. I might not work in a shiny office block, or wine and dine clients like you, but it's still work and if everyone else is getting helped up the ladder, then I need to work harder." I pull on a blue hoodie and change into my Docs, fighting with their laces.

"Wouldn't a white shirt be more professional?" Danilo asks, opening the wardrobe, rummaging through my clothes.

My blood boils with his intrusion. "Leave them, I don't need you to manage my life."

"I was thinking a smart shirt might give a good impression."

"That's what my mum used to say, too." I pull his hands from the wardrobe, and slam the door shut. "I've had enough with people telling me what I can and can't do, what I should or shouldn't be wearing, who I should and shouldn't care about. I came to London to get away from all that. I thought you were different."

He shakes his head and sits on my bed.

"What?"

"I can't work you out sometimes, Harri. One minute you're all over me in bed, the next you seem sick of the sight of me. Me and Jack are over, long over, but it seems you and him ain't."

"He's just a friend. It's you I care about. Just give me some time." I stare at the ceiling and count to four before joining him on the sheets. "I'm sorry, okay. I do appreciate you, just I've had a lot on with the move, the queens and…"

"And Jack."

I nod. "He does care about me, regardless of what he says, and I care about him. Look at everything we've done for Eric."

"What *you've* done for Eric," he corrects. "He's using you but you're too blind to see that. Do you believe he drove around the country for your benefit and not his? He would've known Richard had bought the paintings. Jack only went to make more money."

"That's not true," I say, hoping I'm right. I roll over until my head is on Danilo's chest. "I have to constantly try and please everyone and it's impossible."

Danilo takes the flyer for our exhibition from the pinboard above the bed and flips it in his fingers. "You're going to show everyone how amazing you are this week, so long as you keep focussed. Let's scrap today, but let me take you for dinner Wednesday evening?"

"That's press night."

"I know a cute Greek place on Bayham Street. I'll book a table for 10pm." He squeezes my hand tight and pulls me closer. "You deserve to celebrate with the people who genuinely care for you."

Growing up having your home life constantly ripped apart and taped together should've taught me not to trust anyone. The exhibition has been a lifetime in the making and I want to share the night with those who have made it happen, but that still includes Jack.

Some of what Danilo says is right though. I do need to obsess more about him. He's the one who has been there for me through all of this, and what have I given him in return? I lean across and kiss his cheek.

"How long is your flat free for?" he says, smiling.

The want of the gallery is calling, but the gravitational pull of Danilo is stronger. I push him flat to the bed, his shirt unbuttoned in record time, his jeans soon tossed to the floor. It's about time I gave him my full attention.

20.

Echoes of a Life Mislaid

I stand outside the back of the gallery, high on the steps above The Stables market. The summer weather has been replaced by a westerly front, the clouds heavy and gun metal grey, the punters near the Chinese food stalls pulling their jackets tight. The gallery entrance one floor down has the red carpet rolled out and my nerves are unreal, my right leg bouncing, my body thirsting for a stiff drink.

Danilo stands at the bottom of the steps looking forlorn, kicking the floor expecting to be invited in early, but I have to break free. He's stayed at the flat for the past two nights and I'm yet to catch my breath after the suffocation of cabin fever. My only invite still sits with Daria. The article he helped create will appear in *Soho Now* this weekend announcing the official return of The Dragnificent Seven.

"I'll call you when I need you," I shout down. He leans back against the wall and lights a cigarette – the first time he's smoked in front of me. I guess we're only together through coincidental timing. Me, craving attention as the search for The Dragnificent Seven stagnated, him wanting a new project to keep boredom at bay.

I press the silver bell on the right of the wooden door. Somewhere inside, Jack will be pacing. I can't settle until we've cleared the air, and Danilo cannot be present for that conversation. His guidance could ruin it all.

"Should be open," comes Gloria's voice from the speakerphone. I twist the handle and step into a long white corridor more at home in a hospital. The yellow wet floor signs are the only burst of colour, the bleach still fresh on the stone tiles.

Gloria pulls me into a hug. There's something motherly in her grip, holding me close, knowing the emotions are forming a cocktail inside. "You deserve tonight to be about you," she whispers.

A short man powers through the door at the far end and covers his cheeks with his hands. "My darling, my darling, the rumours are true. My Gloria is home."

His hair is blonde, styled to portray someone a decade younger than the age his crow's feet reveal. His t-shirt is baby blue, tucked into high waisted chinos and sitting well with an aubergine suede jacket.

"Justin, babe, lovely to see you as always," says Gloria as she air-kisses him. "This is Harri. He's in Room Two."

"A pleasure," Justin says, gripping my left hand in both of his. "Magento has told me *everything* about you. I was Eric's number one fan."

"He tells all the queens that," laughs Gloria. "Anyway, we don't have time to gas. We open in an hour. Justin, take Harri down will ya?"

Gloria disappears into a glass-fronted office and immediately talks animatedly at the three shocked young women working inside. As she moves paperwork between desks, I follow Justin to my room.

The three gallery spaces all lead from a central foyer, the ceiling domed with cut glass dripping from the light fittings. A dark-haired woman in a stunning floral evening gown sits behind a piano, running through the scales. She sits back at the end of each run and cracks her knuckles, the sound echoing across the open space.

To my right, a serious-looking older man with a clipboard and earpiece instructs cloakroom workers to keep out of sight, the waiting staff behind prepared to load their trays with flutes of golden champagne. This is the world I wanted, but to have finally landed doesn't feel real. The press questions will plunge into the thoughts behind my artwork, but how deep will they want to scratch beneath the surface of my personal life? I'm out of my depth, treading water to save myself from drowning.

Room Two is small, but the six works I've chosen glow in the soft lighting. From the entrance, only one can be seen. It'll be the first thing Jack sees when he enters. I hate how he'll never know he inspired it.

I began painting it shortly before my birthday, the grey and black borders spiralling towards the centre, the nucleus never completed. Like my life at that moment, something was missing, a hole in the shape of Gloria and Jack. They plugged that gap. The central sunshine orb is purely Jack, a beacon of hope, yet tonight I must pretend I did it for Danilo.

Guidebooks sit in a plastic holder on the wall, and I pull one out and sit on the sole bench, taking in the moment. Miss Kennedy would be so proud of the troublesome boy who sat in front of her during those afternoon detentions. Like with every other deadline, I left sending the names of my pieces to the gallery until the last minute, scrabbling around to find the middle ground between amateur and pretentious.

"*Echoes of a Life Mislaid*," says a voice from behind. I twist on the bench, Daria's silhouette from her slim-fitting dress blocking the light. "Guess you'll always be that nerd."

I pace across the room and hold on to her biceps. "You came?"

"I wouldn't miss this for the world."

She leads me back to the bench, leaning her head on my shoulder as she takes in my work. "They're really great."

"You're only saying that cos I'm your brother."

"No I'm not. I actually like these ones." She punches me gently on the arm, and then places a hand on my knee. "Do you remember our tenth birthday?"

Her question catches me off balance. "Was that the one with the cake incident?"

"That was our ninth."

The birthdays blend into one. We used to argue constantly about when our party would be. With only four weeks between us, we were pressed to share, forcing our separate groups of friends to cramp into the lounge, all sitting atop a stretched-out bedsheet.

Each year may be the same for me, but Daria has always been built different, compartmentalising memories into a mental filing cabinet.

She grips my hand tight and swallows. "On the morning of our tenth party, you came into my room, desperate to open the extra presents, despite it not being 5am. There was one you couldn't wait to open. Do you remember, Harri?"

I'm sat on her princess bedsheets, drinking a glass of milk, dropping crumbs from a cookie, shaking with excitement. The memory is as clear as day. "The day I got my watercolour set from *WH Smiths*."

"You were obsessed with it," Daria says as she strokes my forearm. "You dragged us into that bloody shop every time we went into town. I didn't mind of course, because it allowed me to play with the giant Barbie dollhouse they had on display."

"That thing was always taking over our front room," I say.

"Until *someone* decapitated my Safari Barbie and threw her out the upstairs window."

I can see the blonde hair and khaki cap of the doll head flying into the rosebush below, her torso remaining bent and broken on the bedroom floor. The screams. Mum's grip on my collar so tight my feet barely touch the floor. I'm there now, being dragged into my room, the headless Barbie in Mum's hand, waved in front of my face. And then the aftermath.

"Mum took my brushes," I say, tears falling down my cheeks.

Daria nods and grips me tighter. "I can still see her, red-faced in the kitchen, snapping each brush in half, leaning over the sink, washing away the paint. Stamping on the box."

My shoulders slump, never knowing they were discarded so furiously. "I guess it's no wonder I'm a bit fucked up."

Daria tosses her designer handbag to the floor, and sits facing me, legs crossed. I mimic her, as if we're pre-teens. "Look around you," she says. "Despite everything, despite *her*, you've made it. I know you aren't proud of yourself, so I'm double proud to make up for your personal shortcomings."

"You're not just saying that, are you?"

She smiles, touching the side of her eyes to stem the tears fighting to come out. "Mum's been awful to you and I should've done more, but I was too tied up with my own life and lost sight of what was important. But look at you now. You've found Eric's queens, you've found a new group of people who want you, and we're surrounded by all this amazing work you've created. I fucking love you, Harri Forrester."

Our foreheads rest together, collecting ourselves before the champagne corks start popping. As the pain of my formative years subsides, so do my nerves. She's right, I have made it. All that's left to repair is my friendship with Jack.

"Does your being here mean my invite to Fashion Week is still on?" I ask.

She runs a hand through my hair, wiping her now greasy palm on a tissue. "As long as you promise not to sleep with my model friends."

I hold out my little finger. "Pinky promise."

Classical music fills the foyer as I lie prostrate on the floor, staring at the ceiling, finally exhaling after a lifetime of holding my breath. The door to Room Two opens slowly, causing the volume and chatter from outside to increase.

"Gallery spaces open in thirty," says Gloria, sticking her head through the gap. She walks across and crouches next to me. "You alright?"

I sit and give her a hug. "Thank you. For everything."

She pushes me away and pulls out two nicotine patches from her clutch bag, blue to match her eyeshadow. "Stop being soppy, you deserve this. Get off the floor and come have a drink with us."

I follow her into the foyer, taking a glass of champagne from the nine out of ten who's dressed in a semitransparent white shirt. A month ago I'd be planning how to take him home. Instead, I've a boyfriend waiting outside, and someone who I thought would have that title hiding in a gallery of his own nearby.

"To us," says Gloria as she clinks her glass into mine.

"To us," I reply. "Should I be more nervous?"

"Don't be daft, it's only for the press."

"*Only*," I say, nodding towards the cloakroom. A photographer is already messing with various lenses and calling instructions down her phone.

"The queens couldn't make it by the way. Probably for the best, cos the last thing we need is for them to cause a scene with their fucking bickering. If they keep on like that we'd have to cancel the performance before one of them commits a murder. Had to put a fifty-quid deposit down at the Nelson and I'd quite like not to lose that, thank you very much." She takes another glass of champagne, swilling the bubbles around her gums. She swallows, nods behind me and taps my arm. "I best leave you to it."My heart jumps a little when I see him. Jack's face is pale, his hair glowing less than the last time we were together. But he's here.

He meanders across the room, kissing Gloria on the cheek before standing in front of me, eyes focussed on the floor. "I'm sorry, for what it's worth."

I down my drink in one before reaching for a second. "It's good to see you."

I'll leave it to a jury to decide if I mean that statement or not. Jack picks up a salmon canapé from the trestle table behind, tossing it into his mouth whole. I've not been able to bring myself to look through to Room Three. Jack Montague this, Jack Montague that. He's the main draw of this event, everyone knows it, and seeing what he's created may make myself doubt my own abilities more so than I did this morning.

Instead of lengthening our stilted conversation in public, Jack takes hold of my right cuff and pulls me towards his room. I look to Gloria to save me, but she smiles like a proud parent. To follow Jack is to go against everything I'd promised Danilo in the taxi, but my feet take me there regardless. He closes the door and sits me on a chair at the edge of the room. The heavy light switch clunks, the spotlights popping in turn to reveal his work.

"I've done these for you. For Eric." His hands are buried deep in his pockets, his face turned away. The five artworks side by side on the far wall are larger than the others of his I've seen, at least double in width and height. The base colours build a pride flag, brightening the plain walls from which they hang. Gone are the slogans, the anger, the pain of his protests. In their place is the simple black outline of the crown from The Duchess' bonnet.

They're wonderful, of course they are, but I can't bring myself to tell him. He doesn't deserve to know, not yet. I allow a long silence to play out before fishing for the answers I need. "Where did you go?"

"When?"

I look at him as he squats beside me. "I know you're not stupid. When do you think?"

He shrugs. "I just needed some space."

"Gloria was worried sick."

"And you?" He tries to take my hand, but I brush it off.

"You haven't the first idea how much your disappearance tore me apart." More silence. "I know you and Danilo had a thing, by the way. No need to hide that anymore."

A gentle, defeated nod. "He told you then?"

"I found the pictures."

He rocks on his heels, punching his thigh. Two punches, then three. His eyes have lost their spark as he glares at my chest. "I should've told you."

"You think? After everything that happened between us at the farm, after you knew I was with Danilo, you still chose silence."

As I stand, he raises a hand and takes hold of my lapel. "I wanted it to happen too, y'know, me and you. I pushed myself away because I was scared to get close. When I was away I realised how much I needed you."

"Well you've a funny way of showing it."

"I'm trying, Harri, really trying."

I shrug him off. "You were right before. We weren't friends, just acquaintances, and I'm done trying. Every time I got close, you walked away. Everything I did was for your benefit, but you never learnt to reciprocate."

"That's not true." He downs his champagne and grabs

the door handle. I hold it shut, blocking the base with a firm stamp of my left Doc. He clutches his hair and spins to face the centre of the room. "Harri, grow up."

"I've spent a lifetime being told to grow up, to fit in, to hide in the shadows and not be problematic. I wish I were the one with the wealth, the ski holidays, the five-bed house. I wouldn't have thrown it all away."

Jack pushes past me, our shoulders colliding. His breathing is heavy as he smashes his glass against the gallery floor and leaves, with me following, just like a puppy would. He strides down the short horseshoe corridor leading back to the foyer, Justin standing back against the wall, hands raised as we pass.

Jack races across the foyer, his mood juxtaposed against the notes of Mozart floating from the pianist's fingers, the entrance door slamming against the interior wall. We spill onto the red carpet, pushing through the assembled press, where Danilo is waiting for me. It's like he knew this would happen. He grabs my waist as I pass, using his full weight to restrain me.

"I need to speak to him," I spit, but Danilo laughs sarcastically. "Danilo, please."

"Your show is about to start."

"This is more important right now."

Danilo's grip is firm on my collar, my heels off the floor as I fight against him. As I try to break free, he pushes me back against a wall, a finger pointing to my face. "We spoke about this Harri. He's using you, just like he used to use me. Anytime I didn't let him get what he wanted, he ran away."

"Yet you still chose him over me for *ArtReview.* This isn't about you, Danilo. You're just as much as a hypocrite as the rest of us so stay out of it." He pushes me away, and we face off as I brush my blazer down. "Just give me five minutes, that's all I'm asking."

"I won't let you ditch me for him after everything I've done to make tonight happen."

"I've made this happen," I reply, my hand slapping against my heart, my voice sharp, firm.

Danilo widens his stance so my route is blocked. "He doesn't care about you, Harri. Why can't you get that into your skull? If you go after him now, don't expect me to be waiting when you come back."

The rain is coming down heavy, but the choice is easy. Danilo glares as I walk away, making it onto the pavement. Jack is in sight, the orange glow of restaurants and bars illuminating his every move. I turn the collar of my blazer up and break into a jog as he powers onto Camden High Street.

"Jack!"

My call goes unanswered, his head remaining down. On the left, a group of drinkers huddle together under an awning, like bees in a hive, the ashtray their queen. Conversations stop as I pass, the eyes of bus passengers waiting at red lights all fixed on my plight. Drinkers snigger as I run, the water from my soaked hair dripping mascara into my eyes. Rainwater fills my shoes and flicks up to my hamstrings as I sprint.

Jack turns down a narrow street, the heavy traffic giving me a chance to close in, his body central in the crosshairs of my vision as he heads towards Mornington Crescent Station. He battles through the tourists, walking against the flow, but when he's in reach, I make a grab for his shoulder. I hold his top tight and force him to face me. Eyeliner is streaming down his cheeks with tears, like ink blots on ivory parchment.

"Leave me alone," he says softly, his voice hidden beneath the sound of tyres through puddles.

"No." I lift his chin to force eye contact. "We came into this together, and we need to finish this together. We don't even have to pretend to like each other if you don't want. Tonight isn't for you, nor for me, but for Eric, for Gloria."

"I've tried, Harri."

"Well try harder. You'll never know how I felt when you were missing, or thinking it was you that they were dragging out the Thames."

"Stop, please," he begs.

I won't allow myself, not this time. "I thought leaving Stonemouth would solve my problems. Stupid, I know. There was me thinking a new city, new people, would extinguish all the pain of my past. I thought you would be part of that, but anytime there's the smallest inconvenience you'd disappear, pushing me away. Danilo was right, maybe you can't be trusted."

"You don't understand the first thing about me," he screams, pushing his hands onto my chest.

"Fine," I say, stumbling forward, leaning my full weight onto him to stem his movement. "Have it your way. Gloria will have the door on the latch because she's good like that. Too good for you if you ask me."

"I'm off, maybe see you later."

"See if I care. Just go, like you always do. This is my life Jack. This is all I have. I don't get to dip in and out whenever I choose."

"I don't either!"

"Bollocks. Everything is fine in your world."

He changes direction and heads back the way we came. The rain and wind are in my face as I stalk behind. He gives me the middle finger over his shoulder and quickens his steps.

"Fuck you Jack," I scream. "I should never have believed in you."

"Fuck you back," he calls through the storm.

I need to let him go, break the chains of unrequited love that have bound me prisoner for the past month, but once again, he's won and I'm left in the gutter. He has the final glance, but I need the final word. "Why don't you do us all a favour and fuck off back to your family for good this time?"

He stops dead, completely statuesque, the rain bouncing from his body, his shoulders slumped. His crying is harder now, unrestrained and guttural; the mask he's been wearing cast aside, the bravado gone, his spirit broken. His knees buckle as he approaches me, cracking like glass under pressure. I take a step back, waiting for him to lash out, but instead he reaches for my hand as his body crumbles.

"I can't do this. I can't run from you anymore."

"Why? Is it because your family are tired of your bullshit too?"

His shoulders fall further as he stares into my eyes. "It's because they don't exist, Harri."

Everything falls silent.

His chest moves in rhythm with his breath, and for the first time, there's no anger in his face, just a look of defeat, his eyes dark and hollow against his pale skin. The outside world fades, the revellers disappearing, the rain no longer having an effect.

The street is nothing more than a film set, our worlds fictional. He squeezes my hand and rests his head gently on my chest. "My parents, Harri. They don't exist. They never have, and they never will."

I wrap my arms around him, holding his shivering body close to mine. He sobs hard and I hold tight to stop him collapsing onto the damp surface below. "You mean none of it's true?"

"None of it. My whole life is a lie." He presses his head to mine. "I'm so sorry."

"So there's no ski trip? No house in Wimbledon? No dog called Noodles?"

He wipes his face, the saltwater of his tears mixed with the freshwater of the rain. Our bodies are close, his heartbeat transferring itself onto mine as he nestles into my shoulder. "It's all made up."

"Maggie and Lisa?"

He takes a deep breath. "I chose *The Simpsons* cos it's easy to remember."

"And then there's Maplewood. I guess that was a lie too, and you were looking into my background all along.""That's my only truth." He looks back into my eyes and this time I know he means it. He pulls his sleeve to reveal his scar. "This did happen in the beehive. I played rounders, I picked fruit, I spent evenings in the meadows. I loved it there too, just like you."

I place my hands on his temples and lean my forehead into his. "You're a care kid too, aren't you?"

He nods. "And I always will be."

I release my grip and we move to a nearby fire escape, our bodies covered in the dark. The satsuma glow of streetlights barely illuminates his face. "I wanted to tell you, honestly, but having made up stories about this ideal life for so long, even I started to believe my lies."

Footsteps approach, running, but slowing to a halt

nearby. Danilo is metres away on the other side of the traffic, eyes fixed on us. Cars flash their lights to allow him to cross, but his feet remain planted to the spot as he stares at me and Jack together.

Nothing I can say to Danilo would make a difference. Like Mum, giving an ultimatum was his way of snaring me. I'm done with his love bombing, dictating who I can and can't see, keeping me wrapped in cotton wool.

I grip Jack's hand. "You're safe now."

He sinks into a squat. "I never found the family I wanted, not until I came to London anyway. I was a tear-away, running from every chance they gave me, running from the carers, the foster families, every single time. They thought sending me to Maplewood would fix me, but I guess I'm so broken I can't be repaired."

I remember being talked about like a cracked toy, social workers in strange buildings talking in hushed tones to the next family who had taken me in. I learnt early not to trust any figure of authority, knowing if I acted up someone else might wash their hands of me.

"When you were away, I found some newspapers in your satchel."

Jack nods. "At Maplewood, they used to keep the rubbish bins in this room off the dining hall. The Chokey we used to call it."

"So did we."

"They locked me in there once to keep me quiet. I can't remember now what I'd done. What I do remember though is the lighter in my pocket, the flame licking the edge of the wastepaper. Creating a scene would get me out, allow me to break free, and, well, you know the rest. When I disappeared last week, that's where I went. I went back to Maplewood, Harri."

"Were you recognised?"

He shrugs. "I've longer hair now and grown into my features a bit. They've been fundraising for years to rebuild it as a retreat so families with kids can go, you know, kids who are ill, or kids who don't have as much. Each time I sold a painting, I'd send money to them anonymously. Last week was the grand opening. I needed to close the circle, Harri."

"Does the name Charlie Baker mean anything to you?"

He's silent for a while. I don't encourage him to talk, instead allowing him room to find the words naturally. "When I came to London, I couldn't let people judge me. Only Gloria knows my old name."

"Jack's a nicer name anyway," I say.

He chuckles. "Someone had scratched Jack into a stone near The Afterglow Vista. Saw it when I was hiding from Benedict Busby one afternoon. I was gonna call my first kid Jack, but I think I suit it better."

If my memories hadn't blanked out that symbol, his tattoo would've revealed his past to me long before now. I only ventured to the stone circle at Maplewood once, but that was enough to creep me out. The wind used to whistle through the willows and the air felt colder.

Jack takes my hand. "And I *am* glad you're here. I mean that. You'll never know how much Eric meant to me. I haven't shown it, I know, but I'm pleased you succeeded in finding the queens."

"We succeeded," I correct him.

The rain eases, the bars coming back to life. We make our way back towards the gallery, our rooms likely full of potential buyers and critics by now. We'll make a great advert arriving late and looking like we've been dragged through multiple hedges backwards.

As we cross the bridge of Camden Lock, Jack stops again. "Sorry for being a dick."

I nudge him gently with my shoulder. "You don't have to apologies *every* time you're a dick, you know."

"You're so good at letting people in, but me? I push them away. You included."

"I only trust people because of my lifetime of rejection."

Jack lets out a laugh. "And I force them away for the same reason."

I stroke the back of his hand with my thumb. I need Jack in my life, *want* Jack in my life, regardless of what I promised Danilo.

"How did you end up in London?" I ask.

He picks at some loose stonework and drops it into the

ghostly water below. "After I came out the young offender's, I'd just turned seventeen. They sent me to this house in Oxford."

"But you didn't stay?"

"For a bit, but it was horrible. Damp, dangerous, loud. It would've led me down an even darker path. One autumn night I packed a bag and went to the station, boarding the first train I saw. London was easy to hide in, living rough for a bit, moving between areas. Spent a week not too far from here once. Then, after about two months, I slept on the right doorstep."

"And someone gave you a chance?"

"I was lucky." He slides an arm around my waist. "They cared for me from the moment we met, allowed me into their home, treated me like a son. They saved my life, Harri, and I owe them everything. They made a promise on my first night to fight for me, to never let me down."

"And did they?"

"Never. And Gloria will never let you down either."

21.

Lighting the Fuse Might Result in a Bang-b-b-bang!

Gloria stalks my bedroom, examining the firework propped in a holder on the bedside table. It's over a foot in length, and the fuse's proximity to her lit cigarette forces both me and Daria back against the wall. One false move and the whole flat will turn into a giant Roman candle.

"Are you sure this is what Eric would've wanted?" Daria asks, now examining the Eternity Rocket closely. "Isn't it a bit, I dunno, too cheerful?"

Gloria nods. "Out with a bang. Not all of his ashes are inside, but enough to scatter over the Thames."

"Wouldn't he have preferred to have been a tree?" I ask. The screwed look Gloria gives me shows there would be no chance. "Was only an idea."

Daria flops onto my bed in her oversized grey tracksuit, her hair scraped back and face make-up free. She'd invited me to a Vogue Gala in Kensington last night, but Gloria insisted I stay to finish outfits for The Dragnificent Seven's reunion show this evening.

To my surprise, Daria arrived shortly after eight, a Tesco bag full of snacks and three-quarters of a bottle of gin under her arm. Our fingers are still raw from gluing sequins to skirts and adding googly eyes to Boo Karky's props.

She takes an Alka-Seltzer and fizzes it in a glass of ice-cold orange squash. I look at her, smugly clear-headed myself. She drinks half the effervescent liquid and suppresses a burp. "I've not had a proper drink since before

New York. The bosses frown on it, of course."

"What about the two trays of chocolate fingers you ploughed through?"

"Let's say they're often replaced on the menu by salads and unseasoned chicken breasts."

Gloria places the firework carefully back inside its aluminium box, before lighting a cigarette and clearing last night's empties. "You two should get ready. Jack'll be here shortly. I'll go make a flask."

"Do we have to come?" I ask.

"He's dropping her off on the way," she says, pointing at Daria.

"I've promised to have lunch with the girls from work at London Bridge."

I look her up and down disapprovingly and she gives me a V sign in return.

"We're the same dress size so it doesn't matter if I arrive like this. We always share clothes."

"Can't Richard get the tube? It's only ten minutes from Euston."

Gloria chuckles and switches my small television on, leaving it mute as normal. "This is Richard we're talking about. He'll have at least four suitcases of outfits and will step off the train in eight-inch heels. On the phone last night he said he's bringing fifty shimmer curtains. In his head it's still the late eighties and we need to decorate the Nelson ourselves. Even for a trip to the off licence he'd never travel light."

I move my six unsold artworks to the side and throw open the wardrobe, pulling out the most garish top I can find, ready for tonight. The invitation states 'dress to impress'. With the queens ninety per cent polyester and sequins, there's no way my generic black jeans and Bowie t-shirt combo will wash.

Daria joins me on the floor as I lay out my clothes. "I wouldn't put you down as someone who'd wear purple." She holds the silky shirt from the shoulders and side-eyes me as the bright sunshine reflects off its material. "This is gross."

I give her a smug grin. "It's Grainger & Grainger."

"In that case, I love it."

I pull it from her hands and throw it at the black bin liner containing the other clothes destined for Oxfam. I take the royal blue shirt I wore on *The One Show*. "How about this one?"

"It brought you luck last time."

"There we are then. What are you wearing?"

"Gloria says a queen has a suitable outfit I can borrow."

I almost roll on the floor laughing. "You want to be on the cover of *Elle* and *Cosmo.* You won't get booked if you get caught strutting around London in arseless chaps and a studded harness."

"Would keep me cool," she retorts. She moves back to the bed and holds her glass to her forehead.

"Still feeling rough?"

When she doesn't answer, I join her, just like all the times from our youth. When either of us had nightmares, we never went to our parents, instead clutching each other close, squeezed into the same single bed with multiple stuffed toys.

"Mum called me last night." Her voice is quiet, almost defeatist. I look across and she stares to the ceiling. Her pose is identical to the tragic evening in Year Nine when she admitted she'd kissed Duncan Lightbody from the year above. The same boy I'd told her I fancied the previous evening. "Mum actually apologised."

I prop myself on my elbow and look at her. "For what?"

Daria lets out a sigh. The lack of foundation allows her eye bags to be visible. Her eyeballs are bloodshot and her skin dry. "For the way she treated Eric."

"It's too late now."

"She was pleased your art show went well last week."

"Exhibition," I snap. "And if she cared she'd have apologised to me, not you. And she'd have apologised a long time ago and been in Camden. I've moved on and she needs to as well. Life is better without her interfering." Daria falls back flat again but I stare down at her. "Was she expecting me to accept her apology and pretend like nothing happened?"

"Not immediately, no."

"Not ever. I pity her more than anything." I grab a towel and throw my socks into the washing, before taking Eric's picture from the dresser. "Send her a copy of this. This is who she should be apologising to."

The first sign of Jack arriving comes in the form of The Duchess backfiring. The noise smashes through the flat, and my first thought is that Gloria has smoked too close to Uncle Eric's rocket, leaving nothing but a set of curlers and two smoking slippers on the rug in the front room.

I slide open the window and throw a mini pork pie from my lunch plate at him. It bounces off the car and towards Roberto's Café, narrowly missing Jack's head as he pulls himself out the driver's seat. For some reason he's half naked, not that I'm complaining. He's hot even from a distance.

"Where's your top?" I shout.

He wraps his arms around his body to hide his skin. "The Duchess had a little accident."

"What did you hit?"

"Nothing! It started throwing out windscreen washer for no reason so had to use my shirt to clean it off."

"Couldn't you have used the wipers?"

"Wiper. Singular. The other fell off somewhere near Dartford."

Gloria follows me and Daria from the flat, throwing my backpack onto my lap as I slide into the backseat. She takes the passenger seat so the one remaining working window can be cracked to release her tobacco clouds. It takes five attempts for Jack to get The Duchess going. After kangarooing to the junction with Berwick Street and almost taking out a trio of cyclists, the car cuts out.

"Not again," says Jack as he twists the key in the ignition. "Three times this morning this bitch has done this."

"No swearing in front of The Duchess, remember?" I say.

"When did this last have an MOT?" Daria asks, picking foam from the ripped seat cover.

"Eric had it done at the start of the year," Jack replies, the wing mirror disconnecting with magnificent timing and bouncing on the tarmac.

"His friend is a mechanic," says Gloria. "Eric slipped him a fiver and a ticket to see Erasure. She passed the MOT with flying colours, funnily enough."

We clamber out as Jack twists the ignition key once more. The engine clicks, but instead of a smooth purring sound, four loud bangs come from under the bonnet. Steam floods out, and within seconds of Jack escaping, it's replaced by thick, black smoke. My knowledge of cars isn't great, but even I know this isn't a good sign. Orange and red flames dance around the exterior, , catching the material of the seats inside and engulfing our ride.

"Could be worse," says Jack as he crouches on the kerb next to me, pulling out his vape.

Gloria barks instructions to the fire service from her phone as we can do nothing more than watch The Duchess burn. Paddington stares back through the front windscreen, his fur charring and eye melting until it drops from his face. Less than ten minutes later, the whole car is nothing more than a twisted clump of charred metalwork.

I sit in the Lord Nelson, halfway between the stage and ticket booth. My eyes itch with the glittery eyeshadow I allowed Richard to apply over an hour ago, and my flares are slowly cutting off the blood supply to my legs.

A cute technician is doing another test of the stage lights, casting Cynthia in alternating purple, blue, and green hazes as she marks the floor with masking tape. The budget for the show increased somewhat once Danilo's article on The Dragnificent Seven appeared in *Soho Now*. All references to me were cut, not that I'm surprised, knowing it'd be the case after he blocked me from both Instagram accounts.

"Get us a Bacardi would you, love?" Cynthia calls down through a squealing microphone. "And a pint of IPA for Lynden. It might get his hands away from the switches for five seconds and stop blinding me with these lights."

Lynden looks crestfallen as he steps away from his tech desk, the stage dimming as he falls into a seat. As I wait for the bar staff, the front door flies open. Jack is dressed in a sharp dark blazer and crisp white shirt. A subtle layer of make-up allows his cheekbones to become magnets for the little sunlight that's seeping in. He brushes back his flicked fringe, a gold ring now around his right thumb. Behind him, Daria enters through the haze, looking like a million dollars in a hugging red dress. As the vapour around her settles, another beaming face presents itself.

"Michelle? You made it?" I say, hugging her tightly.

"I took a leaf out of your book. Told Craig I was going to the bins this afternoon and never looked back."

"About time," I reply.

"We bumped into Jack in KFC," says Daria.

"You didn't give him my Instagram," says Michelle. "I told you to snatch me a hot grungy guy."

"I'm not grungy," says Jack.

"Or straight," I add.

"The best ones never are." Michelle throws her rucksack on the table and sprays *Jane MacDonald: Ocean* perfume liberally to hide the particles of caffeine and stale pastries clinging to her hoodie.

"I'll get some drinks," Jack calls. He slinks behind the bar and grabs a pint glass from the shelf. "IPA, right?"

"Please. Oh, and a 1664 for Lynden."

He stares at me, his mouth dropping. I nod towards the stage. "He's the techie."

"Is Lynden straight?" asks Michelle. She's like a dog on heat, not that my track record is anything to be proud of.

I lick my thumb and remove rogue eyeliner from her face and give her a pint. "Go and find out."

She approaches him cautiously, pulling the back of her top down with each step. Within seconds, he's showing off the lighting deck, Cynthia once again being flooded in spotlights.

"Grab a Bacardi for the girls," I tell Jack.

He takes a bottle from the fridge and sticks it in a bucket, taking a plastic scoop to fill the remaining space with ice from a chill box below the bar. "It's easier to give performers a whole bottle, trust me."

I take my drink back to the table, my heart rate slightly faster than expected. My foot bounces involuntarily on the wooden rest halfway down to the base of the stool.

"Are you nervous?" Jack asks as he takes the seat next to me.

I shrug. "What if we let Eric down?"

Jack takes a deep breath, and under the table he links his fingers through mine. Hopefully, he won't care about my sweaty palms. "He would've loved this, Harri. You did everything he wanted. I'm sorry for nearly messing it all up."

He looks away but I squeeze his hand tighter. "It was inevitable there would be bumps in the road. I should've taken a step back but I can be too self-centred to realise."

"It isn't your fault." Jack twists until we're face to face. He makes eye contact for the briefest moment before they flash back to somewhere behind my right shoulder. "I hate admitting I'm wrong, but I want you to know Soho is better with you around."

"Even as an acquaintance?" I say, giving him a sarcastic look with gritted teeth.

Jack takes a deep breath, before two large sips of wine. "Harri, acquaintances are people who flash in and out of your life. They're the people you can use, casting them aside when their worth drops. You put yourself on the line for me, stood up for me when I didn't deserve it. You'll never be just an acquaintance."

"Friends it is," I say.

A piece of fluff falls from the roof and I reach to remove it from his shoulder. He catches my arm and brings it back to my lap. I rest my forehead on his, praying I'm not misjudging his signals. He swallows hard.

"How about friends who date?" he asks, tapping his thumb on the back of my hand. Two taps, then three.

Gloria bundles into the Lord Nelson, shouting over her shoulder as she pushes through the twinks in 'Power Bottom' t-shirts forming a queue at the ticket booth, all wanting to see the reunion of the century, thinking there would be space this late. With fifteen minutes until the performance, it's already standing room only. Gloria air-kisses some of Soho's Elders, as she's insisted on calling them, before making her way across to our table. Her eyebrows raise when she sees me and Jack hand in hand.

"About bloody time too." She throws a bin bag onto the table. "Can I have a word, Harri?" I kick out the chair we've reserved, but she nods towards backstage.

"Be back in a sec," I say to Jack and go to kiss him on the cheek, but he leans back in his chair. His smile shows he doesn't mean any offence, and Michelle chews his ear off immediately. The music pumps from the ceiling speaker, but I still manage to catch her barking the words *Lynden* and *hotel*.

Gloria powers through the swing door in a dark corner and paces down the toilet corridor. The air is thick with rancid bleach, and a suspect stream of yellow liquid seeps across the torn flooring. She throws open a silver curtain, revealing the cramped area behind the bright lights of the stage.

Like I'm entering a camp Narnia, I step over the threshold and squeeze into the last space not occupied by a drag queen. Richard has a leg on a desk, using tape to tuck things into the correct place, whilst Vincent is clutching at the rear zip of Boo's swan outfit.

"I told you it'd fit," Boo says as he's hoisted up with Vincent's firm tug.

Vincent releases his grip. "I give up. It's like trying to force custard into a condom."

All surfaces around the four queens are covered in a light sprinkling of glitter, and my hand slides on dropped Vaseline when I lean casually in front of the large lightbulb-framed mirror.

"Give us a sec," Gloria says to Cynthia. She drops her lipstick into her make-up bag, and Gloria gives her a shove, Cynthia's wheely chair heading at pace to the far end of the room. As she hits the back wall, Gloria grabs my earlobe and brings my head close.

"I need you to look after Jack," she says. We're so close I'm able to breathe in the garlic lingering from her lunchtime bolognese.

"Me and Jack will be fine, I promise. We're gonna take things slow."

She takes my hands. "I mean tonight. We have a problem. Ivana is back." I pull the stage curtain back an inch and stare across the crowd, scanning for the final piece of the jigsaw. Gloria grabs my arm, her nails digging deep into my biceps. "She ain't out there and never will be."

"What about seeing this lot?" I say, nodding to the queens.

"She had her opportunity." Gloria's words are curt, venom hiding behind each syllable. "I'm so glad you never went to Limehouse."

"She was there the whole time?"

Gloria nods. "Still hanging around with Dai White. Since he came out of prison, he's snared her again. When Jack went sniffing around, Dai was the one who threatened him, Ivana the one who chased him with the pool cue. He told me a few weeks back. Recognised her from some article he saw on the wall at Boo's place."

"Why doesn't Dai let Ivana do what she wants?"

"Because he's a bastard, Harri. Dai has a track record of treating people this way, hence his sentence. I won't let him get within fifty feet of any of us."

"Am I at risk?"

"Come with me." Gloria pulls me across the hall and into the accessible toilet. She wedges the faulty lock shut with a bit of tit tape. "At Eric's funeral," she says. "That was the last time we saw Ivana."

"She was there?"

"They both were, but never made it into the crem. They sent threats to Jack after his visit. He saw them stalking the car park."

"Dai wrote to Mum too," I reply, thinking back to Mum's accusations in Craigs café. They seem a lifetime ago now.

"If you spread your shit wide enough, some of it will land on the seeds," Gloria says. "Dai was in the same group as your mother for a while, before it went sour between them. Even your mum had her limits. He organised more aggressive countermarches, gave them the weapons they needed to fight us."

"So why did Ivana go with him?"

"He promised he'd supply what she needed to stem her cravings. Anyone can have their vision clouded by addiction. Once she went with him, we were cast aside. Dai came out of Holloway shortly before Eric left us. He may have seen a letter from your uncle and was expecting a visit. When Jack went, Dai had to put out a warning."

"Did you see him at the funeral?"

"I did, but I was too late to stop Jack seeing them too."

Gloria pulls the chain when a tap comes at the door. "We have to look out for him tonight, okay? The bouncers know who Dai and Ivana are, and as long as we stay inside, we should be safe."

I sit next to Daria at the table, Jack reaching for my hand again, desperate to be saved from Michelle's monologue. Behind us, punters are clambering onto the bar to get a better view, and bouncers are struggling with a one-out, one-in policy. Fire regulations must be being pushed to their uppermost limit.

Four microphones stand across the front of the stage, each with a different coloured boa hanging towards the floor. The sound of *Like a Virgin* is faded out by Lynden and the lights in the venue dim to black. Jack grips my hand tightly as the roar from the crowd continues to rise. It's borderline hysteria, Romans waiting for the gladiators, albeit now dressed in heels instead of sandals.

Stage left, the glow from a cigarette is the only indication someone is about to become the focus of our intention. It moves slowly, like a firefly in a poppers-scented forest, and towards centre stage. The voices in the crowd stop, the soft footsteps echoing.

A clunk and a flicker later, Gloria is illuminated. She's holding a photo of Uncle Eric. He's dressed as Wilma, wig not fitting into shot. Gloria takes a deep breath and looks in my direction. The hours of driving, the fallout with my family, the pain of nearly losing Jack. I hope Eric's here somewhere, looking down on us and feeling as proud as we are. His final wish realised.

Gloria nods to Lynden, the first bars of *Kids In America* starting up. Lights burst on behind her, one by one. Under each, a queen stands. Gloria smiles widely and kisses Eric's photo. She moves her mouth near the microphone and waits for the cheers to die down.

"He's, she's, theys and gays. Let me re-introduce you to The Dragnificent Seven."

On my fifth birthday I blew out my candles and wished for the perfect family. Eighteen years and one and a half adoptions later, I'm so thankful it's come true. My body is screaming, desperate to crawl back into bed with Jack and sleep peacefully. I bend over the kitchen sink, my eyes sore as I furiously scrub away last night's thick eyeliner. If I don't get rid of this, I'm guaranteed to look like I've two black eyes in photos later.

I pick up the top of a gear stick, the only surviving piece from The Duchess inferno, clutching it tightly as I stare outside. The sun's rays deflect into my eyes from neighbouring skylights as birdsong filters through. It's the ideal day to blast Eric off on his final journey.

"Good morning, you," comes a tired voice from behind.

I jump and catch my arm on the table's edge, causing a stack of make-up to tumble to the floor. We should've left the Lord Nelson much earlier last night, not that I can remember what time Jack finally dragged me home.

"I thought you wanted a lie in?" I say as I wrap my arms around Jack's naked torso.

"The bed got cold without you in it, and it's nearly 6pm." Jack kisses me on the shoulder before pouring ground Colombian beans into our percolator. "I wanted to get some painting done before we headed to Greenwich, but it can wait. I can't let you get too big-headed now you're a superstar."

"I haven't sold an artwork so I'm hardly Andy Warhol. Someone was interested though."

"Was it to the creepy guy in the flat cap who clearly wanted to sleep with you?"

I gyrate my hips in his direction. "Not my fault my body is too bootylicious."

Jack points a teaspoon at me. "Please never say that again."

"Deal. And anyway, it wasn't. It was some rich bloke from up west."

I sit at the table as Jack goes through his breakfast routine, despite it being nearer supper. "Is Daria coming?" he asks as he swigs milk from a four pinter. "Said she might have clothes for me."

"I thought I got first dibs."

The percolator churns like a steam train heading uphill, causing the conversation volume to rise with it. The only words I can pick out are 'crushed velvet' and 'lilac' but those are enough for me to discard it. Those colours don't suit me at all, even if Daria has got them for free.

A smash comes from the front room. We run through and find Gloria on her back in the centre of the carpet. We each take an arm and pull her to the sofa, Jack sliding a cigarette between her lips.

"I think I'm still drunk," she says.

"How?"

"Might've had some gin at the Nelson for lunch."

"We have to get the train soon," Jack says.

She laughs, coughing phlegm up in the process. "Wrong. We're driving in fifteen minutes."

I fall next to her. "We don't have a car, Gloria."

She raises one finger, waving it in my face. "I might be, very well be, drunk, but your carriage awaits. Look outside."

I look to Jack, and he shrugs. I throw back the curtains and Gloria nods her head until her shades fall over her eyes. I grapple with the window lock until it comes loose in my hand. Tossing it to the floor, I lift the frame. A familiar sound powers across the room.

Jack looks at me with wide eyes.

"Phil Collins," I say with a smile. The four queens are leant against an old minibus, all in their most flamboyant stage outfits. At the rear of the bus, Michelle and Lynden stand, waving sheepishly from behind Daria.

The rust on the roof of the bus is peeking out around the edges but this is hidden by wide pink and yellow stripes across the bodywork. A large black crown has been daubed in thick paint across the bonnet.

"We got it from a dealer this morning," says Gloria from the sofa. "This lot have spent all morning painting. What do you think?"

I hope the curse of The Duchess isn't passed on to our new rescue vehicle, but what sits in front of me is fitting for Eric's final journey. I crouch next to Gloria and take her hand. "It's perfect."

Greenwich Park is cold even with the summer sunset still visible, the skyscrapers of Canary Wharf breaking the horizon. I lay back on the picnic blanket with Jack as disco music blasts from a sound system. Most queens are dancing, dragging Daria, Michelle, and Lynden into their circle.

Cynthia is sat on the floor, making sure the launch tube for Eric's rocket is secure, batting Gloria away when she pulls out her Sterling Duals.

"Is this even legal?" I ask Jack.

"Eric did many things that weren't." He twists his body until his head rests on my stomach. I play with his hair as he closes his eyes. "Life is boring if you only play by the rules."

One thing that's definitely illegal is the position of the new Duchess, Gloria insistent on it being parked at the top of the hill. One fault with the handbrake will take out the National Maritime Museum, but the gaudy vehicle forms a fitting backdrop for this pantomime. I'd run in front of a truck for any of the people stood in front of me. Just like myself and Daria, being blood related is not a requirement to qualify as true family.

And then there's Jack. If the timings of our childhoods were shifted by a few months, we would've met in Maplewood's beehive, able to spend multiple summers together, but some people are worth waiting for.

"Quickly, he's about to go up," shouts Gloria, waving from behind The Eternity Rocket.

Richard extends his cigarette holder onto the fuse, and we huddle as the spark bounces in the fading light. The rocket fizzes on the ground before firing high above. A loud bang reverberates and we're showered in golden stars. Small embers float, catching on the breeze coming down from the Thames estuary.

I grab hold of Jack's hand and he buries his head into my shoulder. As the last pinprick of sun falls beneath the horizon, Gloria joins our huddle, followed by the other queens. Night has fallen over London, over Soho, over us.

Although we may be together in darkness, I'll always believe in the sunrise.

Acknowledgements

Thank you to my agent Anna at Intersaga who believed in this book from the start, calmed me down, listened to my rants, and let me get away with much more than I thought!

Thank you to Spectrum for all your support and for continuing to promote diverse voices in publishing.

Thanks to those who read this book in its various stages and provided feedback to make sure it went in the right direction, especially David Brown and Zoë Partyka.

Thanks also to Saffron at Indiosyncrasy for your hard work in promoting indie authors, and for giving them a much-needed platform.

Thanks also to my fellow members in the Rat Race Discord, a community with members who support each other, review each other's words, and generally tell us to get a grip when we feel something isn't working.

And if you have read this book, thank you. It really does mean a lot. If you are just reading the acknowledgements in a book-store, please pay at the counter.

About the Author

James was born in Oxford, and now resides on the South Coast. He is the author of HALF THE WORLD AWAY (SRL Publishing), a semi-epistolary YA novel set during Section 28, and OUT IN GREENWOOD (SRL Publishing).

Previously James worked with actor Bradley Riches (Heartstopper, Celebrity Big Brother) to adapt Riches' stage script "A" DIFFERENT KIND OF SUPERPOWER into a novella. The novella centred the topic of autism and was featured in publications such as British Vogue, Gay Times, and Attitude, as well as being discussed on Sunday Brunch.

James was schooled in a non-diverse market town during the Section 28 era, and this has driven his passion for writing novels which centre LGBTQIA+ characters, history, and themes. Outside of writing, he is a keen runner, and supports Oxford United FC. He has appeared on podcasts, local radio, and on panels at events hosted by independent bookstores.

James is represented by Intersaga Literary Agency Ltd.